The Lost Sister

Also by Robert Love Taylor

LOVING BELLE STARR

FIDDLE AND BOW

ROBERT LOVE TAYLOR

· ·

THE LOST SISTER

A Novel

ALGONQUIN BOOKS OF CHAPEL HILL

1989

PUBLISHED BY

Algonquin Books of Chapel Hill

Post Office Box 2225

Chapel Hill, North Carolina 27515-2225

a division of

Workman Publishing Company, Inc.

708 Broadway

New York, New York 10003

Design by Molly Renda.

LIBRARY OF CONGRESS CATALOGING-IN-PUBLICATION DATA

Taylor, Robert Love, 1941–
The lost sister:a novel / by Robert Love Taylor.
p. cm.
ISBN 0-945575-10-6
I. Title.
PS3570.A9519L68   1989
813'.54—dc 19   88-23800

FIRST EDITION

for Willie Merle Davis

CHAPTERS

· · · · · · · · · · · · · · · · · · · ·

Little Brother

Mama didn't want Daddy taking Little Brother to Arkansas. How would she visit the grave, see that it was kept clean. It was too far away. And how would he get Little Brother there.

On the train, Daddy said. I'll carry him myself on the train.

How do you mean to carry him, she said. In a suitcase?

I'll make a coffin. Don't you worry. It'll be a dandy.

Daddy was a small man and Mama was big. They never argued for long. Daddy was quiet, he liked things calm. He worked hard and had deep dark eyes. He had moved to Oklahoma City, and that meant something. His younger brothers and sisters stayed behind in Arkansas and did not care to leave, but Daddy did. He had to make his own way, no kinfolk to help him.

Mama and Daddy had Johnnie first. Daddy had wanted a son, but Johnnie was born instead. Then came another daughter, Cora Mae. That was in 1916 when he and Mama left Arkansas and moved to Oklahoma, after Cora Mae was born. In Oklahoma City they first lived near the packing plant in a small frame house on Agnew. The smell from the slaughterhouse was something that Mama complained of. They had lived in Oklahoma City five years, and then Little Brother was born. He lived only three and a half months.

Mama worked hard keeping the house clean, making clothes for the girls, and making quilts from the clothes they outgrew or wore out. She made do, and though they were poor they never knew it. That was Mama's gift. Daddy's too.

To Cora Mae, Mama seemed to grow larger over the years, while Daddy got smaller. Cora Mae wondered if the same thing would happen to her and Johnnie when they got their husbands. Mrs. Perry next door was a good deal larger than Mr. Perry, and Mrs. Furman at the grocery store had a tiny husband who always winked at them when handing them their change.

Girls, Mama said that day of Little Brother's death, sit down and be still.

Johnnie and Cora Mae sat on the floor, their knees crossed. They waited. Cora Mae had goosebumps all along her pale arm. Mama sat in the rocker without rocking, working her hands back and forth over the smooth arms of the chair. Cora Mae had never seen Mama cry and thought that this might be the time, but it wasn't.

Mama leaned forward in the rocker and stared hard, first at Johnnie and then at Cora Mae.

Pray, she said, reaching out and putting her hands on their heads so that they could not have looked up even if they had wanted to.

Dear God, she said, make a home for our sweet baby boy in heaven. He was never any trouble, the sweetest baby a mother could want. Thank you for sending us such an infant to bless our days and to cherish in memory. Help the rest of us to live up to his promise. In the name of Your Son, crucified that we might have eternal life, Amen.

She didn't take her hands off their heads yet. To Cora Mae it seemed a long time, the heat of the afternoon and not a breeze blowing, Mama's hand hot and heavy, and Johnnie breathing deep as if she might begin to cry. Then Mama's hand lightened, and instead of gripping began to stroke.

• • •

No doctor had come. Mama never placed much faith in them, and Daddy used to say if they knew as much about healing as about feathering their own nest, why, there would be no sickness on the face of the earth. Mama and Daddy never had time to think how to prevent what was happening to them.

There was no undertaker either. Johnnie knew that Mama would lay Little Brother out, bathe him and dress him and tuck him in when it was time for him to leave. The burying part of it was Daddy's business. Mama did not approve of his taking the baby to Arkansas, family graveyard or not, but she would not stop him.

Cora Mae's death eleven years later is another story. Cora Mae went to a funeral parlor, Street and Draper's, and had a regular funeral and was buried in Oklahoma City, Sunnylane Cemetery. Mama wasn't going to hear of any more trips to Arkansas with a homemade coffin.

It was a virus that took them. We would say a virus now. Then, it was just another mystery. One day they were alive, the next dead.

When Johnnie thought about it, everything seemed amazing. At the time, it was just what happened. They knew nothing else, had no other life to compare theirs to. Told to make themselves useful, they did. They went to the kitchen. They shucked corn, they snapped beans, they wiped the table, they swept the floor. She and Cora Mae were certainly not helpless. They had never been waited on and they knew what they could do when told to get busy. Johnnie was nine then, Cora Mae eight. They were Daddy's girls all right, but if their mother said jump, they didn't wait for her to say how high.

Johnnie did not care to sneak into Mama and Daddy's room and see what Little Brother looked like dead, especially since Mama was in there with him.

Go yourself, she told Cora Mae. I'm staying right here.

Too many times she had let Cora Mae persuade her to do something she knew better than to try to get away with. This was not to be one of those times. She scrubbed the tabletop, then scrubbed it again.

Mama had swaddled Little Brother in blue and made him clasp his hands. Cora Mae saw him with her own two eyes. Mama sat across from him, a strange look on her face. She might have been asleep, but she sat up and her eyes were wide open. She sat in the straight-back chair, her large hands folded in her lap.

Mama?

Mama didn't answer. Cora Mae stepped closer, on tiptoe at first, but then she thought how silly that was, the baby surely not going to wake up and Mama in such a trance. She walked right up to the crib and touched Little Brother on the cheek. He was smooth and cold. He smelled minty, like the sachet Mama put in her clothes-drawers. She heard hammering out on the back porch. Daddy was making the coffin.

Little Brother's eyes were open, big blue eyes, light blue like the sky, but Mama said that would have changed. Babies' eyes didn't stay the same color. You had blue eyes too, she told Cora Mae. Now they were a grayish green color that Daddy called hazel. Daddy's eyes were so dark they looked almost black. Somebody had reddened Little Brother's cheeks with rouge. Mama must have done it, though it was certainly hard to imagine, Mama never wearing rouge herself, not one dab, her face as white as it could be.

Cora Mae felt afraid. She looked at her mother, so pale and still and large, and at Little Brother, no more real-looking than a doll though as alive as you and me just hours ago. She never felt so afraid. It seemed that she could not get out of that room. He's no doll, she told herself. He's real, he's just gone from his skin, he's not in this room at all anymore. I'm the one that's here, and

I'll be here forever, though not always in this room, Lord help me to get out of this room, Lord help me stay always in my skin, forever and forever, Amen.

That night Johnnie woke to the sound of wood being sanded. Then she slept again and woke to the smell of the paint, just about daybreak. At breakfast Mama told the girls they were not allowed to go back to the porch where Daddy was working. The paint wouldn't be dry. They would get their hands on it and make Daddy have to do it all over again.

No, we won't, Cora Mae said.

Don't go in there, Mama said.

They didn't. They didn't see Daddy until dinnertime in the middle of the day. He walked right past the table as if he didn't even see them sitting there.

Where are you going, Marshall, Mama said.

To work.

Today!

Yes.

And he went out the front door. Later, people came calling, Mrs. Perry from next door and some of Mama's church friends, and the preacher. Told to sit still, Cora Mae and Johnnie sat on the straight chairs in case any of the visitors wanted to sit on the sofa. Mrs. Perry sat for a while, stirring the air with a fan that was lavender-colored and had a picture of snow-capped mountains on it. When Cora Mae expressed her admiration of the fan, Mrs. Perry said that it was made in the Orient and you could get one at Walgreen's.

The church ladies came in groups of two or three and didn't stay long. They dabbed at their eyes with lace handkerchiefs and told the girls that surely such well-mannered young ladies were a comfort to their mother in her time of adversity. If one sat down, Johnnie had to offer a glass of ice tea and go get it while Cora

Mae made pleasant conversation. None stayed long. One lady, as big as Mrs. Perry and with a black veil over her eyes, pressed a dime into the girls' palms. For being such sweethearts, she said.

All afternoon Cora Mae kept saying, Let's go see the coffin.

We can't, Johnnie said. Mama said not to.

Who'll know.

Don't you go back there. After yesterday, I'd think you'd not want to push your luck.

What yesterday.

Didn't you sneak in and peak at Mama and Little Brother?

I want to see the coffin. I never saw one before.

You'll see it soon enough. It's not finished. The paint's not dry. Didn't you hear?

I won't touch it. I just want to see it.

To distract Cora Mae, Johnnie got her to playing checkers.

When Reverend Wiley arrived, the church ladies had been gone for some while, Daddy would be home soon, and Cora Mae and Johnnie should have been thinking about supper. Let's play one more game, Cora Mae kept saying. They were in the middle of a match when they heard the porch steps creak and saw Reverend Wiley standing there in his blue serge suit and black felt hat. He walked right in and handed his hat to Cora Mae as if it were a prize. He was a tall, heavy-set man, as unlike Daddy as a man could be, with a thick, short neck and grayish face, a thin line of a mustache that ran along the edge of his mouth, and hair that looked pasted to his head. Johnnie was always a little afraid of him and glad that she didn't have to sit through the church service and hear what he preached about. Cora Mae and Johnnie always went home after Sunday school and helped Daddy get the Sunday dinner ready while Mama stayed the whole morning. Daddy said church was Mama's business, not his, and that God would surely forgive him for not attending, because there were far worse sins to look out for.

Is Mr. Monroe in? Reverend Wiley asked. He leaned towards

the girls and spoke in a loud, deep preacher's voice. Cora Mae let his hat drop onto the sofa.

Daddy's at work, Johnnie said. He had to go to work.

Bless his heart. No rest for the weary! A cook, is he.

Yes, sir. It's his own restaurant.

Seeing to one form of sustenance, that of the body.

Ribs, Cora Mae said. His specialty is ribs. He makes them with a special sauce that he invented.

Well, well. And which way—

Little Brother's in there, Johnnie said. With Mama.

Reverend Wiley shut the door quickly behind him, and in his deep voice said to Mama, Dear Mrs. Monroe. The Lord provideth and the Lord taketh away.

Damn him, Cora Mae said.

Be quiet, Johnnie told her.

Daddy came in.

What's this, he said, pointing at the Reverend Wiley's hat on the sofa.

Reverend Wiley, Cora Mae said.

And this, he said, pointing at the checkerboard.

Checkers, Cora Mae said.

I might have known, Daddy said, and he tossed his own hat down next to the preacher's. Daddy's was a blue-striped engineer's cap, given to him by the friend that Johnnie was named after, Johnny Barnett, who died of the flu epidemic a few years after she was born. The cap gave Daddy a devil-may-care look, but really he cared about almost everything.

He went to the kitchen, Johnnie and Cora Mae following him.

Well, he said, I see supper isn't on the stove yet.

It isn't time yet, Cora Mae said. We were just getting ready to come put the potatoes on.

It was almost the truth. They weren't all that late in getting started. Daddy was upset and needed a way to let off some steam. Johnnie knew it at the time, but didn't feel any the less guilty. If he so much as hinted that she had done something to disappoint him, she felt as though she could go crawl in a hole. He never had to take a switch to her like her mama did. Just a look did the job.

You girls run along, he said to them. I guess I'll have to see to our supper.

Mama said for us to do it, Cora Mae said.

I know that. But you're not doing it now, are you.

We were just about to.

Run along.

It's our job. Johnnie and me are supposed to do it.

I'm telling you run along.

Daddy had begun to peel a potato. Now he stopped. He carefully set the potato peeler down on the counter. Next, the potato. Next, he was gone.

Well, you can help us, Cora Mae called after him. We'll let you help us, Daddy.

He didn't come back though. He left supper to Cora Mae and Johnnie. Johnnie was so mad at Cora Mae she could have screamed, but she didn't say a word to Cora Mae, just as Daddy would have done. She worked at those potatoes.

Reverend Wiley stayed for supper.

A shame Mr. Monroe has to work so late, he said, especially in a time of bereavement.

The restaurant never closes, Mama said.

Mighty good cornbread, Mrs. Monroe.

The girls made it.

Bless their hearts. They'll make a man happy some day.

I suppose they will, Mama said.

Oh, yes. They certainly will. And please the Lord too.

Please themselves, most likely.

The Lord dwelleth in us all, Mrs. Monroe.

No, he doesn't, Cora Mae suddenly said. Not in me. He doesn't dwelleth in me, not a lick.

She got up so fast she almost knocked over her chair.

Spiteful child, Mama said.

Cora Mae ran through the kitchen, and then the back door slammed.

She'll be back, Reverend Wiley said. They always come back. And full of contrition.

She'll be back all right, Mama said, and that one in there, the sweetest child ever took a breath, he's gone forever!

We're all mortal, Mrs. Monroe. Gone forever from this world, every last one of God's children, in our own time.

He might have been an ugly man, but he spoke the truth when he said that, the living truth, and Johnnie knew it. She knew it so bad that she had to excuse herself from the table. She said she had a stomachache, and then she slipped into the bedroom where Little Brother lay.

She had expected to see Little Brother still in his crib, but there he lay, already in the coffin Daddy had made for him. So the paint must have dried by the time Daddy had to go to work.

She had pictured Little Brother washed shiny, in his blue gown. She thought if she looked carefully she might see a halo around his reddish curls, and that if she bowed her head before him and told him she was sorry for all the bad things she had done, she might look up and see her own image there in the crib and feel in her heart the blood of Little Brother and walk away in his perfect skin. It would be her soul that Daddy would carry to Arkansas, and Little Brother's would stay here in her.

The coffin rested in the middle of Mama and Daddy's bed. Dust motes sparkled in the light that shone through the room's one window, the window sat crooked in its frame. The coffin was painted white, and the paint had not been applied thickly, so that you just could make out the grain of the wood beneath and see how smoothly he had worked it, the corners gently rounded. Another paint probably wouldn't have let you see that. And all around the edge, just beneath where the lid would be fastened,

Daddy had tacked on a swatch of cloth, like a tiny curtain. No more than six inches long all the way around, it was uneven everywhere, blue in places, green or red or brown or even plaid in others. It was not one piece, but many—scraps, Johnnie saw, that he had taken out of Mama's quilt box. The scraps had not even been stitched together, just cut into rectangles of varying widths and tacked to the edges of the coffin. He must have tried to even them up along the bottom, but given up. She recognized pieces from a favorite dress she'd only recently outgrown, some from Cora Mae's dresses, some from Mama's. It was really beautiful. Daddy had made a pretty coffin for Little Brother, a dandy, just as he had said he would.

A Stroke of Charcoal

Returning from the burial of Little Brother, Marshall had felt dead himself. Jane kept to her side of the bed, breathing deep. Sometimes she moaned from her dreams. Days came and went, all a grayness. At the cafe the griddle seemed to hiss at him, the customers, few as they were, slumped over at the counter, dabbing at their food as if they weren't sure what it was for. Late in the afternoon Johnnie and Cora Mae came in, helped him scrub pans, peel potatoes, get ready for the supper trade. Ordinarily the presence of his daughters would have cheered him, but during this time he resented them. They were only playing at helping, they only made more work for him.

I'll do that, Johnnie said.

No, Cora Mae said, it's my turn. You did it yesterday.

Well, it's my job.

You have to take turns.

Don't either. Who says.

You have to take turns! Doesn't she, Daddy!

He'd do it himself, for God's sake. Go on, he would say. Run home and help your mother for a change. Didn't say it, of course. He knew how they would sulk, how it would hurt them if he so much as raised his voice to them. And he wasn't about to hurt them. They would have plenty of sorrow in their time without his adding to it.

Jane took to her canning, then to her quilts, her mending. Often as not, he came home and found her in the steamy kitchen, sitting at the table, her head bowed.

The newspapers was full of talk about the oil discoveries. Everywhere boomtowns sprang up and fortunes was made. You saw photographs of the gushers, the oil-splattered faces, you read reports of the wildcat rigs striking paydirt. He began to think a fellow with sense should go to one of those towns—Bowlegs, say, or Wewoka—and set himself up in business.

The idea just lay there in his mind for a time, but then he thought: Why the hell not?

You'll lose your pants, Jane said. That's why.

And then one day a man carrying a fiddle case came into the cafe. He wore a black Stetson, patent leather shoes, and pants with silver stripes up the side. When he took a stool, he said, Tell you what, bud, I'm going to tell you the secret of life. And you know what? All you got to give me in return is a plate of hash, a side order of grits, and a cup of coffee, black.

That's all, huh.

Hash, grits, coffee. And johnnycakes for the little lady.

Marshall didn't see any lady.

She'll be along directly, don't you worry.

This was late in the morning. Nobody was in the place but Marshall. He had the breakfast dishes done. He had greased the skillets and griddle until they shone. The hash was, in truth, only lukewarm, but well on its way. Now and then somebody like this came along that was down on their luck. He fed them. So why should he turn away this fellow, who promised nothing more than any of the rest, but called it the secret of life.

It'll be a minute before the hash is ready, he said.

I've got the time. All the time in the world for what I got to do.

The woman came in then. She had red hair and pale smooth skin.

I take it that this is the secret of life, Marshall said.

Name's Argenteen, the man said, and I'm her husband Pink Miracle. We're pleased to meet you.

They stood out from the usual run of customers he had in the cafe. After that, they were regular, coming in late in the mornings, before the blueplate-special crowd came in. Grits and gravy, they said. Biscuits and butter. Eggs and bacon. Could they ever eat! And, after that first week, they paid up on the spot.

They had them a job playing at the Arcadia Ballroom on Grand and Walker. Plowboy, Pink called himself, Plowboy Pink Miracle, who learned himself the fiddle on the sly out in his daddy's barn back in Arkansas when he should've been milking, taught himself "Sally Goodin," which he had heard his Uncle Laclede play a hundred times.

Argenteen was a singer. She sure didn't look like anybody's wife. In Arkansas, for example, she would have stood out like a sore thumb, and even in Oklahoma City she was pretty unusual. It wasn't just her red hair, nor the way she clipped it short and set it in smooth waves that gave her motion. Nor was it entirely in her manner of dress, the short skirts coming to be common enough, and the fringed shawls, the rows of beads, the rhinestone brooches, the turquoise earrings. No, it wasn't something you could put your finger on, it was the whole woman, her voice as if always close to singing.

Marshall had music in him too. He could sing and he could play the piano. Only he didn't have a piano at this time, and Jane didn't care for his singing. Even when it was a hymn she didn't like it, said he made it sound sorrowful.

It was lively being around Pink and Argenteen Miracle. On Saturday nights he closed the cafe early and went with them to the Arcadia Ballroom. I'll tell you, Marshall Monroe, Argenteen said, you better be glad you're attached.

One day, when he was alone with her in the cafe, she said: Marshall, come here. I want to show you something. Have you got a mirror in this place.

He did not. What use did he have for a mirror in the cafe.

It's all right, she said. I've got one. Look here.

She took a small mirror from her purse. It was round, in a gilded frame.

Look in it, she said. Tell me what you see.

Myself, he said.

Sure. Now look at me.

She took something from the depth of her purse, and before he knew it, she had touched him with it, touched his eyelids.

Hold still now, Marshall. This ain't going to kill you.

She had come in that evening by herself. Pink was playing his fiddle, she said, he was rehearsing. She needed no rehearsing. What I sing, she said, I sing from the heart. It has to be taken by surprise. Otherwise it hides, it sulks.

What she held was like a thick pencil with black lead. Just charcoal, she told him, stroking his eyelids. Now look.

He looked into the mirror.

Ain't that a sight better, Marshall? Now look, I'm going to show you another trick.

And she took the pencil, blacked his thin mustache, had him look again in the mirror. His eyes stared back at him as if from dark pools, black jewels shining, the line above his lip like a strand of jewels too, aglow in its improved blackness.

Damn sight better, she said, ain't it.

How white his teeth looked, how pink his lips.

It's nothing to be embarrassed about, she said. It ain't that you wasn't lovely to begin with. Now you are lovelier, that's all.

She gave him the charcoal, told him he could do it himself thereafter, and he did, every Saturday night before going to the Arcadia Ballroom, leaving straight from the cafe, where he had tacked up a mirror in the back room and made a little shelf beneath for the blacking pencil. Before he went home, he stopped by the cafe and washed it all off in the dish sink, rubbing with a dishrag and drying with a dish towel.

You smell like soap, Jane said one night as he settled in beside her in the bed. But she made nothing of it, turned over once and fell back asleep, breathing heavy. She knew he went out Saturday nights. It was no secret and why should it be. There was no harm in it.

It's your soul, she said, not mine.

He dreamed he sat in the center of a cave. Next to him was Little Brother—his only son, dead not even a year—only bigger than in life, his long feet planted firm on a flat rock. He could talk, of course, only he would say nothing, no matter what you asked him. Marshall had plenty of questions.

Where you been all this time.

What do you think you are doing.

Who do you think you are.

Little Brother just stood there, him that in life had never grown big enough to stand. A tall fellow he had become on this rock, his shoulders broad, his arms long and lean, too long for the shirt he wore, the sleeves way up on his wrist, nearly to the elbows, the wrists thin and with the twisting veins protruding, throbbing before your very eyes. It was light in the cave, and he wondered where the light came from, then saw his father holding an electric bulb in the palm of his hand. The bulb blazed with light. You ain't seen the last of me, his father said.

He woke and there was Argenteen. It was almost as if she were there with him, warm and soft in the bed. He got up immediately. It was time, the sun breaking through, the room rapidly lightening, Jane already up, he could hear her in the kitchen, her heavy footsteps, the clink of plates. Argenteen! He must not think of her that way, her hands, her bright red fingernails, the curve of her ankle. She leaned close to him, touching his eyelids with the charcoal. Don't move now, she said, and she raised her free hand to his cheek, steadying him. I'm not going anywhere, he said, I'm real steady.

At the Arcadia Ballroom she walked honest to God like a song, the light singing from her silver patent leather shoes. Through the crowd of dancers she moved toward the stage at the far end of the hall, where Plowboy Pink announced through the megaphone what a treat everyone had in store for them, what a special treat, the fairest flower, a sweet bouquet, the honey of New Arlins, Queen of Arcadia, a Looze-anna songbird come down from her perch in the swaying pines to sing for you, just for you, yessir, nobody else but you, so let's give her a hand, what do you say, let's make the little lady feel right welcome!

Marshall clapped so hard his hands stung.

Mornings, standing behind the counter, peeling potatoes, chopping onions, he seemed in the middle of a dream. His mama kept coming to mind.

What do you mean to do with yourself, she had asked him.

I mean, he told her, to study butchering.

You'll not forget your soul, Marshall. You'll take care of your soul, won't you.

It would take care of itself, willy-nilly, he believed, but he told her yes, sure, he would look to its health, see that it don't fail.

Don't be like your daddy, she said, always needing to prove himself. Looking after your soul don't have a thing to do with proving yourself. If you think so, Son, you've got another think coming. You've got it backwards. Look to your soul and you will see what you are made of. Flesh and blood. The better you know your soul, the more proof you have that you count for very little. If anything counts less, it's the good opinion of others. I would like to have a nickel for every time I've tried to explain that to your father. Do you understand me, Son.

I understand, Mama.

He did understand. It was his own heart she spoke of, his own desire, which was why the butchering trade would suit him just fine, whatever put food on the table while the soul of him found its own nourishment.

What counts, Son, is the love that is in you. You've got it in you whether you want it or not. It's what your soul gives you. It's the closest you can come to knowing your soul.

He didn't like it when she talked of love. He was willing to admit she knew something of the soul, but what inkling could she have of love, who had lived with his father the best part of her life. Love was for him, Marshall Monroe, to discover. It would come in its own time and in a way peculiar to him. It might nourish his soul and it might not. He knew enough of it already to know that it might also have something to do with flesh and blood, with knowing his body, with being known in it.

Already in those days, his mama speeding merrily towards her last illness, he had his eye on Jane Bagley. He had known her and her family all his life, but had only noticed her of late. Among the first words he remembered her saying to him was, Have you repented, Marshall Monroe. It was no question. She stood beneath a big maple tree, she wore a white dress and white shoes, she had a grand tortoise shell comb that held her long hair in a rising curve in back. The camp meeting was over, the evangelist gone, the believers standing in clumps beneath the limbs and leaves of the generously branching oak and sweet gum trees, the men tall and stiff in their dark suits, high collars, the women plump and shiny, the shape of bells in their long skirts.

There ain't nothing like a good hymn, he said to her.

Yes, she said, but there's some that can't carry a tune in a bucket, and I'm one of them.

No, he said, that's not true. I heard you singing.

That wasn't me. That was Lavon Belle Ennis. She was standing next to me. God gave her the purest, sweetest voice. And he gave me something that is a cross between a cow and a frog.

You sing just fine, he said, not knowing why he said it, certain that she spoke the truth, since she brought it up, and that he had mistook Lavon Belle's high ringing voice for Jane's. Lavon Belle was as broad as an outhouse, thick-waisted and with short stout legs. The daughter of Octavius Ennis, who owned a good half of Blue Mountain, no small part of Waveland, and some of Danville, Lavon Belle had taken piano and voice lessons in Fort Smith since she was three years old. It hadn't hurt her none.

Well, he said to Jane, you sing with genuine feeling. I know that for a fact.

Thank you, she said. It's a shame that feeling counts for so little. But I know you meant that as a compliment.

He had, yes, for even if it hadn't been her voice that he heard, it was her soul delivered up by the music, the heart and blood of her that came forth when Lavon Belle sang This world is not my home, I'm just apassing through, My treasures are laid up somewhere beyond the blue.

He liked her heft and height and how shy she was, as if nobody never touched her the way he did—and maybe nobody had. There was something else too, who could say just what it was. This world is not my home, she'd sang. Could be it wasn't his either.

It was Argenteen that said, in the fall of that year, Marshall Monroe, look here, what is keeping you in this cafe? If you are making any money at it, I don't see how. You give away as much food as you sell.

In fact, he had begun to tire of the work. What had kept him going all that summer was the knowledge that every morning and evening he would see Argenteen and Pink, and then Saturday night would roll around. The rest of it was not so good. He'd be the first to admit it. He was too far from Packingtown to count on that trade, and Oklahoma City was loaded with cafes and hamburger joints. Last spring, before Pink and Argenteen came along, he had considered returning to the meatcutting business. He was good at that, he knew, and any of the big grocery stores —Morgan Ferrill's, say, or the Piggly-Wiggly—could always use a good meatcutter. It would be steady work and decent pay. He'd be working for someone else though, keeping time by somebody else's clock. That made a difference, a big difference.

Nonetheless Jane had urged him to do it. The cafe would be the death of him, she said. It would work him to the bone.

And Argenteen said, I'd go where the trade is brisk, if I was you.

And she showed him the articles in the *Daily Oklahoman* about the boomtowns out in the oil fields. Fortunes were made daily. Gushers blowing. Roustabouts and roughnecks by the hundreds and thousands swarming those oil fields. Towns went from a hundred souls to a thousand, a thousand to ten thousand, almost overnight. And what was the first necessity for a workingman—food. He wanted a square meal. If he was an oilfield worker, chances are he had the cash to buy him a good supper in a nice clean cafe.

Maybe so, he said, but—

No *buts* about it, nor *ands* nor *ifs*. What a fellow has to do is get in on the ground floor. After that, it's no use. Sign yourself to a grocer and cut up hogs and cows and cows and hogs to your heart's content.

There's more to it than that.

Can you name me one rich meatcutter, Marshall?

I can name you plenty that's making decent wages.

Comes a time you have got to find out what you are made of. Are you of common clay or what.

Common clay, yes, common as it comes. Was there any other kind? Some might think better of theirselves, but comes a time when the truth is told.

You know what I'm talking about, she said. What makes one man sink, another rise. The will to do something, that's what. Wanting more than you have—now, hear me out. You know I'm not just talking about money. It's the same thing makes Pink play such a pretty fiddle. Listen to that music. Where do you think that sound comes from. Not just from the horsehair and the catgut and the pieces of wood. I draw the very same bow across the very same strings, and the sound I get sure don't sound like the sound Pink gets. You try it sometime and see.

Pink's not rich, is he.

Doesn't matter. There's some things you do, you don't worry about money. The money will take care of itself.

Meatcutting isn't one of those things.

That's right. Neither is running a cafe the way you do. Running a cafe and not caring about money would be like playing the fiddle and not worrying about how it sounds.

There's a lot of things Pink doesn't worry about.

I'm not talking about Pink. I'm talking about you.

You were comparing me to him, if I remember correctly.

Just to make a point. And what do you mean, there's a lot he doesn't care about?

Worry about. I said worry about.

What are you getting at, Marshall Monroe.

Nothing. Not a thing.

If you mean he don't care about me, you're dead wrong, mister.

Okay.

Because he certainly does care about me. Yes, he does.

Okay.

Why would you think such a thing anyway.

Never mind. I never said I thought it, did I?

Just because he leaves me alone from time to time, is that it. Just because he leaves me alone with you, is that what you're driving at.

I wasn't driving at nothing.

Don't you think he ought to trust you, a married man and a father of two sweet little daughters. Wouldn't you imagine that he might believe you was a safe companion and a good friend, if anybody was.

You can leave my daughters out of it.

I can, can I.

I'd appreciate it, yes.

Pink came in then. What time was it, so close to midnight? Must have lost track of the time, getting into a argument, what a waste of time with Argenteen. She could out-talk the devil, wheedle her way into heaven.

Hello, kids, Pink said. How's my sweethearts, how's my honey lambs.

Take your hat off when you come inside. Didn't your mama teach you nothing.

Beg pardon, ma'am.

Pink wore a broad-brim, high-crown white Stetson with a Ft. Worth crease and a beaded band, and he lifted it gingerly from his head, holding onto it with both hands, his fingers just touching the edge of the brim.

Fellow give this to me. May you wear it always in good health, he said. Ain't it pretty.

Pink leaned close to the counter, squinting his eyes, then set the hat down carefully.

Clean enough, he said, for a queen's ass.

No plate has touched that counter for hours, Argenteen said.

Well, I'll be. Where's the clientele this evening, Marshall.

Elsewhere, Argenteen said. Same as always.

Never much after the supper hour, Marshall said.

Nor before. Nor during.

Well, now. I'll tell you what, Marshall, you're looking at one hungry old plowboy. What's on the menu.

You can't hit your mouth with the fork, Argenteen said. How do you expect to get food in your belly.

I'm hungry. I'll have the chicken-fry platter. With mash potatoes and gravy. Green beans. What you want, honey. I bet the pork chops is good. Peach cobbler for dessert. Get whatever you want. It's not too late for supper, is it. You'll fix old Pink some supper, won't you.

This kitchen's always open.

That's the spirit. Isn't that the spirit, Argenteen.

You're the expert on spirits, honey.

Well, I say that's the spirit, then. Put on the chicken-fry, Marshall. And a pork chop for my baby. This is a very special night. This is a celebration.

What is there to celebrate.

Didn't I tell you. I thought I told you. Didn't I tell you when I came in the door?

You didn't tell me nothing.

I didn't? Well, can you beat that. Bet I didn't tell Marshall either then, did I.

You came in and put your hat on the counter.

The hat's part of the celebration.

What's going on, Pink honey.

You better sit down. This is big news.

I *am* sitting down. Lord.

You can listen to this too, Marshall. I want you to know. I want to share with you this golden moment.

Golden moment? What on earth are you talking about. What is a golden moment.

Honey, it's when I tell you we're going to California, that's what it is. We are going to the Golden State. Now I've told you and so this is our golden moment, we are in it right now, all three of us. Don't it feel fine.

Marshall couldn't say that it did. Not exactly, no. He began to fix Pink's supper.

Man gave me this hat, Pink said. Told me to keep it as a token of his good faith.

Did he give you any hard cash, Argenteen wondered.

That don't matter, between two gentlemen. He gave me the hat off his head.

Honest deal or not, the next day Pink and Argenteen were gone.

. . .

He stopped going to the Arcadia Ballroom on Saturday nights. Argenteen sent him a postcard from Amarillo, another from Albuquerque. Thank you for the swell times, she wrote on the first one. Signed, Argenteen. The second said, Crossed some mountains to get here. Pink is fine. Yours truly, Argenteen. Then he didn't hear for a while. Business at the cafe was very bad, and he thought again of what Argenteen had said. Some sink, some rise. She would go out to one of those oil-field towns, she would, and set up her business where there was plenty of hungry men with cash in their pockets.

Later that fall Jane's brother George and his family came through Oklahoma City. They had done with their harvesting and were on the way out to the cotton fields of Grady County, where they all could find good work.

It's good money, George said. I'm as fast as anybody alive, and Mildren and Monroe here are getting pretty quick theirselves. There's four or five harvests in this country, you know. A good long growing season. Cotton likes hot weather.

We got plenty of that, Jane said.

Maybe we ought to go along, Marshall said. Maybe we ought to get some of that easy money.

Well, Marshall, George said, if you don't mind my saying so, those two girls of yours, they are not going to be worth as much in the fields as my Mildren and Monroe. They are mighty sweet girls, but they are city girls.

I bet I can keep up with Mildren, Cora Mae said.

Mildren sat cross-legged next to her on the pallet they had laid down on the floor. He and Monroe had a red rubber ball that they rolled back and forth to each other, and now and then Cora Mae tried to intercept it.

I'd sure like to see them two out in the fields, Mildren said. Wouldn't that be a sight. Cora Mae, you'd get your hands dirty.

Who cares.

There's snakes in them fields too.

That's enough, Mildren. This is grownup talk.

George thought, after considerable talk, that the risk of the oil-field camps might be the better risk for Marshall. You had to take risks, no matter what your line of work. A farmer knew that better than anybody else.

This isn't farming, Jane said.

She had read about the killings and the robbery in those oil towns. No one was mentioning that. No one was saying a word about the low life that went on in towns the likes of Bowlegs, Maud, and Cromwell.

You know what they say about Maud, Mildren said.

What? asked Cora Mae.

You have to go through Bowlegs to get to her.

Mildren, not another word out of you!

Things go on in them cotton-field camps too, Sister, George said. It's not always the best people picking cotton. They bring them in by the truckload. Some're from Arkansas, I guess, but you can't imagine where they drug up the rest.

He's not going, Jane said.

He did go, for all that, though lessening the risk by not selling the cafe. He let a boy that hung around a lot run it for him. One thing to be said about cotton picking, George had said, it cleans out your mind. A few hours in those furrows, that sack slung over your shoulders, you don't have a thought in your head except to keep moving, keep picking, and how hot that sun is and how good it is to have a hat on your head. Years later Marshall would remember that. When Cora Mae ran off and married Don Temple, Marshall remembered George's words and went to the cotton fields. Went down to California Street where the growers had their trucks, stood in a line of men that was a block long. One of the lucky ones, he got signed on the first day. But it wasn't as George had said. Hot, yes, but no sooner did he start moving down those long furrows than he thought of Argenteen. The slant of her ankle. Her red hair, short and wavy.

And then he remembered Blue Mountain, Arkansas, the little house up high on the ridge where Johnnie was born, Jane screaming as if the pain would kill her, later swearing there would never be another, a man could never understand, a man could never go through with it. And right then, at the very moment Johnnie came into this world, a cloud, white and cool, the edge of it anyway, passed through that house, from window to window, blown by a breeze. Johnnie Monroe was born. And her father, himself, Marshall Monroe, felt struck down with the pain and beauty.

He remembered the light beneath the closed door, the angle it made across the planks, light so mysterious and remote it might have come from a star. Get the water ready, the women had said. This woman, the midwife, had arrived atop a mule so small that her feet almost touched the ground. When the mule had stopped, she stayed in place so long that he began to think she meant for him to lift her off of it. Perhaps then she would walk into the house, perhaps she would require carrying. She wore overalls and men's boots and had thick white hair tied into a fist-sized knot at the nape of her neck. She had a mighty chest and broad shoulders and not a tooth in her head. When at last she removed herself from the mule, she walked right to the door without a word. She smelled just like a pine tree. Wait a minute, he said, what am I supposed to do.

You done your part, she said, but you can get the water ready if you want to.

It wasn't the same with Cora Mae, born in Danville. No cloud passed through the house, not even a breeze. No midwife arrived, but a doctor drove up in a shiny Oldsmobile and stepped down from the running board like a shot, his black bag in hand, his spectacles in place. He wore a black suit that smelled like coal oil and a derby hat that he handed to Marshall as he entered the house, breathing so heavily you would have thought he had run all the way. This time the water was ready. But he still wasn't ready for the scream. It blistered, it tore at him.

As soon as he saw Jane with that baby in her arms, he wanted her, could have slipped inside her in a minute, pushing the baby to one side, wasn't it asleep anyway, what would it care, dead to the world on its mama's milk.

He could never do that though. He knew well enough what Jane would have to say about such behavior. Oh, but that baby was sweet, not a thought in its head but when to suck, how much to take, how soon let go.

III

. . . .

Pit of Iniquity,
Distant Thunder

When Uncle George and Aunt Billie visited from Arkansas, bringing along the two boys, the twins Monroe and Mildren, all the cousins slept on pallets in the living room, close together on the hard wood floor. Cora Mae wondered at the twins. They were not like Oklahoma City boys. They talked with a thick slur, as if their teeth were in the way. They carried big jackknives and were always taking them out of their pockets, opening them up, tossing them into the trunks of trees. They chased Daddy's chickens. Why is it, Mildren said one night, girls don't seem to know nothing. They were stretched out on the pallets in the dark. You're the one that don't know nothing, Monroe said. Now this Cousin Johnnie, I believe she knows a good deal.

Well, said Mildren, if it comes to that, I'd say Cousin Cora Mae comes closer to knowing *something*.

Cora Mae, Johnnie said, do you think all Arkansas boys are rude, or just our cousins.

Just our cousins.

When you come visit us in Arkansas, I've got something to show you.

Oh, Mildren, I know what it is.

What is it, said Cora Mae. I don't know what it is.

See, Mildren said. See how dumb she is. Here I was just bragging on her too.

Shut up, Mildren. Go to sleep.

You go to sleep yourself, Monroe. I want to get to the bottom of this.

You are at the bottom, boy. Rock bottom.

You're so smart, Johnnie, then tell me what it is I'm going to show you when you come to Danville.

Same thing you always show us. A snake. You always say you have something to show us, and that's what it always is. Some old dead snake, hanging from a tree.

Maybe I got something else this time.

Oh, I doubt it. Same old thing, I'll bet.

We're not coming to Arkansas this summer anyway, Cora Mae said.

Yes, you are. We're taking you back with us. Ain't we, Monroe.

I'm not talking no more. Go to sleep, boy.

He don't know nothing anyway. I'm the one Daddy told. Said to me, Mildren, he said, how'd you like to take those two little cousins of yours home with us.

What'd you say, Cora Mae asked.

I said that'd be just fine. And Daddy says, You think you can teach them a thing or two. Yes, sir, says I. I believe I can.

Cora Mae lay awake for the longest time. The boys breathed heavily in their sleep, if in fact they were asleep. The floor was hard, even with the pallet, and it was not easy getting comfortable. Johnnie, she whispered, but Johnnie didn't answer, had already fallen asleep. The room was dark, and yet you could see just fine, even the crack in the ceiling, the cord hanging from the window shade, its little circle turning, and the rocker that Mama had fed Little Brother in. Cora Mae wasn't afraid of the boys. She could look at them and not be the least bit afraid, turn on her side so that she could see them clearly, their long legs, their feet sticking off the pallet, such skinny toes, she could easily touch those long skinny toes with her own if she wanted to, once she was sure the boys were sound asleep. Mildren had just been teasing about taking her and Johnnie home with him. And the snake—Johnnie was right. Cora Mae remembered last Thanksgiving, when Mama had taken them to Uncle George's on the train, Daddy staying home to keep the restaurant open, and Mildren had said, Cora Mae, come here quick, and it was sure enough a snake, right there in the barn, but before she could think to scream, he swung a hoe and cut the snake in two. Just a old black snake, he said. Won't bother you if you leave him alone. They're all over the place. You have to look where you're stepping all the time.

Poison?

Naw. He's a pretty one. And awful nice to touch. You want to feel of him? He can't hurt you now. A fellow over in Waveland has him a shirt made out of a rattler's skin. Says it won't never wear out.

He was four years older than her. I'll be taller than my daddy, he said. I know it. I'm already taller than he was my age. He told me so himself.

She wondered why Mildren didn't look more like Monroe if they were twins. They had the same color hair, light brown with a reddish cast to it in the light, and were about the same height, but Mildren was skinnier, so that he looked taller even though when the two of them stood next to each other you could see that he wasn't. Monroe had a fuller face, his nose flatter and his lips bigger. They neither of them had the Bagley hazel eyes. Their eyes were blue, like their mother's. In a foot race Mildren always outran Monroe. So lean, he just looked faster, and walked with a long brisk stride whereas Monroe ambled, dawdled.

They aren't identical, Mother said. Some twins are identical, some aren't. Mildren and Monroe aren't.

Uncle George and Aunt Billie had four other children, three

sons and a daughter, but these were grown up and married, with farms of their own or else, in the case of the daughter Georgi-anna, a nice house in Little Rock. Mildren and Monroe were the babies of the family, Aunt Billie was fond of saying. Maybe once we was, Mildren said, but we are steadily improving. Uncle George laughed and cuffed him on the back of the head.

Cora Mae didn't mind all Mildren's teasing. She guessed she liked him all right and didn't mind tagging along after him when, the summer after that, she and Johnnie rode the train to Arkansas all by themselves and stayed at Uncle George's farm for three whole weeks. And when he called out, Come here, Cora Mae, I got something to show you, and led her into an empty stall in the barn, dark and musty and cool, she didn't mind that either.

It's taking a risk, all right, said Uncle George on that earlier occasion, but sometimes you got to run a risk if you want to end up with anything at all.

He spoke slowly, his speech thicker with Arkansas than even that of the twins.

Farming's one risk after another, you know, Marshall.

This isn't farming he's talking about, George.

I know it isn't, Sister. It's similar, is all I'm saying.

Nothing at all similar. I've heard of them oil-field camps.

You've heard—what you've heard, Daddy said, is what the preacher's said, that's what you've heard.

Tell me it's not greed that keeps them going. Tell me it's not avarice keeps them oil-field camps alive.

I won't tell you nothing at all. You already know it.

Now, Marshall, Sister's got her point of view.

Don't she though.

Daddy went out to the oil-field town of Cromwell, Mama's point of view or not. Cora Mae didn't care for the idea of Daddy going away, leaving her and Johnnie alone with Mama. Two fool things he's done in the last year, Mama said, buried Little Brother in Arkansas and chased off to a God-forsaken place called Cromwell. If Mama was so against the place, it must be at least interesting, Cora Mae figured, and she wished that he might have considered taking her along. Instead, he had called her and Johnnie out to his garden, sat them down on the bench he'd made out of the interior of the old commode, and said, Girls, I want you to be good to your mama. She will need all the help you can give her, and no hindrance, hear. You're big girls now, young ladies, your daddy's pride and joy.

Johnnie started to cry, and so Daddy took her in his arms, there among the pole beans and tomatoes, and it was such a pretty thing to see, Daddy holding back the tears himself as he stroked Johnnie's head, that Cora Mae began to feel the tears coming to her eyes too. Daddy reached out and took hold of her hand, gave it a nice squeeze, Johnnie still sobbing on his shoulder. It'll be all right, Daddy wanted to say, but his eyes—those black eyes set back deep—his eyes said he knew better, nothing ever came out all right, one thing after another, honey, might as well get used to it, this is only the beginning.

That was a long autumn, 1924, the wind gusting up so hard it might have been March instead of October. Daddy had a man working the restaurant for him, but it was Cora Mae and Johnnie's responsibility to take care of Daddy's garden and feed his chickens. Long into October the heat kept up, the crops kept coming in, and dust might blow up into your eyes while you weeded around the potato hills or carried water to the turnip greens. At last Mama had them canning string beans and black-eyed peas and tomatoes, putting up Mason jar after Mason jar out on the enclosed back porch, where Little Brother's crib served as an extra shelf and it was dark and cool. Mama pickled red beets and cucumbers, the kitchen steamy and vinegary, and showed the girls how to make a sweet relish out of peppers and onions.

It was not as bad as Cora Mae had imagined, Daddy's being

gone to Cromwell. Mama didn't seem as short-tempered as before. She was quieter, even gave orders in a softer voice, and once said, You girls have been a blessing. Your daddy would be proud of you.

In school Cora Mae did her lessons but also fell often to daydreams. She tried to imagine Daddy in Cromwell, behind the counter of his restaurant in his white apron, serving platters of ribs and creamed corn to the oil-field workers, who would have muddy boots, streaks of oil on their hands and faces, and dusty bandannas around their necks. It was a thrill when letters from Daddy came, but the letters never told her enough. Girls, Mama called, here's a letter from Cromwell come today. And she had the girls sit on the couch while she, in the rocker, read aloud the portions of the letter that concerned them. Is that all, Cora Mae asked. Didn't he say more than that? The rest is not your business, young lady, Mama said, but she said it softly and almost smiled as she refolded the letter and tucked it back away in its envelope. A few times he wrote directly to Cora Mae and Johnnie. Today it was mighty hot, Daddy wrote. Yesterday we had a hard rain. There are more cafes than you can shake a stick at. A lot of the roustabouts are camping out in tents. It is a rough town and no place for two sweet little girls. Your daddy sure does miss you. Be good and help your mama.

The weather turned cold and rainy, Christmas three weeks away.

He won't come home, Mama said one morning, why then we'll go see him.

When? Cora Mae asked.

Bring me your clothes. We'll pack right now. Don't just sit there like bumps on a log. Run on now. We're going to Cromwell.

In one letter Daddy had written, It won't do for you to come here. Cora Mae didn't remind Mama of that. She wouldn't have brought up the subject of school either, didn't need to. What about school, Johnnie asked, and Cora Mae could have yanked

Johnnie's hair out, but Mama just said, There are things more important than school.

They walked to Avenue C to catch the streetcar downtown, Cora Mae and Johnnie taking turns holding the suitcase, Mama carrying the box of fried chicken. The wind was brisk and had sleet in it.

Can get you only as far as Seminole, the ticket agent at the train station said. You'll have to get somebody to haul you out to Cromwell from there.

If we get that far, Mama said, I imagine we can get the rest of the way, even if we have to walk.

Cora Mae and Johnnie had seats to themselves. Mama was one row up and across the aisle. She sat very straight and still, the shoebox in her lap. The train jerked to a start and then, once they were out of the city, made a high humming sound. Other passengers were mostly men. Many wore blue work shirts. They leaned back and puffed on cigarettes. Some went to sleep, even though it was the middle of the day. When one saw Cora Mae looking at him, he said, Want a smoke, girlie, then grinned, pushing his tongue through the space where his two front teeth should have been.

Roughnecks, Johnnie whispered. These men must be roughnecks.

Or roustabouts, Cora Mae said.

What's the difference?

How should I know?

Soon you could see oil derricks, the horizon filled with them in some places, black and tall against the gray sky, pointed at the top. Then the derricks were closer to the tracks, and you could see the big hammerlike bars off to one side, pumping steadily. What would it be like to climb to the top of one of those derricks, Cora Mae wondered. There seemed to be a little platform near the top, with a railing around it like a porch so that you might stand and see a long ways.

The sleet had stopped by the time they got to Seminole and the air had warmed. It must have been about three in the afternoon. Almost everybody got off the train there and now milled around in the station, which was small and crowded, with a coal stove in the middle and only a few benches. Sit here, Mama said, and don't you move an inch. She put the suitcase under the bench but sticking out enough so that Cora Mae had to rest her feet on it. The shoebox of fried chicken she handed to Johnnie. Eat something, she said, while I see if I can find us a ride to Cromwell.

Didn't that chicken hit the spot! But no sooner had they begun than Mama came back. Come on, she said, we've got a ride. Get a move on, it won't wait forever.

Mama and Daddy didn't have a car—would never get one even if they had the money, Cora Mae knew for a fact—and so riding in one was almost as thrilling as the train. This was a spacious car with a snug-fitting cream-colored top, a broad running board, and a long low front end. You might see Douglas Fairbanks in such a car, on his way to the ball, where Clara Bow awaited him, silken and languid. Hop in, ladies, their driver said to Cora Mae and Johnnie. He had cinnamon-colored skin and wore a dark blue jacket with short red fringe at the bottom. Is he an Indian, Cora Mae whispered to Mama, but Mama just shushed her. Sitting in front with the driver was one of the roughnecks. He wore a low-crowned felt hat with the brim turned down all the way around. Any day now, John, he said to the driver. Had to strap down the ladies' luggage, John said. We'll get there soon enough, friend. They ain't sucked up all the oil yet, fella, no siree.

The road was bumpy at first, then muddy, the car sliding from time to time, and soon they felt the rear end sinking, the tires spinning and whining. The roughneck had to get out and push, then run up alongside and jump onto the running board, which he accomplished, Cora Mae thought, in a dashing and graceful manner.

Godamighty, John, he said, you'll have us off in a ditch.

May be some oil there, fella, hey!

Three more times the car got stuck in the mud. Godamighty, the roughneck said each time he hopped back into the car.

At last the driver said, Here we are, ladies. Cromwell. Used to be nothing here at all, no road, nothing. Now, look what you see.

It was a wide Main Street, deeply rutted and muddy, lined with cars. All along on both sides were narrow frame buildings, one right up against the other, mostly single story, and in back of some of them you could see oil derricks, so close they looked as if they rose up clear through the roofs. Such a lot of buildings, and so small, with tin awnings extending over a plank sidewalk, big signs above the awnings: O. K. Casing Crew, Tulsa Cafe, H. S. Drugs, Palace Hotel, Club Cafe, Jennings Casing Crew. The entranceways looked dark, shaded by the awnings, the day itself fast darkening, the sun somewhere back of the thick clouds setting as it always did, earlier and earlier. There was motion in the shadows, plenty of it. Climbing out of the car, stepping across the mud and onto the plank sidewalk, Cora Mae saw that the dark motion was made everywhere by men such as had lounged about in the Seminole station, lean and tall, certainly taller than Daddy, grim-looking, some with thick mustaches that hid their mouths. A lot of them smoked, or else spit, propped themselves against a post and looked across the street at other men doing the same. Bootheels thumped against the sidewalk. There was a muddy smell in the air, almost sweet, and a chill, but the wind had died down and so you did not feel the cold.

Mama gave the driver some money, and then he unstrapped the suitcase from the back and set it before them on the sidewalk.

Take care of them two little girls, he said in a low voice, and you find you that man real quick, hear, before it gets dark.

I know where I am, Mama said.

Cora Mae saw the sign that Mama must have already spotted. Johnnie's Restaurant, the same name he called his cafe in Okla-

homa City. Ribs, the sign in the window said. Cornbread and
Buttermilk. A little bell sang out when they entered.

Daddy was back of the grill, sure enough. Well, I'll be, he said,
turning towards them, his face catching the light. The place was
smaller than the one in Oklahoma City, just a countertop with
stools, six or eight of them, and behind it the grill and sink. One
man sat at the counter, at the end closest to the grill. He had a
coffee cup before him and smoked a cigarette.

Marshall, said Mama.

Well, I'll be, Daddy said again.

He looked smaller than Cora Mae had remembered him,
shorter and thinner, and he had dark shadows around his eyes
and silvery bristles on his chin and cheeks. His thick black hair
looked shiny, pressed flatter and running across the top of his
head as if without benefit of comb or mirror, the part angling
this way and that. But his white shirt and black bow tie looked
fresh as ever, and she knew that if you touched that shirt you'd
see how stiff with starch it was, just like always.

We've come to see you, Mama said.

So I see.

I know you didn't want us—

I said not to come, didn't I. I said stay away, this is no place
for a family.

Yes, you did.

Where do we put our things, Daddy?

Well, I'll tell you, you can put them right back onto what they
came here on, and then put yourself there too, because you're not
staying.

We're not.

That's right. That's what I said.

He looked away from them, seemed to see something out the
window.

It's no place for women, he said. It ain't safe.

That's God's truth, the man at the counter said. Sure as you're born. The ladies here you don't want to associate with. I can tell you aren't their kind, ma'am. And look at these sweet girls here. I'll say! Marshall, are these yours?

They're his all right, Mama said, and they're not going any-where.

Home, he said, that's where they're going.

Show me where to put this suitcase, Marshall.

He showed her. Directed them around the counter and into the back of the restaurant, where he had a cot just like the one he had in Oklahoma City. There was a wash basin—no mirror, sure enough—and a chifferobe shorter on one side than the other. An oil lamp sat atop a crate that had a picture of palm trees on the side of it. The floor planks had wide gaps between them. A door was bolted shut, and through the single window, a tiny one that ran alongside the ceiling, wider than it was long, you could see a thick dark pole, going up and down: an oil well, Cora Mae was certain. She was seeing an oil well up close for the first time, and if she stepped through that door she would be able to see all of it and perhaps climb to the top of the derrick. You could hear it pumping, steady as your heart, going deep and deeper into the bedrock of the earth.

We'll spread a pallet on the floor, Mama said. We won't in-convenience you.

You'll be gone tomorrow, Daddy said.

Then Mama was in his arms, a sight to see, him so much smaller, you almost couldn't see him, just those thin little arms around Mama's broad shoulders, and the sobbing starting up, no telling which one or if both, it didn't really matter, Cora Mae figured, loving them so much at that moment that she believed her heart might burst from the joy of it, and Johnnie tugging at her hand, saying, Come on, we better watch the restaurant.

I want to show you something, Daddy said the next morning. He had locked the door of the restaurant and left the Closed sign in the window. He held onto Johnnie's hand, and with his other gripped the suitcase. Mama carried the shoebox, packed now with a supply of Daddy's cornbread and ribs, along with the leftover fried chicken. In the next block, he had a car waiting to take them to Seminole.

I want you to see what kind of place this is.

They followed him on the sidewalk, past the clusters of staring men, the wind stiff and cold, stinging your cheeks. At the end of the block, Daddy stopped. Look there, he said, nodding his head towards a lone tree that stood just back of another cafe on the opposite side of the street from where they looked. Cora Mae saw more men, all in a line that began at the tree, maybe a dozen of them. Except for their being in line, Cora Mae didn't see anything unusual about these men. They looked pretty much like the others, their hats pulled down low, boots muddy, but then she saw the chain. They were all connected by a chain that ran along the ground from the tree and up to the wrists of each man, held on there by thick iron cuffs. The men huddled close together, must have been cold standing in the open like that.

Last night's crop of thieves and murderers, Daddy said. They're rounded up like that every month or so if somebody remembers, and then marched off to Wewoka to jail.

Why aren't they put in jail right here, Mama asked.

No jail. Not in Cromwell. Dance halls and taverns, but nobody's had time to stop and build a jail. Did you see that oil tank on the edge of town when you came in yesterday?

Didn't notice it, Mama said.

Found a man dead in it last week, pulled him out of there and he was black as pitch, coated with oil.

The pit of iniquity, Mama said. I told you what you was coming to, Marshall.

Oh, it's awful all right. You dassn't step outside for a smoke at night for fear of some mischief.

It's greed does it. I told you, Marshall.

Yes, and I told you to stay away, didn't I now. I told you it was no place for a woman and family.

And he led them to the waiting car—it was the same driver as before—and saw that they got in it and stood there in the street waving goodbye. Cora Mae watched through the back window until she couldn't see him anymore, and then she watched the oil derricks, which with the motion of the car seemed to be striding right back to Cromwell as fast as they could.

Pit of iniquity or not, the whole town of Cromwell went up in flames not long after that. Too much oil, all at once. It came gushing out of the wells and rained back down, thick and dark and shiny, on all the shanties that made up the town. Once the fire started, it spread fast. So Daddy was home by Christmas.

If I had been a driller, he said, it might have been different. Fortunes were made there, I know. You could almost smell the money.

Brimstone, Mama said. Brimstone, that's what you could smell.

Cora Mae remembered the men on the streets of Cromwell, the dark motion they made, shaded by the broad tin awnings, back of them the tall oil derricks. She dreamed of the men chained to the tree. In her dream she was chained with them, and the chain led from the oil vat in which the dead man floated, to a tree that rose taller than a derrick into the flaming sky.

In the autumn of the year after Daddy's return from Cromwell, two years after the death of Little Brother, Sarah Jane was born. She cried a lot at first, and Mama was glad to have Johnnie or Cora Mae take over the rocking, feeding, and amusing of the baby, whereas she had kept Little Brother to herself. Cora Mae didn't like taking care of Sarah Jane nearly so much as Johnnie did. You would have thought Sarah Jane was Johnnie's own child instead of her baby sister, and Daddy called her his little mama. Oh, Johnnie was his favorite, no question.

The boys flocked around Johnnie. What was her secret. Cora Mae studied her and learned from her. She was pleased to note that her own eyes were very nearly the same color as Johnnie's. Their hazel eyes had come from Mama's side of the family. Grandma Bagley had them. Look at her close, Mama said, and you'll see. You've got your Grandma Bagley's eyes. But look at Grandma Bagley close and she was like as not to wink at you and then pull her false teeth out to scare you, see if she could make you run away, then laugh until she almost choked and you thought she would die then and there.

You've got Mama's skin, Johnnie told Cora Mae. It's so white. I'm like Daddy. Swarthy. I wish I had skin as fair as yours.

She could very well have it, as far as Cora Mae was concerned. It did her no good, not when she had the Bagley nose, little more than a stub, and these sad excuses for lips, the lower puffed out and the upper sucked in.

Cora Mae studied the way Johnnie would smile at a boy and then look away, usually at the ground. She studied the way Johnnie walked, so briskly, almost like a man, no mincing swing to it, as if she knew exactly where she was going (she seld m did, though—Cora Mae knew this for a fact). Johnnie's hands, too, always seemed to know exactly where they were supposed to be, brushing back a strand of hair from her forehead, ever so delicately grazing her hip as she walked, or resting calmly in her lap when she sat, as if her fingers longed to touch each other and could do it only on the sly and softly, it was their secret.

None of this was done on purpose, understand. Johnnie could never have tried to control her charm, turn it on or off. It was who she was. She always knew just what to say, and said it in a way that made boys listen. In school she asked the question the teacher wanted to hear, gave the answer no one else could think of in time. With boys, she spoke when they hesitated, hesitated when they spoke.

Ain't it a fine day, one said to her, edging close, trying to let his dangling hand nuzzle hers as if accidentally.

I've known finer, Johnnie said, veering away from him. I like a day with clouds in the sky.

Oh, yes, he said. Clouds, sure.

Not just any clouds.

Oh, no. Some clouds are good, some bad.

Bad clouds? What do you mean, bad clouds?

Well, he said, rain clouds, for instance. I don't much care for rain. I don't care what the farmers say. Just muddies things up, in my opinion.

But don't you like the big thunderheads, the way they roll up and up, silvery domes rising in a blue, blue sky. And then comes the distant thunder, stately and grand. And the whoosh of wind with the smell of rain in it.

Blue skies I like, wind and rain I can do without.

The weather, honest to goodness, they were talking about nothing but the weather, and they would go on and on about it and at last the boy—Paul or Phil or Billy or Joe Ed—would drift away believing that he'd just had the most enthralling conversation. That Johnnie! Wasn't she some little talker, he'd say to his friends, and cute as she could be.

Cora Mae, Johnnie said later, I don't understand it. You know that Hill boy, Tom Bob? Well, we were walking along, carrying on a pleasant ordinary conversation about nothing in particular, just down the block from the restaurant, where Daddy was waiting for me to help him scour the pans, when out of the blue, Tom Bob grabs hold of my hand and squeezes it so hard I thought a bone snapped. And that's not all. Before I could catch my breath he yanked me close to him and actually, oh, Cora Mae, he actually kissed me.

Where, Cora Mae wondered.

Why, right there! Right in the middle of the sidewalk!

Johnnie, are you sure it wasn't nearer to the curb?

Oh, I don't know. Maybe it was. I don't remember.

Johnnie! On the cheek or on the lips?

Why, Cora Mae, what difference does that make. On the cheek, I think. Or maybe the neck. I think he meant the cheek, but hit the neck. I moved.

What difference did it make! Well, but no doubt Johnnie was right. It really didn't make a difference, the effort itself what counted. And how you went about inspiring such an effort.

You won't tell Mama, will you, Cora Mae?

She wouldn't, no, nor Daddy either. *Silvery domes, big thunderheads like silvery domes.* She would commit that to memory. *The distant thunder stately and grand.*

A handsome fellow in a suit and tie sat at the end of the counter, sipping on a Coke and eyeing Johnnie. He looked like he might have been Daddy's age until you noticed the peach fuzz above his lip. Cora Mae watched him from the sink in the kitchen. Johnnie wiped the counter as if she didn't see him— Cora Mae knew better. Grease sizzled on the grill where Daddy had pork chops going.

The man said to Johnnie, Say there, sweetheart. How're you anyway.

Oh, I've been better, Johnnie said.

Yeah?

Oh, yes. Maybe you can tell me the difference between a verb and a predicate. It beats me.

Well, now. I'll have to think about that.

Cora Mae bet he would. Her hands sunk in hot dishwater, she couldn't take her eyes off him. His bow tie was crooked, but he had the prettiest mouth and such eyes. He was making a loud noise with his straw in the Coke.

I don't know nothing about verbs, he said. I've given it some thought. I believe I heard of them, but that's as far as I get.

They're a part of speech.

Really.

Action words.

The best kind, in my book. Say, what's your name anyway, honey.

Johnnie.

Johnnie. Pleased to meet you, Johnnie. That's a nice name— Johnnie.

And who are you, mister.

Name's Don Temple.

Cora Mae thought he wasn't really looking at Johnnie now. He had seen her and was looking right past Johnnie. She hunched down, embarrassed, and looked down into the soapy water, but then had to glance up again to see. Looking right at her, yes, he was, grinning from ear to ear.

And who might *that* be, he said. Who is that sweetheart with her hands in the dishwater?

Cora Mae, Daddy said. Come over here.

He put her to work on the potatoes, in the back of the kitchen where she had to sit on a low stool facing a cinder block wall. Too late, though. The meaning of Don Temple's look was not lost on Cora Mae. What was to happen had happened.

A prisoner, she told herself, peeling the potatoes. A prisoner of love.

She was twelve years old.

Once or twice Daddy took Cora Mae and Johnnie downtown to the Criterion Theatre, where the lights on the ceiling twinkled high above like stars, the organist played "Sugar, Sugar" and "Satin Eyes," and then on the screen you saw men in tuxedos, black bow ties, patent leather shoes, and glazed black hair. They drove about in long low motorcars, danced in huge ballrooms, and loved women who were sleek and furry like cats, now clinging, now flitting away. All this took place elsewhere—never once in Oklahoma City.

Mama would never go to a movie. It's for them that's got no better task to do, she said. And then when Sarah Jane came along, she had that excuse. Johnnie offered to stay home with Sarah Jane, let Daddy take Mama to the movies, but Mama wouldn't hear of it. Picture shows was for them that had time and money to waste.

By the time Cora Mae was in the ninth grade, in 1929, she had had about enough of school. Johnnie got to quit because Daddy closed up his restaurant for lack of customers and then got so sick that he couldn't even look for other work. The day after quitting, Johnnie found work at Woolworth's downtown, and the money she brought in from that job put the food on the table. Cora Mae had to stay in school another year at least because she was the younger one. It was her privilege, Mama said. Seemed more like punishment. Johnnie got to rouge her cheeks and put on lipstick every morning, and then ride the streetcar downtown. Cora Mae had to walk to Capitol Hill Junior High, sit in hot rooms lorded over by frail, powdery ladies who would as soon have your head as not. She had to traipse the halls among a crowd of skinny boys and gangly, dazed girls who wouldn't give you the time of day. Queen Cora, they called her, when they troubled to notice her at all, mean-spirited, the lot of them, and worthy of her contempt. Johnnie had always had a bunch of girls around her, boys too, of course, but Cora Mae kept to herself, dreaming of Don Temple. A new high school that looked like a castle had been built on Grand Boulevard, but she hoped not ever to have to go there.

After Daddy's restaurant shut down, she saw Don Temple now and then on Avenue C, at the soda fountain in Goodner's or maybe standing in the doorway at Taylor's Billiard Parlor or looking at the movie posters in front of the Yale Theatre. He was always alone. He looked at her out of the corner of his eye and then, when he knew she saw him, tipped his hat, said, Nice day, Miss Monroe, as if she were responsible for it. He wore two-toned wingtip oxfords, navy blue and white, and favored white

straw hats with striped hat bands. When it turned cold, he wore a
thick blue serge ulster, a gray felt hat with the brim turned down
above his eyes, and a white scarf richly draped about his neck.
His mustache, so wispy and pale when he first came to Daddy's
restaurant, now had darkened to a nice reddish-brown strip as
pretty as a ribbon above his fine pink lips.

One day he was waiting for her after school, and then he was
there every day.

Nothing better to do, he said.

Sure I work, he said. I'm a working man. I pay my keep.

I live where I sleep, he said. I don't stay there long.

Little good it did her to ask him questions, she saw that. He
walked her home—as far as Shartel anyway, didn't want to make
her mama worry—and she told him what she wanted out of life,
happiness, was that too much to ask for, happiness for a time
anyway, even if only a short time, because once you'd had it you
could stand most anything, it would give you strength, didn't he
think so.

He did. You bet.

Only you had to take it, he said. It would not come to you of
its own accord. In fact the opposite would happen if you wasn't
careful.

Why was that so.

It was the way things was, and forever would be. He knew
that for a fact.

Once she asked him point blank if he came by his money
honestly.

No, he said, but I'm not a thief. I take the bread from no man's
table.

By then, she was beyond caring. She loved him and would have
loved him whether he robbed banks (which he did not) or sold
apples (he would never do it). That is the nature of love. Not
very rational, is it, when you stop to think about it.

IV

· ·

Transients

A mystery was Don Temple, even to himself.

You're no son of mine, his daddy told him. I rue the day you were born. A father's curse I place upon you. May you wander the world, homeless to the end.

I was considering leaving, Don said.

He was seventeen years old. It was Christmas Eve, 1927, as good a time as any to move on out into the world. He wasn't going to end up in no shoe store like his daddy, lacing up hightops for farmers, smiling like it thrilled him. He wasn't going to no church every Sunday either, sweat through sermon and hymn, then put his pocket money in the collection plate.

Your soul, Daddy said. You must look to your soul.

What was that anyway. Maybe he never got one to begin with.

So he lit out. He had the idea he might go to Oklahoma. He had a granddaddy lived there, also disowned. A wastrel, Don's daddy said of his own father. A profligate.

Couldn't be all bad, Don figured. But where was Oklahoma. He had no notion of the whereabouts of places.

Go to hell, his daddy said, but he didn't provide no map.

He lit out. He had saved up a little money, and when he told his mama how it was, she handed him some more, fifty dollars,

more than twice what he had. It was plenty. He could have paid
his fare and boarded a train, but he decided to hang onto the
money for a while and hop a freight. Proud of himself in the dark
swaying boxcar, though so cold he feared freezing to death, he
hardly slept a wink. Then morning came and he was found out,
clubbed, and thrown to the ground in a strange place.

What the hell.

At least it was someplace, with buildings taller than he'd ever
seen and a big train station. He went to the station and stood in
line at the ticket window. When his turn came, he said, Where
am I, mister.

Oklahoma City, the man said. Where do you want to go.

Nowhere in the world. I'm here.

Then step aside, son.

It was a miracle. He had begun in Missouri and now here
he was in Oklahoma. It was fate. A miracle. He would find his
granddaddy, a wastrel like himself, a profligate, but first he must
rest his head, which ached from the clubbing, and stretch out his
stiff throbbing body.

He stopped a man and asked where a person might find a place
to sleep. The man looked him over.

You are a transient, ain't you, the man said.

I might be, and I might not, Don said.

The man puffed on a cigar and kept it in his mouth when he
talked.

You know what a transient is, son?

Don did not like it that the man called him son. So had the
ticket clerk. Why did they do that when he was nobody's son.

Transient means homeless, the man said. It means on the way
to someplace else. It means passing through and never settling
down.

He paused, taking the cigar out of his mouth.

It means not having a pot to piss in. Does that describe your
situation more or less accurately, do you think.

To a *T*, mister.

Well, then, you just might find you a cot down on California Street. Two blocks thataway. Look for the sign in the window. Transients, it will say.

He found the California Dormitory for Men easily enough. Three floors of Clean Cots. Shower Bath Privileges. Laundry Privileges. Locker Service. Checkers and Dominoes. Ten Cents a Night. The Largest and Most Modern Cot House in the Southwest. All this information was painted on the big front window, and it had a sign hanging over the door that said, Transients Welcome.

The checkers and dominoes he could do without, but the man said the price was the same, player or non-player.

He was put on the third floor. The cot felt okay. Don slept a good sleep. When he woke up, he knew right where he was. He remembered that his granddaddy lived in the vicinity, but realized that he had no address, did not even know the name of the town Granddaddy lived in. He didn't believe it would be Oklahoma City, but even if it was, where would a person begin to look.

He was on his own.

Here I am, he told himself, and then rose from the cot and stretched. It was dark. He had slept through Christmas Day. In the darkness he could make out the forms of the sleeping men all in a row, there was a ton of them, breathing steady. The man closest to him made a whistling sound. He slept on his back, his hands clasped across his stomach, his mouth open. Through the big window at the other end of the room the moon shone just like it would do back in Carthage, Missouri. Daddy would see it too, Don thought. If Daddy was to wake up at this very minute and look out his window, he would see that same moonlight, coming from the same place.

But this was not Missouri, was it. No, sir. He had got himself to a whole other state.

He went to the window, stepping lightly, and looked out on this new place where he was. He saw a wide street, paved with bricks. He saw streetlamps. The light from the moon was from those streetlamps. One was right below the window and another directly across the street. A taxicab was parked beneath the light. The driver appeared to be hunched over at the wheel, asleep. It would be cold out there, Don figured, for it was cold from where he stood, wasn't he shivering in this dark room, the coal stove giving off little heat, the men wrapped in their blankets, warm in their covers. Still, he would like to be out there. How much better to sleep in that cold cab than to stand at this window! He seemed to see himself there, waking in the driver's seat, rubbing his eyes, stretching his arms. Now he started the car, revved the engine. He knew how to do it, sure he did. He had driven his father's Chevrolet coupe, taken it out into the country on Saturday afternoons while Daddy worked in the store and couldn't know any better. He liked the knobs, the dials, levers and pedals, and he liked the wind whooshing in by the wide open windows, the dust riled up behind him, the road stretching ahead of him and the farmhouses going by, farmers in their fields, the mules stately and calm, the crows on the telephone poles.

In Oklahoma City he would drive up and down the broad streets, the streetlamps regular as breath, marking time and distance, the streets smooth and straight, nothing ahead but sky. That engine hummed and the wheels rolled and rolled.

Lord, where was he, what was he come to.

He would not think of his daddy's curse. What did that mean —nothing.

New Year's Day, 1928, Don shivered in his cot all morning. Around him, most of the men had already gone off to wherever they went to. A few slept in the daytime and was gone all night. One of these spoke as Don at last climbed out of the cot.

Come here a second, the man said.

At first Don hadn't placed the voice. Then the man, three cots down (all between them already vacated), raised his hand and motioned for Don to come to him. Don went. The man slept in blue silk pajamas, not in his clothes like most of the others, or in nothing at all, like Don. Underneath his cot lay a canvas bag, next to a pair of slippers aligned neatly with his shoes and socks.

I've had my eye on you, the man said. I judge that you are of a different grade than the rest. There's some that are here by choice and others by necessity. Do you follow me? I believe you do. I am one of the choosers, and you, if I judge correctly, are too.

Yes, sir.

You were reared in the South, I take it.

In Missouri.

In Missour-uh. Well. Good as the South. You have Southern manners.

All right.

You think I'm going to Arkansas you, don't you.

Beg pardon.

Deceive you, trick you, cheat you, swindle you. Arkansas you. You're right to be wary in a place like this, sharpsters and ne'er-do-wells at every hand. I'm wary myself. In the long run it pays.

Yes, sir.

Adolphus A. Greer here.

Pleased, Mr. Greer. Don Temple.

The name means nothing to me. I said mine as a formality. Might be an alias and might not. My middle name you can trust, however. I don't tell it to everybody but I will tell it to you. It is America.

No fooling.

Maybe it is and maybe it ain't. A name means nothing. You are wondering why I called you to my bedside.

You was just being friendly, I figured.

There's not a friendly bone in my body, boy. Listen, a man says he wants to be your friend, keep a good grip on your wallet.

All right.

I have a proposition to make, a deal to offer. You may walk away now, or take a seat on that cot and listen to what I have to say.

Outside, sleet was starting up. One of the other day sleepers, his cot pushed into the darkest corner of the large room, tossed in his sleep and now and then said something that you couldn't understand, as if he was arguing with someone in a foreign language. In the middle of the room the coal stove sat like a plump dog. It gave off little heat, the coal bucket beside it empty, the ceiling above it blackened. Adolphus Greer sat propped up by pillows, his hands beneath the blanket.

Okay, Mr. Greer, Don said, taking a seat. Tell me your deal.

Imagine, my boy, a country lad like yourself. He has lived in the city, earned good money, started up a family, and, seeing his little son playing on the city sidewalks, constricted on every hand by streets, he wishes for that little son the life that he, the father, had in that pastoral village in Missour-uh so many years ago. Self-reliance was what he learned there. The love of freedom. Dusty paths, leafy bowers. This man, you see, has begun to tire of the city amenities. It is not exactly as he had hoped. An office in a stuffy building. A thirty-minute car ride each way. Maybe he will have a seat, maybe not. The boss expects him to carry work home. Paper work, dull as socks. His wife, once a village maiden, takes on city ways. Abrupt with him at supper. She opens accounts at Rothschild's, at Kerr's, takes a fancy to gemstones, gilded gimcrackery, gives away money to the poor and the milliner, devotes her time to the orphanage and the corsetiere. Whewee, he says, I never had such a damn hard day, and she replies, Please pass the corn on the cob. What is a fellow to do. Run off, you will say. Hit the road. Scat. Kit and kaboodle. But no, that is not in the cards for our young gentleman. He must change his life, yes, but he has made his bed and must sleep in it. Ah, *but he can move that bed!* And you, my friend, can help him do it. You, my designated agent, authorized by implication of the Katy Railroad and Mr. A. G. Nix, can sell this country lad a lot in Chickhoma Park. Chickhoma Park! Picture it. Located on the northeast quadrant, a matter of minutes from the State Capitol Building, Chickhoma Park will be no ordinary tract. No, sir. In the country, yet near a streetcar line, each lot will consist not only of a fine home, but—here is the stroke of genius—the lot will have upon it a chicken coop. The rooster crows every morning. The hens lay eggs galore. A cooperative will be formed —a poultry colony. A Few Months from Eggs to Dollars, that's our slogan.

We will share the profits, fifty-fifty, Adolphus Greer said. Think it over. Now I must rest.

He had to think about doing something, didn't he? His seventy-five dollars would not last forever, even with such inexpensive accommodations.

Adolphus Greer took him out for training the next afternoon. As they walked, Adolphus pointed out prime prospects.

Try to look in their eyes, he said. If you see restlessness there, combined with weariness, there's your man. Latch onto him. Just remember this: complacency and desperation are kissing cousins. Where is the happy man? Nowhere, son. This nation was founded by the desperate, for the desperate. Remember that, whenever you grow discouraged. Everybody is a customer.

Don tried to remember it. But he had no luck. He did not like talking to strangers. After three days of trying he told Adolphus Greer he was through.

Are you a drinking man, Adolphus asked. If you are not a drinking man, I can offer you another opportunity.

In that way Don Temple became a whiskey runner. He found it to his liking. It put him in a car, driving fast.

. . .

On a Saturday of that spring Don stepped into a cafe in Capitol Hill and saw the prettiest girl in the world, helping her daddy with the dishes.

There was two girls, one dark, one fair. The dark one was older, but the fair one looked at him in a way no female ever had. It wasn't claiming a thing. It was announcing something, however. It was saying, Here we are. She was just a little thing, no more than twelve, thirteen years old, but grown into a woman in her soul.

Still, her daddy would never hear of her going out with a man such as Don Temple, seventeen years old, run away from home, and a whiskey peddler.

She'd get older though, and then she'd have a mind of her own. He made up his mind right there that he could wait. What was his hurry anyway.

He began to go to the cafe every chance he got, just to hope for a glimpse of her. She wasn't always there. When she was there, generally her big sister—he had figured out they had to be sisters —was there too. Their daddy was a small, dark-haired man that never let your coffee cup stay empty for long. He wore a white shirt under his apron, and a black bow tie. The dark sister took orders, though there weren't ever many customers, and the fair one washed plates. You were most likely to catch them there late in the afternoons, after school was let out, and on Saturdays.

That little one, the fair-haired sister, would be his sweetheart one day and know it.

In the fall he moved out of the California Dormitory for Men and into a boarding house on North Hudson. He hardly ever saw Adolphus Greer anymore after the first couple of weeks of doing business. Now Don was making good money, he was on his own. He paid down on a car, a Reo roadster, which he kept parked in front of the boarding house and polished often.

He didn't think much about his daddy's curse, but he did miss his mama. Son, she had said to him, your life is your own, it is in your own hands to make of it what you will.

That seemed to him the truest thing anybody could say to him, and he kept those words in the front of his mind and said them to himself often.

One day, a mild sunny Indian summer day, he was washing the red dust from the Reo and preparing to polish it when a taxicab pulled up alongside him and let out a customer. He heard the door slam and the trunk lid open, and he went about his business, rubbing down the front fenders of the Reo. He liked to be able to see his reflection in it.

Then he heard a voice.

Joseph Donald Temple, it's you, isn't it!

There was no mistaking that voice—it was his mama, Lord help him.

Mama, he said, what the—

I just went away, she said, hugging him. I left, same as you.

All One Road

Clara Slade Temple freely admitted it: she was not a good woman at heart. But maybe John Temple, whom she had married in good faith, believing in his love for her and fond of his broad pale hands and his pink elbows, his firm virtue and his stern passion, maybe John was too virtuous for his own good.

Married young, knowing nothing, she stayed married for twenty-eight years, learning some things. Each time she brought her sons to term, she had been full of herself. Leroy amazed her by the pleasure he gave her, as if the seed of him grew in order to teach her to savor taste and scent, how to see and touch and hear all over again. Trained to believe childbirth holy but a curse, she was shocked with its beauty. Then that tiny mouth nursing at her breast—she was the one that had to be weaned.

John Temple, after working all day in his shoe store, came home expecting a prompt and filling meal. Let there be meat, let vegetables be the proper colors. Evenings he read his Bible until he fell asleep, then lugged his sleeping body to the bedroom.

She told herself she shouldn't want more. Let women learn in silence with all subjection, Paul wrote to Timothy. In sorrow thou shalt bring forth children, God confided in Eve. Clara had learned these lessons. But in time their force diminished, at last disappearing altogether, and in their absence a strength grew up that had no name. She was a large woman who had been a little girl. Much had frightened her, she now realized, that should not have: her brothers' fists, her sisters' angry eyes, the ways of men, the ways of the world. All the time she had had this strength, a small thing that awaited her discovery of it. Once found out, it would grow and grow.

Then came a time, some years after the birth of Leroy, that John Temple found out this strength in her. And he came to her, touching her, this chaste husband, professing nothing but to yield to the heat of her, let his blood (he put it this way) have its head. For would not flesh be flesh. Yes, by God, he said, pressing against her, his hand on her breast, yes, this human heart must have its way, by God, let us consecrate our love, live deep in the sweetness of our skin.

Wasn't this a switch.

He began to talk to her. He felt himself escaping, he said. Out there, where he was headed, danger lurked, death hid. A damnable redemption! Dark grace!

She was pleased by his attention. Presence beat absence all to hell. He might aim for his own soul, but it was her that he hit.

One day he came home in the middle of the afternoon, his dinner pail hanging from his hand like something he wished to be rid of. He set it down on the kitchen table. She had beans soaking, greens awaiting the pot, hamhock readied, cobbler cooling, and now she sat at the head of the table, her place at this time of the day, before Leroy's return from school, John's from the store. The September sun slanted through the kitchen. Seating himself in Leroy's chair, placing his grand, pale hands before him as if to offer them to her, he began to speak:

A man asked for a pair of oxfords, he said. It was Woodrow Hinton, you know, has the feed store. He sat down and stuck out his foot. A pair of oxfords, he said. Black. Church shoes. He has a long foot, Clara, and a wide one. I looked at it, set it on the footstool, took off his shoe like always, measured his foot. But then something come over me. I went to the stockroom, but I felt weak and had to sit down. I began to think of my father—I don't know why. I imagined Elzick Temple walking out the door of his sod house. Come in, Son, he said. He was very old, and Mama, he wanted me to know, far from being dead, sat inside waiting for me. I felt warm and short of breath. Then I put my hand on the box that contained Woody Hinton's church shoes— this calmed me.

I took Woody his shoes. He looked asleep, but when I drew near, he aimed a foot at me. Fit this one, John, he said, it's the big one.

Now I done something I never thought to do before, Clara. I set that shoebox down before him and I said to him, Woodrow, I said, have you ever noticed how a shoebox greatly resembles a coffin. Why, no, John, says he. And the foot, says I, how like the soul.

I saw that I had brought the wrong size shoe, but I began to work it onto his foot.

Woody, says I, I believe you are growing.

Brother Temple, he says, this shoe ain't my size.

But it was, I said. It was when I brought it out. You've already grown, Brother Hinton.

The devil you say.

Yes, I told him. Some get bigger, others lose ground. I am one of the latter. Perhaps you've noticed. One day I will fit in that shoebox. You, on the other hand, why, your toes, sir, will squirm and fatten like hogs.

He took back his feet, re-shoed them, and hastily departed. I locked the door behind him. It was time for dinner, and I went to the stockroom with my dinner pail. How long I sat there, the pail open, sandwiches untouched, I can't rightly say, Clara. I had lost ground. I would not need as much food as I once did, would I. I closed the pail. Then came here, as you see.

Clara, what is to become of me!

Whatever was to become of him, in the weeks that followed he became someone very fine to Clara, and out of that fineness was conceived their second son, Don Temple.

But then his sternness came back, his jaw hardening before her very eyes as he sat across from her, the Bible on his lap, his eyes moving from side to side, his fingers pressed against the gilt-edged pages and his knees close together and still.

After all, he never missed church, not once, and now he returned to his small sorrow even as she quickened with the child of his brief sweetness.

The year Halley's comet crossed the night sky, 1910, Joseph Donald Temple came into the world. By that time John was wholly himself again, good and cold as the devil. She concentrated on her sons. Leroy might be lost to his father's influence, but Don was another story. On his feet and walking before his first birthday, he raced from chair to table, settee to davenport, an impish grin on his face. The meaning of the word *no* seemed hard for him to grasp, and from his crib, gripping the railing with his pink but long fingers, he stared at his father as if he could not quite place the man.

His mother was forty-three in 1928, Don calculated, and a good one hundred seventy-five pounds. She made herself a pallet on the floor of his room, and he recalls having to step across her in the night, for he was just starting out and likely to be called at any hour. The room was tiny, and he worried that he might step on her. The first time, she grabbed his ankle. It's business, he told her. I make deliveries, Mama.

And what do you deliver, two o'clock in the morning.

Medicine.

Within a week she had her own room. He helped her carry her satchels and made a special trip for the trunk that held, she said, her mother's silver and her father's saber, the Slade family Bible and the Book of Knowledge encyclopedia, in addition to a few personal items of her own. Don't strain yourself, Son, she said as he lugged it down the narrow staircase. The Reo rode low under the weight of his mother and the trunk, and they had a ways to go, over on the northeast side, not so far from the capitol, to a three-story brick building with a broad front porch, a hand-lettered sign above the door: The Osage Arms—Clean Rooms.

She had got herself a job serving tables at the coffee shop in the Huckins Hotel downtown.

Come see me now and then, she said.

He did not see her as often as he might have. It seemed he had to be in the Reo all the time, driving out into the broad open land that he came to think of as his territory. He loved the car—it might have been a dream, that smooth straight driving through the state of Oklahoma. He noted the tilt and heft of the land, its gullies and washes, the wind-bent grasses and the gristly trees, the red-banked winding creeks and the unpainted farmhouses, windmills and lean-tos and cropless fields. Sometimes as he drove he liked nothing better than to say the names of the towns he had come to, in the order that he'd passed through them—El Reno, Calumet, Geary—as if the names alone were enough. Watonga, Kingfisher, Dover, Hennessey, Lacy, Okeene. He traveled in broadening circles, loops, often on dirt roads and sometimes lighting out across open fields. At night it was just as good, the teeming stars and the lights flashing dim from windows at the edge of the world.

In Oklahoma City he had ridden the streetcars to the end of the line and back, he walked up and down Broadway, Robinson,

Main, crossed the Walker viaduct to Capitol Hill. In Capitol Hill he patronized Johnnie's Cafe, where if the two sisters were not present he could always get their daddy to talk about them. He learned that the fair one, his sweetheart, was named Cora Mae, and the dark-haired older sister was Johnnie. Their daddy, Marshall Monroe, had named the cafe for Johnnie because she was his firstborn and meant good luck, the apple of his eye.

In that way the yellow grass came to be green again and the trees once more laden with leaves. The chilled wind lost its bite and the spring sky piled high the storm clouds, dark and lush like huge flowers. Rain came suddenly and in torrents, and hail the size of your fist. You heard rumors of winds traveling a hundred miles an hour, of tornadoes touching down and carrying away rooftops or even entire houses. Then in the wink of an eye the rain ended, hail ceased, wind stilled, and the great sky opened up into a clear washed blue that broke your heart.

One day it was summer. It might have been early April, but no matter. This was summer heat, summer dust, and it would not let up.

During that summer, calling at the Osage Arms, he often found his mother seated in one of the low-slung canvas chairs on the porch, next to her a pale, long-legged man who, rising immediately and giving a stiff little bow towards Mama, said in a soft voice, You will excuse me, please, somebody's got to mind the store.

Certainly, Captain, she said.

Oil derricks were springing up everywhere. The derricks could be seen rising up beyond the roof of the OK Cleaners across the street, two of them taller than any tree in sight, as natural as could be.

Have you got a girlfriend, Mama asked him. A boy your age might have him a little girl he's taken a liking to. I don't mean a woman like Maud Ward. That's another thing. When Leroy was eighteen he was married. That was a mistake, but a natural one.

I was twenty myself, and your father twenty-five. The wait didn't kill us. The marriage, however, might have.

Mama, Don said before he knew what he was saying. Mama, I am in love.

Well, that's just fine, Son, she said. Love is just fine as long as it lasts.

The porch was the only place you could bear the heat. Tenants sat cooling themselves in the wicker chairs, the ladies stirring the air with paper fans. Sometimes Clara Temple closed her eyes and listened to the thumping from the oil wells, the occasional whine of a passing car. Sometimes people talked.

A scorcher, one said.

A humdinger.

Can't remember it ever this hot.

The voices went on and on, the crickets started up, and all the time the oil wells back of the OK Cleaners thumped and thumped. Dozing, Clara remembered how when Leroy was little he would come to her in the summertime and say, Mama, I do love you so much, won't you get me a glass of lemonade? In the end, he marched off to Sunday school in his knickers, his spit-shined shoes matching his daddy's, his boy's lips tightening before their time into the same grim line as his daddy's. If religion did that to you, she'd stay bad.

Her mother had been a religious woman, but her daddy, even though going to church every damn Sunday, remained immune. Asleep from start to finish of the sermon, he woke up for the hymns and sang them so loud that Mother nudged him in the ribs. But you couldn't quieten him. Large-boned and firm of flesh, he was a farmer that sang to his mules and let his hogs run.

She was the baby of the family, with three sisters and five brothers. At Mama's funeral, the next-to-oldest sister, Celestine, who once pushed Clara into a mud puddle, now looked ancient, her mourning dress as shiny as a shroud. Come see us, Baby

Sister, Celestine said. And her brother Lucius, the red-haired boy who had teased her so many years ago, was solemn now as a bedpost and just as bald.

Mama had outlived Daddy by thirty years. Sold the farm and moved to Joplin, where she had herself been reared and where, after six years, at the age of sixty, she married a banker ten years her younger who took her on a tour of the Holy Land for a honeymoon, caught pneumonia on the ship back, and died in the port of New York. A widower with six grown children, a deacon in the First Baptist Church of Joplin, he left his money to the Baptist Missionary Fund, his house to the six children. No doubt he meant to change his will promptly upon their return from the honeymoon. Mama had to move in with Gabriel, the eldest son, who had never married. This would have been in 1904, Leroy not even in school yet, and that cowboy Teddy Roosevelt President of the United States.

It was late now, dark and sultry on the porch. The moon, a pale sliver, had risen up above the oil derricks, and one by one the porch sitters excused themselves with a sigh and passed through the screen door of the Osage Arms. Captain Lovell stayed. A pallid wisp of a man, tall but wasted-looking, Captain Lovell had long legs and had adorned his long feet in two-tone wing-tipped oxfords such as her son liked to wear.

I like a woman has some meat on her bones, he said to her.

I like a man of some heft, she said.

I like a woman can joke with you.

I like a man knows the difference between a joke and a fact.

Some facts is jokes, way I see it, and vice versa.

He then invited her to supper in his room, where he had plump pinto beans simmering on the hotplate and a beverage that he hoped might please her palate. The beverage turned out to be bathtub gin, which she could not stomach, but the beans were most tolerable, and his company beat all to hell the competition, which was flies.

I am a gentleman, he said.

I see that, she said, regretting the fact.

I am sixty years old, he said, however I ain't dead yet. I been out to Bolivia with Alfalfa Bill Murray and was personally acquainted with Tom Slick. I'm from Texas. Gainesville, just across the Red River. Daddy raised cotton. Was nineteen when they opened up Old Oklahoma. I didn't care to enter into the sweepstakes, never had a hankering for land, seen enough dirt in my time, but there was considerable excitement in Gainesville among fellows of my set, and a friend persuaded me to accompany him. Santa Fe Railroad would take you right up to the line, and then on the day of the opening carry you on into the Territory. Oh, sure, I'd've been smart to get me a quarter section, sit on it and then get rich on the mineral rights. But you had to improve it, you know. Wouldn't let you just hold on. So I went along, vowing only to observe, for I was a curious lad and eager to have a grasp of human nature.

And did it give you a grasp, Captain, she asked, taking hold of his hand. He didn't withdraw it.

Damn right, he said. Came down to this: greed.

Was that when you went into the militia.

What militia. I never went into no militia.

How'd you get to be a captain then.

Why, it's my name. The name my daddy give to me. Captain Quantrill Lovell, that's the whole name.

Did you ever marry, Captain Quantrill Lovell?

Yes, I did. Twice. First one died. Second one I run off from. I ain't suited for matrimony.

Maybe nobody is, she said, giving his hand a squeeze.

Oh, yes, he said. I believe matrimony is fine. It is human beings that is rotten. Present company excepted, of course.

Of course.

You don't mean to marry me, do you, Clara.

I don't take you for a fool, Captain.

Good thing, because I ain't one.

He pulled her to him and kissed her as if for dear life.

Later they crept downstairs in the quiet house and again sat together on the porch. The night sky glowed in the southeast.

A well's out of control, Captain said. No telling how long it'll burn. It's a great waste.

But beautiful, she said. Like another sunset.

Up close, you wouldn't much care for it.

He reached over and took her hand.

How fine, she was thinking, to be here on this porch, living in a rooming house in Oklahoma City, her two sons grown, John Temple left behind in Missouri. She still thought of him, yes, she thought of John Temple, that poor solitary soul, and she missed him even as she wished he might come to miss himself.

Clara, Captain said, let us flee together to California.

Why not China, she said.

She knew exactly how much such talk meant. Nothing. He would flee nowhere, because he had already got to the place where nobody could find him. That place was inside himself.

We're far enough, she said. We're a long ways from where we started out.

Can't get far enough away, in my opinion, he said. My daddy one time, why, he beat me to within a inch of my life.

My mama remarried, you know, after Daddy died.

Some folks is crazy that way. A woman wouldn't come close to my daddy after Mama died. They all knew he'd work them to the bone and live to bury them, one after the other, like a crop he expected to harvest one day.

The moon rose higher, took on a deep gold color, and the oil field fire in the southern sky kept glowing. Occasionally a car passed.

Then one of the cars stopped. It was Don's Reo roadster. He came running up the steps, almost breathless, in his seersucker

suit, the bow tie undone. My, but her roving son had broad
hands, just like his father's, and broad shoulders like her daddy's.
Why, he might have been her daddy, big and sweet, coming in
from the fields. *Where's Daddy's little girl!* But he was no more
her daddy than she was her own mother. It was the darkness that
did it.

Mama, he said, catching his breath, Leroy's here. Leroy's come
all the way from Missouri.

Leroy? Your brother Leroy?

Leroy, our Leroy, your firstborn son Leroy. He's here.

Excuse me, said Captain Lovell, rising. Nobody's minding the
store.

He leaned down and kissed her lightly on the cheek, then was
gone.

First Mama, thought Don, and now Leroy. Would Daddy
come next? Maud Ward? No, Daddy had settled in for good,
and Maud Ward for nothing. To those two, desperation didn't
signify. But what about Leroy.

Leroy hadn't really left. You have to understand that. He had
not, that is, come to stay. Almost falling, he had appeared at
Don's door, his shirttail out, shoelaces untied, cheeks red, forehead sweaty.

Brother, he said, can you shelter a weary traveler.

Don had just come in from a run down to Ardmore and was
not so fresh himself, but Leroy looked in need of instant support.
Don led him to a chair. Provided with a cup of coffee, he sipped
loudly from the saucer, rolled his eyes, shivered, looked around
him, sipped again and shook. Whew, that's good, he said. Boy,
that hits the spot.

Then he said: It ain't forever. It ain't like it is with you and
Mama. I'm going back. Yes, sir. I'll be going back shortly. A
man's got a obligation, he's got a duty, there's a certain responsibility. He's got people that depend on him. Where's Mama. Oh, I

forgot. She's got her own place. I've got the address wrote down somewhere. A Indian name. Wasn't that something, her leaving that way. I tell you. Folks took notice. With you it was—well, you know, a young fellow like you, there's some head-shaking, but Clara Temple, that's a horse of a different color. How is Mama, Don. Hefty as ever? You know what I want to do, I want to find our old grandpappy Elzick Temple. You seen him yet? No, well, we'll go see him. He's a character, you know. You don't remember him so much, I imagine, but I got some recollections. Oh, he's nothing like Daddy. They come from different worlds, you'd think. Father and son. It beats all.

He paused. He asked for more coffee.

I know, he said. Look at me and you think there's good old Brother Leroy, trodding the straight and narrow, obeying the Ten Commandments right and left. Holy Leroy—that's what they called me in school. And all the time I wanted to be just like them, mean and not care who knew it. Our granddaddy, now there's a mean old son, I'm here to tell you. We'll go find that old son.

Then he said: Take me to our mama. A man needs his mama when he's in trouble. I got her address here somewhere. You know where she lives. Take me to our mama.

He began to sob. He laid his head down on the table and shut his eyes tight.

No, he said into the table, I don't want to see her. Not yet. I've been drinking, Don. I guess you can tell. It's took me three days to drive three hundred miles. I'm not a drinking man, but I couldn't help myself. I drive down the road a ways, and then it's like the world is losing hold. Oh, it goes on and on, the world, don't it, there's no getting around it. I have to stop—I tell myself just a sip from the flask, that's all. Or else I'm afraid to stop, and I can't go on, and so I turn around, or turn off onto roads that stop at some poor dirt farmer's front porch. It's all the same.

It's all one road, Brother. It's a wonder I ever got here. Go get Mama, Don. I want to see my mama.

Don had helped Leroy to the couch, where he could almost stretch out. Leroy was out like a light, and after spreading a blanket over him Don went to get his mother.

First thing she thought, seeing Leroy there asleep on the couch, was how like a baby. But he was no baby and she knew it. So should he. A grown man and in trouble. Well, trouble wasn't always such a bad thing. Worse was not to know you were in trouble.

He appears to be sound asleep, she said. Conversation don't go far when one party is not awake.

I gave him plenty of coffee, Don said. He probably just thinks he's asleep.

Believes it with all his heart, looks like.

Should I try to wake him up?

You might try.

Don shook Leroy's shoulders. Hey, boy, he said. Mama's here. Wake up now. Mama's here.

Leroy didn't stir.

He's been liquoring up, hasn't he, she said.

Mama, he came in here drunk as a skunk. I never gave him a lick.

Good for you.

Don shook him again. Leroy's eyes blinked open.

Say, he said. Is that Mama.

I been called worse than that.

Leroy sat up. He looked bad, hadn't shaved in God knows when, and his eyes seemed sinking deeper as you looked at them. There was trouble in those eyes all right, and she couldn't help herself, she went to him, took him in her arms, Lord what a smell, sweat and whiskey.

Honey, she said. Leroy, baby boy. What is it, sweetheart.

He couldn't begin to say, not any more than his daddy could explain what had happened to him that time he came home early from the store and wept over his lunch pail. They just was wound up so tight, it seemed, and then they had to spring loose or bust. If you were lucky, you came to your senses, you understood what your blood was saying to you. You couldn't teach your children that luck, wasn't it a shame, they either came into it or they didn't.

You go back to sleep, baby, she told him. Lie down there and Mama will pull the covers over you.

I'm awful tired, he said, bless his heart, and she kissed his bristly cheek and whispered, Sleep tight, honey lamb. Your mama's here. Don't you worry about a thing.

If only she could dream his dream, live in his skin, take his trouble unto herself, she would do it in a minute. She brought him into the world, didn't she. She had her natural affections.

Have you a cup of coffee, she asked her second son.

He moved like a prince, this boy that had run away, but when oh when would *his* time come and where would she be when it did.

August in Oklahoma had a weight to it, the sky bearing down, gray and fat. Still the long land opened up before the smooth-rolling Reo, the sun-yellowed grasses whipping back and forth in the dry wind, raising up little twisters of dust.

Turn here, Leroy said, right at that fence post.

Then: No, not yet. I guess it's farther on. We're close now. I remember that little ridge, the way the red dirt makes it look ribbed, and the windmill by the dry pond.

They came to a road, just where Leroy said it would be, poorly graded, rutted and eroded, the red dust rolling up thick behind the Reo. Now and then they passed a farmhouse, unpainted and with pitiful outbuildings, barns that sagged, and chicken coops fit for hogs. What had become of the grass. Now it was only clay around the houses, some of it smooth as stone, and stunted wind-bent trees with twisted branches, blackjacks, their leaves already blown to kingdom come. A horse stood in the middle of a field, still as a stick, leaning in the same direction as the trees.

The house sat about a hundred yards off the road. A lane, narrow and rough, led off to one side of the house and on past to a henhouse with a lean-to. Another outbuilding back beyond the coop looked like a cabin made of dirt. Grass grew up out of the roof of this cabin, or seemed to until you looked closer and saw that was old grass, long dead. The doorway was off kilter, though made of thick beams, and the windows on both sides set back deep in the clay wall. The house itself was a common farmhouse, the siding gone gray, pulled loose in places, the porch sunk down on one side, its roof supported by two thin posts set atop cinder blocks. A big dog, gray as the house, lay on the porch, dead to the world. Lifted his head, though, when the door opened, and begun to pant.

It was a woman at the door. Dark complected, forty-five or fifty years old, short and stout, she wore a man's trousers with the cuffs rolled up to her ankles and a man's workshirt unbuttoned a good ways down the neck, where she had a silver necklace with blue stones set in it. Her long black hair pressed so close to her head that it looked like a cup, and the skin of her face was tightly drawn over high cheekbones and a broad forehead.

He ain't here, she said. He's gone a long ways from here.

But the old man stepped out the door from behind her.

I know you from somewheres, he said, looking square at Don, who for the life of him would not have placed this long-legged bald-headed man as the granddaddy he hadn't seen for, oh, how long, ten years or twelve, and who he remembered as having a thick white mustache and iron-gray hair that curled up at his neck and made curls above his ears.

Granddaddy, Leroy said, this is your grandson Don.

And who might you be, sir.

Leroy Temple. John's boy, his firstborn.

I don't recognize you, but him I believe I know. He looks like my son.

He's John's boy too.

I don't mean John. Damn John. I mean Elmer, dead these twenty-some-odd years that made the Run with me. My boy Elmer.

I'm Don Temple, not Elmer.

I'm Leroy. We come to pay you a visit, Granddaddy.

The old man went back into the house. The woman stayed put and began to grin.

So you are John's boys, she said. You are his blood and he don't deny his blood. So come on in here now. Don't kick that dog and he won't bite you.

Inside, she said: I'm Minneola Choate. I been here over a year and he has not made a honest woman of me yet. Sit down there next to Elzick, while I get you something to wet your whistle.

None of the well water, Elzick said. Almost dry. Maybe whiskey. Made on the premises, guaranteed pure.

Whiskey's fine, said Leroy. I don't want to deplete your supply of water.

Water for me, Don said.

No water, Elzick said. Won't have it. Have we a apple, Rose. Maybe the boy would tolerate a apple.

Apple. When have you ever had a apple on this place, tell me that.

Bring the boy what he wants. Looks just like Elmer.

Elzick Temple sat in the wicker chair, looked straight ahead as he talked, the sun from the window behind him edging his bald pate with light and making it hard to look directly at him. Minneola Choate sat in a rocker, nodding her head, commenting now and then, sipping her whiskey from a pewter mug.

Was a Sooner, Elzick said. Yes, I was and don't care who
knows it. I was ahead of the rest. I made my own time. Tents
and wagons everywhere, horses and mules, all awaiting at the
line and more coming in every minute. It was April and already
plenty warm, with a good hot wind and horseflies. I seen others
slipping in, sure, you bet, I wasn't the only smart one. They had
them buffalo soldiers patroling, big black fellows, you know, in
their plumed hats, and astraddle fine government horses.

With their tails bobbed, Minneola said.

What's that, Rose?

Some of the horses had their tails bobbed, you always say.

Correct. What's wrong with them horses, Elmer asked. Nothing, says I. They's government issue, that's all. Elmer was my
eldest son and always a clever one, smartest of the lot.

How many was there, Leroy asked. Daddy never said how
many there was.

Thousands, there was thousands. All in a line, waiting for the
gun to go off.

I mean children. Daddy never said how many brothers and
sisters he had.

Eleven. There was eleven of them. Eight by Sally. Three by
Mary. Now this one, this Minneola here, I don't believe she
means to bear me none. My Rose, my Choctaw Rose, says she's
through with childbearing.

It's God's truth. Forget about your Choctaw Rose. Tell your
story.

Correct. This was the Opening of Old Oklahoma, don't you
know. Before that, it was Indian Territory. You have to know
that. Rose's people was brought out here a long time ago—how
long would it be now, Rose?

A long time, Minneola said. A hundred years.

A hundred years. Brought out here, was Rose's people, and
also the Cherokee and the Chickasaw, the Seminole and the
Creek. Your land forever, the government said. But restless white

folks soon enough fetched their eye onto this Indian Territory. They was called Boomers and they was led by a fellow name of David Payne that operated along the Kansas and Missouri border. He came to Carthage once, oh, this would have been in '80 or '81. I was working in the office of the Carthage *Gazette* at the time. One day in comes this tall, thick-limbed but slender man carrying a beat-up leather satchel. Had black hair, combed slick to one side, and a black mess of a mustache and slab of a goatee —like a straight line down the middle of his chin, this goatee. His clothes hung loose on him. His cheeks was all sunk in.

I am Captain David Payne, says he. Show me to the editor-in-chief.

Well, I done it, and no sooner had I returned my gaze to the font than I heard them two shouting back and forth. If I was lucky, a fight might break out. But I wasn't lucky. Out comes the chief of the Boomers, stepping briskly, a rolled-up piece of parchment in one hand and his beat-up satchel in the other. He headed for the street, make no mistake, in full stride.

Gideon Duncan—that was the editor—said to me, Elzick, he said, that man is a scoundrel. Imagine, selling shares in a colony smack dab in the middle of Indian Territory. Where does he get the gall to claim land deeded forever to the Indian nations.

It beat me. But I heard more about Payne and his Boomers. Gideon Duncan printed the news of his failed expeditions and damned them in editorials. Still, when the time came for opening up the territory, Gideon was there. He snuck in early too, a Sooner. Well, boys, we was all dirt crazy in them days, just like folks is for oil now. It'll play out. Everything plays out.

That's God's truth, Minneola Choate said.

Now, boys, Elzick said. I want to show you something that lasts.

He rose from the chair and moved for the door. Don understood that he and Leroy were to follow. Elzick held the back screendoor open. Watch your step, he said. Some of them planks is bad. A cat, scrawny and gray, jumped from the shadows and bounded across the dirt. Just past the barn, Don saw the dirt house. It looked like it had been set down into a low place—a wash or a wallow—or else the ground beneath it was giving way. The roof was low, almost flat, with a stovepipe sticking up in the center of it. Closer, you could see bits of grass and straw in the roof as well as in the walls.

A house made of dirt, Elzick said. Ain't it a wonder. Step inside. You can go in it. Come on. Watch your head, Elmer.

It was dark inside the dirt house, dark and cool. Light shone through the holes in the ceiling and some light filtered through the windows, dust-caked though they were, but it was mainly gray inside. The walls were made of thick slabs of sod—carved out of the ground, Elzick said, cut only a few miles from here and hauled in by dray. Oh, each slab weighed plenty, he wanted to tell you, sixty, maybe seventy pounds. What else was to be done, wood so scarce, answer him that. Of course 'twasn't *meant* to be permanent, and, to be sure, a heavy rain played havoc with the roof, you was always having to dab fresh mud up there, it could be downright dispiriting, he'd grant you that. Wouldn't want to live in it forever, no, but how much after all did a man need and wasn't it a fine notion, a house made of earth, cool in the summer, warm in winter.

A nice place, Don said.

Leroy shook his head. He appeared faint.

You see how it has lasted, Elzick said. I won't keep you boys. You know the way back. I'll just stay out here a while. It's right pleasant.

Minneola was waiting for them at the car.

What become of my grandmother, Leroy asked her. Tell me that.

Which was she. Sally or Mary?

I don't know.

Don't matter. Both are dead. He wore them out. Now he's about wore hisself out.

You've been with him a year.

Very nearly a year.

And before that?

Before that, I was like you boys. I thought I knew who I was.

My trouble, Leroy said, is I go so far and then I—

The highway hummed beneath the Reo. All manner of flying insects whirled and chirred in the night, lit up for an instant before the beams of the generated light, then brought rapidly to the glass of the windshield. Don did not want to think about Leroy's trouble. He was thinking about Elzick Temple, he longed for the woman that was Cora Mae. Was this love then? Must've been. He had never felt anything else like it. He caught a whiff of redemption, he breathed in the aroma of his doom. In the lighted space of highway that opened before him he seemed to see the brilliance of time itself—his time and hers. It moved as fast as anything and stayed put in brightness.

Back in Oklahoma City, Leroy shook Don's hand.

I'm okay now, he said. It helped some, seeing our granddaddy. I don't know why, but it did. I believe I can go back now. I know where the road goes.

. . . .

VI

The Home of Dust

I used to like oil wells so much, Cora Mae said. I used to want to climb to the top of them and look at the view. I don't know what I thought I was going to see.

Not much, Don Temple supposed, but you expected more when you were a child.

I didn't. No, I didn't, Don, really. I didn't expect a thing except to be hot in the summer and cold in the winter.

What did she expect now, he wondered.

Not a thing, she said. Are you going to ask me to marry you?

The thought has crossed my mind.

Well, don't expect me to say yes.

Why not.

Just don't.

I thought you loved me. I believe I heard you say so once or twice.

You may've just been hearing things. I don't think I know you very well.

You know me as well as you're ever going to know me, honey.

Fine. Maybe it's not well enough.

What is it you think you got to know. Make me a list.

All right. Number one: what exactly is it I mean to you. Number two: where does your money come from. Number three: what do you mean to do with your life.

Well, now. You know, there is one answer covers all your questions.

It'd better be a good one.

I mean to make a living.

That's it?

That's it. Ain't it a good one.

You're going to have to explain yourself, Don.

I mean to make a living. You mean living to me, and since I mean to marry you, that covers two of your questions, don't it. As for the other, where my money comes from, well, that's of no account.

Do you steal it.

No.

Swear to God?

Swear to God.

All right. I just have to believe you, the other answer's so pretty.

I appreciate that, sweetheart.

Where are we going anyway. Everything looks funny without oil wells.

We're almost to Guthrie.

How much is almost.

Five miles or so, I'd guess.

And then what.

Are you tired? We haven't come all that far.

Not tired. Just bored. Nothing to look at without oil derricks.

Thought you didn't like them anymore.

When it's all there is, I like them fine.

We come to a river soon. I want to show you this river. It's the Cimarron.

I've seen rivers before.

This one sometimes has water in it.

So does the North Canadian. It flooded once. Twice in one year. I remember it well, because that was the year that Little Brother died. Nineteen twenty-three.

She stopped talking, then started whistling. Tipperary, it was. It's a long way from Tipperary. Why was she whistling a old song like that. Heard it from her daddy, Don supposed. She was keen on her daddy.

Here came Guthrie, a nice little town, though old fashioned, with its sandstone buildings all turreted like they was meant to be castles or forts.

You want to stop a minute, get out of the car and stretch your legs?

No. I'm not tired.

Past Oklahoma Avenue he accelerated, headed the Reo north. In a couple of minutes, there it was, the Cimarron. Red as the devil in its sandy bank, not so broad as it got to be in the spring, in fact pretty scrawny, such a dry summer, but still it was okay to see it there, twisting this way and that.

Well, said Cora Mae, will you look at that. There's even trees.

I thought you might like it.

Looks like it's seen better times.

Oh, yes, I guess so.

Let's stop. Want to?

Thought you wasn't tired.

I want to get my feet in the water.

He pulled the Reo off the road, not too far, for it got sandy fast and it was a shifty sort of sand that might give the best of cars pause. Cora Mae was out of the car almost before he had it properly stopped, snatching off her shoes and lighting out for the water. He picked up her shoes—skimpy things hardly heavier than a sock, with high heels and straps—and set them on the fender of the car. If they had to walk across miles of desert sand,

and she knew about it in advance, still she would wear high heels. Said they made her look older, and, anyway, didn't he like the way they set off her ankles and calves.

He caught up with her at the edge of the water, as red as it could be and almost still, a trickle.

Come on in, she said, reaching for his hand.

Looks too muddy.

Feels good when you take your shoes off.

She dropped his hand and waded farther out. She could wade all the way across, he was pretty sure, and the water would never rise far above her knees. Wasn't but thirty yards or so to the other side. On that side the shoreline broadened out, extended deeper, cutting a wide curve into the red soil, making a kind of cliff, a short one, maybe ten feet high, the yellow grasses blowing above it and a few cottonwoods leaning just right so as to provide shade. A couple of raggedy clouds lazed about in the sky, little things that could never do no harm. He kneeled, took off his shoes and socks, folding the socks carefully and tucking them into the shoes. Then he rolled his pantslegs up to his knees.

Here I come, he said. Better watch out.

Watch out nothing, she said. What took you so long.

The water wasn't as warm as he had thought it might be, had a cool bite to it, and the sand beneath fast turned thick, like wet clay, slippery, though soft enough when you stood still, as if you could sink in it.

She held her skirt high and waded almost to the middle of the stream, the water deeper than he had imagined, well above her knees, almost to the top of her thighs.

Umm, she said. It cools you off.

Can't come any farther unless I get my pants wet.

Bet they'd dry.

She laughed, then cupped one hand and splashed water at him. He took his handkerchief from his pocket and wiped his face.

Aren't you the neat one, Don Temple.

She had turned and now waded into the middle of the river, holding her skirt high with one hand and skimming the water with the other. The water reached her waist. She gave him a look over her shoulder that seemed to say, Come to me now, Don Temple, or lose me forever. He went fast. Anyway he meant to move fast, but the water slowed him down. She kept moving, and he saw that she intended to cross to the other side.

Here I am, he said, catching up to her as she began, in the shallow water now, to run for the shore.

She wasn't running away from him, no, nor just teasing him. She took his hand and led him to where the riverbank curved beneath the cottonwood trees. The reddish sand felt hot beneath his feet. The cottonwoods with their leaves flickering in the wind seemed somehow his trees. The wind, strong and warm, made the yellow blades of grass above the banks curve like sickles. She sat down at the bluff where there was shade, releasing his hand, and he thought, I don't have to sit down beside her. I might walk on, follow the bend of the river, or I might turn around and recross it, return to the car. I'm going to marry her, he had told his mother last night. This is one happy son you got here. And his mother had forgotten what woman he referred to, he knew, even though she pretended to remember. A beautiful girl, she said at last. True enough. Cora Mae was a beautiful girl. She didn't think so herself, but all the same she was, beautiful from the word go. Those ankles, for example, and that little grin, and the way she walked, as if she was always out for a stroll, never in any particular hurry, her chin held high and her arms swinging briskly. Still, he didn't have to sit down there beside her. She might want him to, she might believe him about to kneel and place himself next to her, he might want to himself, but he didn't have to, he could just as well choose to climb one of those cottonwoods.

He sat down.

Feels good, doesn't it, she said.

He wasn't sure what she meant. Just sitting here? Being soaked to the bone from the waist down? The shade? The warm wind?

He said yes, because that was the answer to all those questions.

You don't feel funny, being with me? she wondered.

Funny? Why, no.

Sometimes I think you must.

Why should I.

Just because I'm so much younger than you, I guess.

Not so much, really. Five years ain't nothing. My granddad is married to a woman I bet fifteen years younger than him.

I thought you said he wasn't married.

Good as married. We was talking about age.

Well, he's old, isn't he. When you get old there's not that much difference.

No difference in being sixty-five and in being fifty?

Some, maybe. My daddy and mama are the same age.

Honey, it's okay. You and me, we're just fine together.

Just fine. Is that all we are.

The best, that's what.

I hoped you'd say beautiful. Lovely. Amazing. Gorgeous.

I was getting around to it. You took the words clean out of my mouth. You're pretty smart, for such a young thing.

Hush up about my age. Didn't you just say it didn't signify.

Didn't say that. Said it was the difference that didn't signify.

I'm mature for my age, I know that.

Sure you are, honey.

I've always felt older. I think I've been grown up all my life.

I know what you mean.

I mean I can't ever remember feeling like a child. Even when I was little, I remember thinking: this ain't me. It was a little girl in the mirror, but it wasn't me. Inside, I was just the same as I am now. That's the honest-to-God truth.

Don't doubt it for a minute.

It's like I'm at the center of my life—here, right now.

Where you've always been, sweetheart.

Yes. And you with me. Even then.

We've known each other a long time.

The longest time. I remember when I first saw you in Daddy's restaurant. You kept coming back, and I thought you had your eye on Johnnie.

Nope.

I was twelve years old, Don Temple. Shame on you.

Didn't you just say you never felt like a child.

Yes, I did. And it's true. You're right.

I didn't see no child when I saw you stacking plates in your daddy's cafe. There's some that can see the truth. I am one of them, honey.

Why is that?

What.

Why is it some can see and some can't.

Don't know. God's gift, I reckon.

More likely the devil's.

Six of one, half a dozen of the other.

Better not let my mama hear you say that.

They stretched out, let the sun and the warm wind dry them. He was thinking about nothing, just admiring the sky, and then he wanted to look at her, touch her and have only the scent of her in the air he breathed.

We'll be late, she said.

We don't have no place to get to.

I don't know. We might go somewhere.

We're there already.

He was touching her hair. It was the color of the sunshine.

Are you going to kiss me, she asked.

I was thinking about it.

I believe you thought long enough.

Two weeks later, they ran off to California, but got only as far as Elk City, still in Oklahoma, not much more than a hundred miles from Oklahoma City. Enough was enough, Cora Mae said. The highway would go on like this forever, across land that looked cold-cocked by the wind. Maybe that straight and flat and dull line always before them would some day be in California, who was she to doubt it, but why put it to the test. She'd take the rest on faith.

Honey, he said, you have a peculiar way of thinking.

Better get used to it, bud.

He was crazy about her, she knew it, and, as for her, she would happily throw herself in front of a speeding freight train to save his life. Who needed California.

He stopped the car, turned it around, right in the middle of the highway, just past Elk City.

Talk to me like that, sweetheart, he said, and you can get me to do most anything.

Yes, but all she wanted was for him to love her and never quit. The way she saw it, they had a long, sweet life ahead of them— in Oklahoma, not California—a loving life, maybe sixty, seventy years. She hoped he outlived her so that she would never have to be alone. In sixty years she would be seventy-five and he eighty. Could you imagine that.

They passed through Elk City again. It wasn't much. But it had a wide brick street and a movie house.

Don, she said, I'm yours forever.

He stepped on the gas and almost ran through Elk City's stop sign. What did he mean by that?

I can't imagine ever loving anybody else, she said. Can you?

He looked like he might be about to say something.

Never mind, she said. If you have to think it over, I guess that's answer enough.

She scooted over to the other side of the car seat, looked out the window at the scenery. Why didn't they have more trees. Goodness, but it got old. Some trees, sure, but flimsy things, whipped nearly to nothing by the wind. It was funny, though, to see it all going past. You could fix your gaze way off, if you could find something to fix it to, an old farm house, a windmill, but still you saw what was closer, the ground nearest the highway speeding by, the house far out there seeming to float, the sky the only thing that stood still, the car engine humming so smooth, and then she felt herself fly out there. There was no car at all then, no highway, just the broad land, ripped into gorges, heaved into hills, herself as if everywhere, shifty as the dust.

Anyway, what did it mean, his forever.

She was no one's forever. Claim her, might as well claim that cloud bank, big with the dust of Texas, on its way elsewhere.

I've been thinking about your question, he said.

Must've considered all the ins and outs for sure by now, she said.

Yep. All the ins and outs.

There are a lot of them, I suppose.

I was just doing what you said, Cora Mae. I was trying to see if I could imagine loving another woman.

Trying real hard, it seems.

It took some trying, yes. But it was no use.

She had lost interest in the question. What mattered now was this endless highway and when they would get off of it. And she told him so.

Hell, he said, is this soon enough for you.

He pulled onto another road, a dirt road, taking the turn so sharp, so fast, that she had to grip the door handle to keep from sliding back across the seat towards him.

Then he stopped the car. Dust billowed up around them. It made her cough. He slid across the seat, pulled her to him, held her so tight she thought she might burst.

Say, was she a machine, or what.

He was sorry. He didn't know what come over him.

Across the way was a farmhouse with a windmill alongside. The door hung loose on one hinge and the windows were busted out.

There it is, she said. Our house.

She got out of the car and the wind struck her full in the face. A little cyclone danced across the road and everywhere tumbleweeds spun, quick as the dust itself. Don was by her side. She took his hand. It was hard and rough, but he did not squeeze too much. He walked slow, always, and she felt as if she must be pulling him along, tugging him towards whatever lay ahead, even if he were the one that had determined their direction.

The blades of the windmill turned like crazy, but nothing connected that propeller to the ground. It made a fierce whirring noise, at the same time clattering and squeaking.

The dust stung your eyes and cheeks.

You could smell it in the house. You'd think this was the home of dust, where it slept or where it paced when it could not sleep, slumped into a rocker when it wasn't in the mood for chasing across the country.

It's like *his* house, he said.

She didn't know what he was talking about. Whose house.

My grandfather's house. Not the one he lived in. He showed me and Leroy a dirt house that he lived in once a long time ago. It was made of sod bricks that was cut from the ground and hauled in on a dray. It was the old times. Wood was hard to come by, it had to be freighted in from far off, I'll bet—Texas or Arkansas. Can you imagine that, honey.

That was exactly what she was trying to do. Imagine such a time. She pictured . . . nothing at all. Then, a man with a dark beard: Abraham Lincoln. He sat in a theater box—but what was a theater box—and was shot by a crazy-eyed actor. She knew Abraham Lincoln was never in Oklahoma, and the next instant she remembered from school that Oklahoma wasn't even a state during the Civil War. There was a run for land, they'd taught her that, thousands of people staking their claims to the Indian Territory, setting up tents on the vacant prairie. Oklahoma City was nothing but tents at first. One day open space and the next, a city of white tents.

He was trying to explain to her: this house probably wasn't as old as his grandfather's sod house, because it was made of wood.

Nobody lives here now, she said. The life that once lived here is long gone.

Well, he said, it *was* here. It is up to us to put it back.

That life is no more, she said. Just look around you, Jack. It's gone.

It *was* gone. How could anyone doubt it. As sure as Abraham Lincoln, it was gone.

It's our life that's here, he said.

Set your foot down too hard, she said, you'll go right through the floor.

Come here to me, honey. We're going to send ourself right through the roof.

If it doesn't fall in on us first.

He was already holding her, his hands so soft, down low on her back, they might have been lips, then pressing, pulling her close to him. His breath felt warm on her neck, and she thought Oh, yes, that's nice, who cares about Abraham Lincoln, touch me there, that's sweet, that's gentle, his lips now finding hers, hold me, please, my Bud, my lovely Jack, my handsome Don Temple, so big now with your passion. Wasn't this as close as you could come to death—let it go on forever. Could he just lift his lips to hers, there, and mightn't he help her slip from this dress. How she loved him! How she loved that ridge of bone down his back, wouldn't it last forever, and did he like it when she touched him there, and my, those hips, no meat on them to speak of, how could he stand it, didn't it hurt when he sat down, those little hips, those straight thighs, and what broad, sharp-boned shoulders, so dear to her that flat hairy chest with its tiny nipples that swell up ever so slightly when touched, would he like it if she touched her mouth to them as he did for her, like that, her tongue on its tip, such a funny little thing and absolutely useless, never will make a drop of milk, will it.

She began to cough. Dust in the air. They were on an old couch, the dust on it thick. She hadn't noticed at first. Of course not.

I'm sorry, she said. Please, don't stop.

But she couldn't quit her coughing, the dust in her throat, in her lungs, in her blood, that's the way it felt.

He sat up. Cleared his throat. Took a deep breath.

Sorry, she said, pulling her dress back on. I'm really sorry.

She kept coughing, couldn't quit. He put his shirt on, buttoned up his pants.

We better go, she managed to say, it's this dust in here.

He stood, took her hand. Outside, it was better, you could breathe again, but still the dust seemed caught in her throat, and not until the car gained speed did she begin to breathe easier.

At the ocean, he said, there wouldn't have been no dust.

Didn't the sand blow.

Jesus God, he guessed it might, sweetheart, but was any place perfect? Could they get to a place where there wasn't going to be something, dust or rain, tornado or flood, hurricane or earthquake. You just had to make do, like everybody else. Dust never killed no one, not to his knowledge, no human beings anyway, a few cows maybe.

We can go to the ocean if you want, she said.

She had a sudden vision of blue water, she could almost breathe the ocean air, cool and cleansing. It was as pure as the future itself, like nothing that ever was.

Some roads Don turned onto ended up dirt, narrow and rutted. Once the road simply disappeared and for a time the car bumped along in an open field, over tufts of weeds, past stands of dead trees.

My granddaddy lives somewhere around here, Don said. You want to go see him?

She didn't care to, no. Didn't they have other business to attend to?

They came to a town—or what used to be a town, a few frame buildings with corrugated tin roofs, the windows broken out, and some squat one-room shacks, scarcely larger than outhouses.

Are we getting anywhere, she asked.

A long time later he brought the car to a halt.

Here we are, he said. Do you have the license, honey.

She did, yes, but did that house really lean to one side, or was it her imagination. Honest to God, it looked as though it could have been in that empty town. An unpainted frame house, dark inside—but there were curtains, there was glass in the windows. A small white sign in a grassless yard:

H. CLYDE EARLY
Justice of the Peace
Canadian County

Mr. Early did not look like a ghost. He was a big, fleshy man with a red face and stubby, flighty hands. He had a big wife and a big sister-in-law, who were pleased to serve as witnesses. This is truly a momentous occasion, he said, ushering them into a drafty, dimly lit room with a badly frayed carpet and two straight-back chairs for the witnesses. I've done this a hunnert times, he said, and still I get a chill.

It's because of the draft, she wanted to say, but held her tongue.

Clyde is as sentimental as they come, one of the witnesses said —the one that was his sister-in-law, Cora Mae thought. The two women might have been twins, with the same small blue eyes, identical tightly curled flaxen hair.

Honey, Clyde said, stand right here. It'll be over in just a minute.

The wallpaper, though torn in one corner, had a pattern of entwining roses, faded pink with black stems. Hanging on one wall, the one she had to face while saying her vows, was a framed sampler that read Home Is Where the Heart Is. Mrs. Early pointed to it and said, Clyde done it.

Passes the time, Clyde said. A little hobby of mine.

You'll never see fancier stitching than that, Mrs. Early said.

. . . .

VII

A Land of Lovely Shadows

It was a man named Doyle Briggs that Johnnie ran off with, two years after Cora Mae and Don did it, in 1932. She was working downtown at Woolworth's, eighteen years old, at the candy counter—not, as at first, in the hardware department. Now she wore a pink and white striped apron, a white cap—nothing to sneeze at, for these were dreary days.

She hadn't talked to Cora Mae in the longest time.

She met him in the store, where he came during his lunch break for cashews. His hands, when he reached for his little sack of cashews, looked as pale and small as a child's. He had a heavy beard, the dark bristles always showing. His boss at Harbour-Longmire Home Furnishings told him he was not enough of a go-getter. He was trying to improve.

Daddy liked him, or at least seemed to, and so did Mama. It was easy to like Doyle. She supposed she had a weakness for men like him, men that would as soon step aside from the fray as not.

He came to supper and praised Mama's potatoes. When Mama asked him what religion he professed to, he answered Baptist.

That is a good religion, Mama said.

He was so shy, it was the longest time before he so much as

kissed her on the cheek. Sometimes they walked to Wheeler Park. The zoo had been washed away in the big floods of '23 and never put back, but you could watch the softball games and then stroll along the banks of the North Canadian, which was a little too sandy for graceful strolling, but okay.

So they had a lot of fun, doing something together every Sunday that summer, and often sitting out on the front porch evenings after work. Then one night he got down on his knees and said he loved her madly and would she please consider marrying him as soon as possible.

Rather than hurt his feelings, she said yes. Maybe this was the way it was supposed to be, and if she passed up her turn there might not be another. She had had plenty of boyfriends, but none had ever asked her to marry them.

But even when she had said yes, she had no idea what she was in store for. Does anybody? She didn't think so. About the relations between a man and a woman in marriage, no one had ever had much to say to her—her mother would say only that a man had certain needs. Then she moved swiftly from a man's certain needs to a woman's lot, which was to bear up to much unpleasantness in life and to tolerate more in a man than should reasonably be expected.

Sex wasn't the whole story anyway. It's just that because the subject was referred to in such an indirect way, with reference always to the dire stakes involved, you had to conclude it was grandly important. You wished for it as much as you feared it, if only to get it over with once and for all. Cora Mae was different. Somehow the fear never seemed to take with Cora Mae, and wishing was as easy as having. Once in Arkansas Johnnie had wandered into Uncle George's stable and found Cora Mae wrestling with Cousin Mildren in the front stall. Oh, she knew it wasn't wrestling. Even at the time she knew what Cora Mae and Mildren were up to. She said nothing to Cora Mae about it, resisting an urge to condemn her and then possibly to ask questions. Cora Mae had not seen her, she was pretty sure of that, unless she had had her eyes only partly closed. And Mildren had been facing the other way.

When she said yes to Doyle Briggs, he had laid his head in her lap and left it there for a long time without saying a word. When he stood up, he said thank you, then turned and was gone. She sat there on the porch swing for a while, listening as his footsteps on the sidewalk grew fainter and fainter, wondering if there was something she should have said besides yes, something he might have added to thank you.

Now all he wanted was to sit in silence with her, there on the porch swing, holding her hand, or on the steps, looking at the stars. This got a little boring. Sometimes they went for long walks.

After a few weeks of this, in the midst of a long walk he squeezed her hand especially hard and said, Johnnie, let's do it tonight.

Do what, she asked.

Get married. Why wait any longer.

Get married tonight?

Sure. We can do it. Why wait.

You mean elope?

I guess that's what it's called, yeah. Let's elope. Okay?

She was astonished. He didn't even have a car. What would his poor mother think. What would *hers* think! Not to mention Daddy. Doyle had never said a thing to Daddy—about marrying her, she meant. She was sure of that.

I can borrow Charlie Bristow's car. We'll drive out to El Reno or some place, find us a J. P., and that'll be that.

Who, she wondered, was Charlie Bristow.

My old buddy, he said. I've told you about Charlie many a time. Haven't I told you about Charlie Bristow?

No, he hadn't. Doyle was full of surprises this evening.

He's just a guy I know, he said. We rasseled together at Central High.

You were a wrestler, Doyle?

Sure. Didn't I tell you that? I must've told you that. It's the only thing about school I liked.

You never said a word about it.

Well, it was a long time ago. Past history.

It occurred to her that there might be a whole lot more about him that she didn't know.

Doyle, she said, I just can't do it. Not yet.

Sure, he said. You've got to pack a suitcase and I've got to see about the car. And we've got to get a license. Tomorrow night then.

No, Doyle. What's the big rush. Where will we live?

Okay, he said. Tomorrow's Sunday anyway. We'll get the license on Monday, find us an apartment, and elope next weekend.

During their lunch break on Monday they met at the court-house and purchased the license. They took the first apartment they looked at. It had a pleasant little kitchenette and was clean and airy, but the bed pulled down from a cabinet along one wall, making an ugly whanging noise when it came down, and a mist of dust rose from the mattress.

Johnnie would be home again in two weeks, Jane just knew it. Didn't she know her own daughter. Marshall had no call to go carrying on the way he did.

In the note, Johnnie had just said, Please don't worry. I'm married. It's legal. All my love, Your loving daughter Johnnie. Well, there was no explaining a marriage. And now here was her daughter marrying Doyle Briggs, who was a nice enough man, but what could you know.

What simple souls! Not a thought in their heads, not a inkling of what faced them.

When Cora Mae ran off, Marshall had gone out to the cotton fields and worked for three days. Now he just went out to his garden, but she saw the same fury. She couldn't get him to come in. He went out there and dug and dug, all day Saturday, from the time in the morning when he'd read the note to sunset, and then he kept on digging in the night. The chill of winter was in the air, and there was certainly not a thing out there to harvest. He shoveled the dirt up into a mound until you almost couldn't see him for it, and then he started another hole.

Marshall, she told him, there's no call for this.

It was true that the cafe work had played out, and for sure there wasn't other work to be had. Johnnie's check saw them through, and would continue to, marriage or not. But there was surely better ways to pass the time than digging a hole that would harbor no seed, yield no crop.

She brought him sandwiches and ice water.

Oh, Johnnie would be back. Jane just knew it. Two weeks at the most. Cora Mae might stay married because she was too stubborn to admit she'd made a mistake. Spite would see her through. But not Johnnie, no. There wasn't a spiteful bone in that child's body. She would be back. Contrite. Begging forgiveness. Sweet Jesus, bless her heart!

In that hole, he was thinking:

First was Cora Mae. He remembered it so clearly, like a bad taste, that time she came to him, said, Daddy, I'm going to marry Don Temple. There wasn't no opposing her. He knew that, just as he had known all along that she would do this, fall in love at age fifteen, Jesus, when he was fifteen he could have loved a bale of hay, didn't he know what she felt.

But Johnnie, his Johnnie. God damn it all. She didn't love that man. Anyone could see it.

Smart as a whip, all three of his girls, and where did it get them.

It got Cora Mae a man that don't know his own mind and never will. Worst of it was, she didn't seem to care. Oh, Cora Mae was a mystery.

And Sarah Jane, born two years after Little Brother died, was seven years old now. In her eyes you could see the sweetness of Little Brother, but then when she grinned it was nobody but herself. Sometimes she looked as though she was laughing at you. She didn't take after her mama except in her broad brow and maybe a little in her gait, the slowness of it, but that would change no doubt, as she came into her own shape and weight.

Johnnie now, why, Johnnie was almost a son to him, they was that close. His little pal, his buddy, trailing after him in the garden. You ought to be in the house, he used to tell her, you ought to be in there helping your mama.

Can't I stay out here with you, Daddy?

He couldn't never tell her no. All right, he said, but your mama's going to be mad at us, you know. You're five years old, big enough to help out in the kitchen.

Then along comes Cora Mae, but she's out there just because Johnnie is.

He gets hell about it later, sure enough.

They've got no business out there, Jane says. You send them in to me.

Come get them.

Playing in the dirt, that's all they're doing. I can see, can't I.

They're just kids.

Old enough they can do a little more around the house. You'll spoil them two rotten, you will, sure as the devil.

She'd not beat them down, she'd not break their spirit. Time would come, soon enough, when the world would make itself known to them. Damned if he'd be the one to do the world's rotten work.

He was forty-six years old. No doubt the world had plenty of mischief in ready before it was done with him. He had no regrets. If you had regrets, you just might as well give up, it was what the world wanted.

Once you had something. That was the trouble. You had something valuable, and then, little by little, you lost it. Nothing material, understand. No. A way of feeling, of seeing. You didn't know you had it until you perceived how little was left.

His mama was a beautiful woman. He had seen the photographs taken when she was a young woman, oh, must have been in 1880, yes, she was eighteen years old, hadn't even met Papa yet. She died the year of his marriage, before any of his children were born. In the photograph she seemed to say: Here I am, nothing can touch me. She wore a dark shawl, her hair was braided and looped on each side, and strength blazed from her eyes.

Marshall, she had said, Oklahoma is wild country. I wish you would not go out there. I wish you would stay put. But I know you can't. Your daddy had to leave Tennessee, come out here to Arkansas, which in those days was also rough country. You have got that same restlessness. But I am telling you, Son, leave this country behind and you will come to miss it. It will become a land of lovely shadows, and you'll never sink a plough into it. The harvest you reap from it won't put food on the table.

Damned if he knew what she had in mind by calling Oklahoma wild. He'd been there. Maybe it used to be wild. No doubt it had been. Sure wasn't nothing wild about it now, why, it was a state of the Union, with a capital city as big and up-to-date as Little Rock. You hardly ever saw a Indian that wasn't wearing a business suit and oxford shoes. This was 1912.

In the mornings he helped his father move her from the bed to the chair by the window. She seemed amazingly light, the smell of lavender sachet sweetly pungent. Father wrapped a silk shawl around her shoulders, covered her lap and legs with a quilt, and then placed the Bible on her lap, asking her what chapter she'd like it opened to. Revelations, she generally said.

Fifty years—she had lived only that long, but she looked far older in those last months, with her white hair, her frail wrists, her trembling hands. She might have been mistaken for Father's mother. Beside her, Father certainly looked youthful and strong, his hair, though graying, still thick and wavy, his chin firm, his shoulders held straight. Yet Father was eight years older and his health would begin to fail rapidly within a few years.

How unlike his mother seemed Jane Bagley. Tall, taller than him by a good half a head, she carried her height gracefully, had a steady, almost stately gait. Mother looked long at you, aiming to see as deep as she could, whereas you could seldom catch Jane looking at you at all. Mother was fragile, dark, whereas Jane was robust, fair. Mother had a sly, secretive air about her. Jane was all openness. If she was often terse, she was always direct, even blunt, whereas Mama, well, Mama went on and on, sometimes the point not so easy to discern.

What would his children have to say about him. He loved them, Johnnie and Cora Mae and Sarah Jane, and loved in memory their dead brother, the son he'd buried in Arkansas. He was too indulgent, Jane said. He left it to her to punish them. But it seemed to him they seldom deserved punishing, such good girls, pretty and smart, and didn't they know when they'd done wrong, feel plenty bad about it. They did. Johnnie most of all, that sweet child, like a little mother she'd been to Sarah Jane. And you could lose one of them at any time, as Little Brother was lost to them so sudden in 1923.

He would give his life for any one of theirs, yes, if God said to him, Marshall, I want to take this child with me, but if you'd care to go instead I'll settle for you—why, he wouldn't hesitate for a minute.

Truth was, he valued the world little. But it might yield up treasures to one of his children, even as it had pleased him from time to time in spite of itself. They had strength in them and joy. Look into their eyes.

As for him, he was done for. In 1912, even in the face of his mother's death, hope sprung up before him like the very shape of life, grand and quick, somewhat like the shape of Jane Bagley no doubt, its blood starting up in the chambers of his heart and running a merry course. He had been out west as far as New Mexico, and, while he hadn't much cared for it, he'd liked what he saw of Oklahoma City on the way back. It had trees and grass. Everything was brand new.

He returned to Arkansas, meaning to stay only as long as decency required, and then come back to Oklahoma City. But Jane Bagley was waiting for him in Arkansas. And then he must wait for his mother's death. Then, the birth of his first daughter, his second. He had stayed and stayed in Arkansas, it seemed, and for a time he believed he might never leave it. On Blue Mountain, where Johnnie had been born, he looked out on the clouds and could well imagine living forever.

Now his back pained him.

What in God's name did he think he was doing. Digging his own grave, no doubt, and already it was of sufficient breadth and depth to contain several of him.

Johnnie was married. The fellow had a job, and Johnnie wouldn't quit hers. They would get along.

He began to shovel the dirt back in, tamp it, bring himself back to earth.

Johnnie's marriage to Doyle Briggs wasn't to be. Something in her just closed off, snapped shut like a drawer. From the first, she felt this repugnance, a meanness in her that made her dislike him. Who are you, she kept wanting to ask, and how do you presume, what gives you the right to think, to imagine that I'm yours. Well, but wasn't he her husband. He was. He was her husband. She had promised to love and cherish.

When on their wedding night he lay by her side and put his hand on her, she jumped out of her skin. It wasn't very dark in the room in the motor court. Big bars of light jiggled everywhere.

Sweetheart, Doyle said. Honeybunch. Don't be afraid of me.

She had to excuse herself. She felt terrible, physically and otherwise. I'm sorry, she said when she came back from the bathroom. It must have been something I ate.

He stayed on his side of the bed the rest of the night, still and quiet.

Long ago, when she and Cora Mae were little girls, they had pretend-weddings. You be the bride, Cora Mae said, and I'll be the groom. No, Johnnie told her, I'm taller than you. I'll be the groom. Cora Mae made a veil from a towel. There, she said, isn't it lovely. She adjusted it so that it came just below her shoulders in back, looked at herself in Mama's dresser mirror, turning from side to side, her hand on her hip. Am I ravishing, she asked. Oh, yes, Johnnie told her. And she was. As for herself, she wore Daddy's cap, his jaunty engineer's cap. Cora Mae took hold of her arm, and then the two of them walked down the hall, stately and solemn, Cora Mae humming the Wedding March. Next they traded places, but Cora Mae always seemed the better bride.

Wouldn't it be fine, Doyle had said in the borrowed car, if we could just keep going, never stop until we came to the ocean.

Where did this highway go, she wondered.

Why, this is Main Street, USA, Route Sixty-Six, and it goes from Chicago, Illinois, all the way to Los Angeles, California.

And how far is it to California.

He supposed it was over a thousand miles. You crossed a desert and then the blue Pacific stretched out before you. He'd never seen the Pacific, but he'd been to Galveston once and seen the Gulf of Mexico. The sand on the beach, he told Johnnie, had been hot. His mother carried an umbrella to protect herself from the sun. His father had run wildly into the water, kicking and waving his arms. Come on, Son, he had said. This is the life, boy.

She began to think about the desert, which she'd seen pictures of. In school—how long ago? she couldn't say except she knew it was a long time ago—she had done a geography report on deserts. Her teacher, Mrs. Manis it must have been, had a big manila envelope filled with clippings, pictures of camels, cactus, silver mountains, toads, lizards, tufts of pointy weeds, clumps of sharp-edged rocks. Arizona, Mrs. Manis said. Arabia, Utah, Egypt. Words to remember: dune, sphinx, pharoah, oasis. Caravan. The veins stood out on Mrs. Manis's hands and she polished her fingernails bright red.

Fifth grade. It was fifth grade at Lee School.

Illusion, Mrs. Manis said. You see it, but it isn't there. A shimmery pool, a blue lake, a winding river. You head for it, full of hope, your throat parched. But nothing is there. Nothing at all.

The Pacific Ocean, maybe it was there and maybe not.

The truth was—she knew it, felt it as sure as breathing—she walked down an aisle, long it was and broad, the bride of her own desire, and the altar she headed for had no cross. Instead, it bore a circle, her soul looping and twisted, its motion perfect, forever bounded by its blood, kept neat even as it tangled with the mess of her heart. A secret, a dark stream, a thousand miles of herself—she knew where she was, where she headed. As if toward a cave. At last, a cave, and in the middle of that cave lay Little Brother in the coffin that Daddy made for him. A pretty baby, he would grow no more, crazy with death, languid in the land of Daddy's birth, beautiful lost Arkansas, his own father's bride.

I couldn't remember, she said to Cora Mae later, when the J. P. said Repeat after me, I couldn't for the life of me remember. Somebody whispered the words, I guess, or else he just kept saying them until I got them right. But I thought—oh, my this is going to sound strange—I thought I was Little Brother. How could I be the bride of Doyle Briggs when I lay at rest in that pretty coffin that my daddy made for me.

The next morning he was so polite. Would she care to have breakfast. They could find a cafe, he was certain.

Every place they came to, closed up, of course. It was Sunday morning.

It's all right, she told him. I'm not hungry.

He took her to his house—his mother's house, that is, where until yesterday he had lived, a white frame house much like her own parents' house.

Mama's swell, Doyle said as he parked the car. Once you get to know her. And my kid brother too.

Hey, Roy Earl, Doyle said as he opened the door. Come here and meet your sister-in-law.

Roy Earl was a grown man, bigger than Doyle. He wore a skimpy undershirt. Little tufts of dark hair grew at the edge of his shoulders.

Sister-in-law? Roy Earl said. What sister-in-law?

Right here.

You married or something.

That's about the size of it, bud.

I'll be dog. Does Mama know?

Naw. That's why we're here, bud. To tell her.

Whew-ee.

It seemed as cold in the house as it was outside. She looked around, saw a frayed sofa, a platform rocker, a low table with a big Bible on it, the pages red at the edges, the black leather cover worn at the corners.

Sit down, Doyle said. I'll get Mama.

She sat on the frayed sofa. Roy Earl disappeared. Across the room stood a radio console shaped like a toe, a big one, painted black. She heard a floor squeaking, a door slammed shut, muffled voices. On the table, beside the Bible, atop a lace doily, lay another book, a small one with a green cover, a scrapbook, and when she opened it, there was a picture of Doyle and Roy Earl, little boys, riding a goat cart.

Well, God damn it, she heard Doyle say, she's my wife.

Roy Earl appeared. He had combed his hair and applied hair tonic. He grinned and said, So I guess I got me a sister-in-law.

Doyle came up behind him in the hallway.

Excuse me, bud, he said. Coming through.

Roy Earl made way, and Doyle walked across the room, sat down beside her on the sofa with a sigh.

Honey, he said, Mama can't see you just now. She's not feeling so well.

You're in luck, Roy Earl whispered.

Hush up, bud, Doyle said.

Cora Mae and Don had moved into a house of their own. It wasn't such a long walk, maybe six blocks, and although Johnnie didn't know the exact address she thought she would recognize it when she saw it. But then she began to have her doubts. Did it have a porch, like that one, with a swing to one side, or had the door opened right onto the sidewalk, like that one.

The clouds had broken up, the wind had whisked them away, and now the sky was blue and clear, the wind cold and strong. The cold didn't seem so bad, and she thought that maybe this was because she was alone now. For sure, nobody else was out walking, a cold day like this, everybody snug in their little houses.

One thing she meant to do: buy a piano for Sarah Jane and pay for her lessons. Daddy could play the piano too. She knew he could play it, though with him it was a natural-born gift, never had a lesson in his life. Maybe that gift had been passed down to Sarah Jane, who had a lovely singing voice and sang all the time, didn't care if anybody listened or not. Sometimes she sang so pretty it broke your heart, old songs that she had heard on Daddy's Victrola such as "Side by Side" and "Over There," or hymns such as "Farther Along" and "What a Friend We Have in Jesus."

Cora Mae's house wasn't much, but it was better than an apartment. There it was, not a shrub nor blade of grass, how could you miss it, no porch, and the steps to the door were broken and splintery. You could see Mount St. Mary's Academy a block and a half up, big and gray on its hilltop.

Nobody came to the door. She knocked again, louder, then thought she heard footsteps.

Well, Cora Mae said. Look who's here.

She stepped into a small cold room that had a big overstuffed easy chair in one corner, next to it a table with a radio on it, the radio atop a lace-edged doily. Opposite it, a gray-green sofa sunk down, lower on one end than the other, in front of it a fringed throw rug that once must have been white.

I was asleep, Cora Mae said. Is this just a friendly visit?

Friendly as ever.

She sat on the sofa. Cora Mae plopped down on the opposite end, the sagging end, and kicked off her slippers. Her toes were polished bright red and she wore a green robe with a red sash.

Johnnie said: Remember, Sister, when we were little girls. What on earth did we ever expect?

Precious little, Cora Mae said.

We were never ones to live for dreams.

It wasn't so bad, in comparison.

We were happy.

You were happy, Johnnie. I had my sorrows.

I never felt sad. That's right. I may have had cause to, but I never did.

Cause has nothing to do with it. You got it or you don't. I do, you don't.

You had spirit. You had such an outgoing nature.

I lived inside myself. The world seemed far away. How would I ever get there.

I stayed put. I wanted to stay put. And now—Oh, Cora Mae, listen. The strangest thing has happened.

Cora Mae straightened up in the sofa.

What is it, Johnnie, she said.

Cora Mae, I got married yesterday.

Cora Mae sat back again. Well, she said, it had to happen

some day. It happened to me. It even happened to Mama and Daddy.

Johnnie had to laugh at that. Cora Mae could always make her laugh. And now she thought, How had it been with Mama and Daddy? Were they married in a church, or by a justice of the peace. Of course there would have been no motor court such as El Reno's Finest, the Valley View. But what would there have been? Mama had never said a word about it.

I'm waiting, Cora Mae said.

I'm so hungry, Johnnie said. He was going to treat me to breakfast in a cafe, but no place was open.

First rule, Sister: get you a good provider.

When I woke up this morning, it still seemed like night to me. I thought I hadn't gone to sleep yet. Then I saw him. He sat on the chair beside the bed. He had on all his clothes. The light was peculiar in the room. Not as dark as I'd first thought. Greenish. I asked him what time it was and when he said nine-thirty I asked him where the light came from, why wasn't it dark outside. I thought it must have been night. How could I have slept so late! He asked me what I was talking about. I told him never mind—

Johnnie. Stop. I don't know what you're talking about either. You've got to start at the beginning.

I'm sorry. I'm not in my right mind.

Just tell me who he is, okay?

Doyle Briggs. I've told you about him. Haven't I told you about him?

No, not that I remember.

Well, it doesn't matter now. I've left him. It doesn't matter. I ran away from his mother's house. I left him there. It's all over before it started.

Honey, Cora Mae said.

Johnnie broke down then, wept in her sister's arms. You could get used to anything, in time—so she had believed—but what if it were the other way around. What if you never got used to anything, what if the more you knew about things the stranger it all got to be, and you never could feel at home anywhere, with anyone, least of all with yourself. What if something in you stayed hid, would never be found, and that hidden thing kept you in place—that is to say, in yourself, no place at all.

VIII

· ·

Blue Mountain, Arkansas

Cora Mae took it into her head that she had to go to Arkansas and visit Little Brother's grave. It was 1932, and she was pregnant, and Don had been gone ever so long, she couldn't tell you where. It was his business, he said.

A couple of days before, Johnnie had come over and told her that she was through with her husband of twenty-four hours.

It's no good pretending, she told Cora Mae. It's a marriage that just wasn't meant to be. Doyle is a good man. A decent man. He'll make some other woman a fine husband some day, I'm sure. Maybe I'm not cut out to be a wife at all. I just don't know.

Cora Mae was living in a house near Mount St. Mary's Academy. In the mornings she watched the schoolgirls troop by in their blazers and pleated skirts, their bright saddle oxfords, and she tried to be on the porch in the afternoons when they filed back towards their homes. It was a pretty sight. Occasionally she walked to the schoolyard and watched the girls at their lunch hour. They stood around in groups of three or four, talking loudly. A nun patroled nearby, like a shade beneath the elm trees, kicking at the fallen leaves with her thick-heeled black shoes. There was a certain romance in being a nun that appealed to Cora Mae. To renounce the world—which meant, of course, Don

Temple as well—to renounce the pleasure of pretty clothes—for
Cora Mae liked to dress, liked the feeling a new pair of high
heels could give her when she first put them on and walked to the
mirror—to forgo vanity, cultivate virtue, punish greed, reward
goodness, all that had an appeal. If you became a nun, you had
to shave your head. They were bald beneath that odd headgear.
That would take a little getting used to. You would have to shave
it regularly, though surely not every day, like men's faces. Nuns
must have to dress with the same care as anybody else, wrapping their shining heads and stepping into who knows how many
layers of darkness before ready to go forth and teach the girls
that were sent to them. The teaching Cora Mae could do without. Any instruction she might give would not be suitable, she
was sure of that. She would enter a monastery, if that was what
you called it, rather than teach in a school such as Mount St.
Mary's Academy. But there were no monasteries in Oklahoma
City to her knowledge, all of them faraway. She could see the
room, nonetheless, with its picture of Jesus on the wall and its
statue of the Virgin Mary on the chest of drawers. She could do
without Jesus and Mary, but no doubt they came with the room,
standard equipment. All over the high surrounding walls thick
lush vines would grow.

She didn't know the first thing about Catholics. It was just that
Baptists had no nuns, and what good was a religion if it didn't
give you a way to withdraw from the world and renounce earthly
pleasures. It was smart of Catholics to think of this.

Except for being dressed the same, the little girls that passed
by Cora Mae's front porch looked like any other little girls. They
would not grow up to be nuns. They would grow up to be the
brides of men, just like herself, then wives and mothers for the
rest of their days.

Doyle just isn't Mister Right, Johnnie said. Mister Right may
be down the road somewhere, and maybe not. I hope he is. But
he's not Doyle Briggs.

Neither is Don Temple. But here I am.

Well, maybe you should leave him if you feel that way.

He brings home the bacon. I've become fond of that bacon.

How do you think our mama feels about our daddy. I mean, it has to be more than bacon, doesn't it.

You're talking to a woman of little experience. I am seventeen years old, and been married two years. I begin to feel the difference between me and Mama most keenly.

Oh, I always felt that. Night and day.

Sure, but I'm talking about something different. I'm talking about beginning to feel alike. Beginning to. And seeing how far you have to go.

Who wants to go there, Cora Mae.

Not you. We've got that straight.

That's something, isn't it.

Yes. Something.

You're swelling right up, I see.

That seems to be the way it works.

How does it feel. I can't imagine. I can't imagine much at all.

It feels all right.

All right? Is that all you can say? All right! Lord help, Cora Mae. I hope to be as calm. *If* I ever get myself in that predicament.

If you want to keep from it, you've taken a step in the right direction.

And so there was her sister Johnnie, sleeping under the same roof. It wasn't like old times, though. There was no getting back to old times, thank goodness. No, this was new, this was something different. Everything was different, when you stopped to think about it. No getting ready for nothing.

Johnnie in the house made Cora Mae think about some things. She thought of Don Temple. Did she love him? She thought of the way he touched her, his hands as if they might forever wander at the border of her nipples—but then, oh my, gently closing the distance. She thought of his sweet hardness, that loving stick she liked to take to her lips before he entered her, came into the soul of her, became her.

No, she could never be a nun.

And now here she was, as Johnnie put it, swelling right up. This was a sweetness too. Nobody ever told her it might feel this way. Her idea had been that it would be a kind of torture, punishment for the pleasure that you had taken. Instead, it was like making up for Don's absence. Some moments she sat at the window, Mount St. Mary's in the distance but not really seen so much as felt, as if she might reach out and there the brick walls would be, the nun in her layers of darkness. I am this moment, she said to herself, there is no other time but this, nothing left to me but that cloud sidling up to the academy tower, these walls no more than skin, good as fingers, toes. The life within her, that was what mattered, the life she would relinquish to the world, deliver with all her heart. She grew big, not just with child, but with its certain death, a perfect end.

She remembered going into the room that you were not supposed to enter. She seemed entering it again and again, Little Brother laid out in his blue shroud, calm in his sudden fate, happy, it seemed, to be so soon shut of his life. Others might have to wait, but not him. His race was run, and run swiftly.

Just as swift, the many departures of her husband.

I will be back, he said. Keep the home fires burning.

The home fires, she understood, might flicker, light dim, warmth go by the wayside, if she didn't stay behind while he pressed forward. It was all right, it was good. Alone, she knew the heart of her stillness, how it returned her to the soul of its secret, how it restored her to the promise of its joy. She was made for love if for anything at all, like the child within her, as if always there, taking its shape, its sweet time in the dark center of her.

Had her mama known this all along? Kept it a secret, if she did.

Would carry that secret to the grave. *No pleasure for a woman in life.* That was a lie, Mama, and you know it.

Little Brother was a pleasure—why else had Mama mourned so. She had even said as much. No trouble at all, she had said, the sweetest baby ever lived. Cora Mae had watched him suck at Mama's breasts, which were big and full, as if she could feed him forever.

Does that hurt? she had asked once.

No, said Mama, it don't hurt.

He's sure going at it.

He's hungry. He's a growing boy. You'll see how it is someday, don't you worry.

Cora Mae hadn't believed it, not for a minute. Grownups always said that. *You'll see how it is someday.* What they meant was, you'll understand all I went through for your sake, the pain, the sacrifice. You'll get yours, they meant. You could hear it in the tone of their voices.

You'd get yours, all right, but it was for damn sure *yours* and nobody else's. That's what she had believed. Still did, up to a point. But just the other day—who can say why such thoughts come to you—she caught herself saying, This world is not my home, I'm bound for a better place, glory hallelujah. This was Mama's thoughts, Mama's words. What business did they have in her own head, her mouth that was like nobody else's.

Don Temple's being gone: was that anybody's lot but her own?

And then: how would it feel, to bear his child, to love every minute of that bearing, to bring that child of love into the world, and then to see that child lose its life, as if it was the most natural thing you could think of, as certain as the breath it gulped for when pulled into the light.

Such things happen. Such a thing happened to my very own mama. How did she feel.

Had Johnnie ever thought about Little Brother?

No, said Johnnie, who was sitting on the arm of the easy chair that was Don's favorite, filing her fingernails. I mean, she said, sure, from time to time I remember, but I don't dwell on it, if that's what you mean.

I don't mean dwell on it. I mean think about it. The *why* of it. How it might have felt.

To die like Little Brother?

No. How Mama might have felt.

Mama didn't cry. I remember that. I believe I would have cried.

She cried. I know that. We just didn't see her.

Daddy would have cried.

Sure he did. You know he did.

I've never seen him cry though. Have you, Cora Mae?

No, but he looks like he's always about to cry.

Yes, but he's not.

I suppose not.

He holds back. You never know for sure what he's feeling.

He wouldn't have cared for Little Brother's dying.

No. You knew that.

He made that pretty casket for him. Do you remember that?

Yes, sure.

Put those scraps from Mama's quilt box all around it.

Like streamers, flags, ruffles, bric-a-brac.

A lovely thing.

So many colors, and the box painted white as a bride's dress.

And he carried it off to Arkansas, all by himself. Do you remember that, Johnnie.

I do. Clear as day.

That was how Cora Mae worked up to the idea with Johnnie, got her to remembering, and then sprung it on her: a trip to Arkansas to visit the grave of Little Brother. Wasn't it time they did it. They could take the train, just like they used to do when, little girls, they had visited at Uncle George's. They could climb the mountain, Blue Mountain, the same way Daddy had, and see where he'd put Little Brother—next to their grandfather, wasn't it.

And then what, Johnnie wondered.

They'd just come back to Oklahoma City, Cora Mae supposed.

But what would we have accomplished, traipsing up there that way.

Christ, Johnnie, I don't know.

You don't have to swear. You never used to swear. Mama'd wash your mouth out with soap.

I don't doubt it.

Just tell me what it is you mean to accomplish, going clear to Arkansas. And in your condition.

I'm not so far gone I can't travel.

I wouldn't know anything about that.

It would just be . . . to do it. For the sake of doing it.

Johnnie laughed. I just had a thought, she said. Remember Mildren and Monroe?

I remember, sure. But I wasn't thinking about them.

I remember Mildren was keen on you.

That is nothing to remember.

I saw him and you one time in the barn. At Uncle George's.

Did you.

Cora Mae, I was so embarrassed.

You didn't have to look.

Couldn't help myself. Listen, would we visit Mildren and Monroe if we went to Arkansas.

We might. If we wanted to.

Would you want to.

They are our kin. I'll bet they're married and have a ton of kids. We wouldn't be going to visit them. We might see them, but that wouldn't be our reason for being there.

I might could use a vacation. But I don't know if I can rightly ask for one.

Just quit then.

Oh, sure. Just quit.

Quit, and get you another job when you get back.

Wouldn't I love to quit that job.

Quit then. You quit your marriage, you can quit your job too.

It's not the same, Cora Mae. You can live without a man—at least I can—but not without money.

Don gives me money.

I know. He brings home the bacon.

That's not all he brings home.

I wouldn't know about that.

He brings home—

I don't want to hear about what he brings home, Cora Mae. I'm just not interested.

I've got enough put back to pay for both our fares. You wouldn't have to pay a cent. Just come along with me.

And quit my job.

If you have to, yes. You'll find another. You're smart and pretty and experienced.

I'm sick of selling little sacks of candy. That's the truth. But I'm good at it.

There's other candy counters. Or live off of Doyle Briggs.

I'm through with him. I told you.

Let's go to Arkansas then. It's high time.

It's crazy, but it would be a change of scenery. I'll admit that. And, listen here. I'm paying my own way.

You'll quit your job.

I just might.

That meant she would, Cora Mae knew, and so she began to plan their trip right then and there, working out the details, which she had imagined so many times that the planning was easy. She could already see them climbing Blue Mountain. Uncle George would provide them with overalls and directions, but they would not permit him to take them farther than the base of the mountain. This time of the year would be lovely in Arkansas, even if the trees were bare, you would see right through them to the other mountains, sharp and clear and blue themselves, the sky bluer yet, with slivers of white clouds. A cool breeze would keep them refreshed while they climbed the mountain, and at the top, where the graveyard would lie like a lovely reward surrounded by tall spirelike pines, they would sit in a patch of sunlight and listen to the wind in the trees. Maybe they would have packed them a picnic dinner, which they could then open up and eat while they rested against the trunk of one of the pines.

Johnnie had to go down to the courthouse and take care of the annulment.

It was awful, she told Cora Mae when she got back. Doyle wasn't himself. I don't care if I ever see him again.

Was he mad?

Wouldn't say a word to me. Asked the clerk where he was to sign. I got the royal cold shoulder treatment.

Well, it's over anyway. We can go to Arkansas.

Oh, Cora Mae. I don't want to go to Arkansas. What business do we have in Arkansas.

Unfinished.

Isn't everything.

Still, Johnnie would go. Cora Mae never doubted it for a minute. She saw the two of them so clearly, ascending the mountain. It was as if she already remembered it.

Cora Mae fixed pork chops the evening of Johnnie's annulment. She knew how much Johnnie liked them, with some of Mama's canned mustard greens on the side, and fresh cornbread and buttermilk. Johnnie said little, was in no mood to talk. They ate in silence pretty much, though Johnnie did compliment Cora Mae on the pork chops, and she crumbled plenty of cornbread into her buttermilk, had two full glasses of it.

I'll take care of the dishes, Cora Mae said. You just relax.

No, Johnnie said, we'll do them together, just like always.

The next day Johnnie quit her job, was back at Cora Mae's house by noon, grinning.

Sister, she said, let's go to Arkansas.

So they were off.

We've got to tell Daddy, Johnnie said, and Cora Mae thought that would be all right, sure, they ought to tell Daddy. Let's just stop by the cafe on the way to the depot, that's easy enough.

Daddy's latest cafe, being on 29th Street just off Harvey, was in a good location, you'd think, in a fine two-story brick building with red-tile trim all along the top, apartments on the second story, shops beneath, the cafe at the very end of the building, next to the alley. Right across the street was the Capitol Hill Ice Cream Company, and the Economy Grocery. There was Loy Anderson's Drugstore and the Dunlop Tire and Rubber Company. A rival cafe was on the other side of the street too, but up closer to Robinson, not as desirable a location, near the ice dock and the Magnolia filling station. The smell from Dunlop's Tire and Rubber must not have been so pleasant, mixing with the aroma of chili and chicken-fried steak. Daddy had the ice cream company right across from him, and two doors down, just the other side of Olen's Shoe Repair, a bakery, with all its warm smells, plump loaves of bread, glazed doughnuts, chocolate eclairs lined up like precious jewels, you could see them through the window as you walked past, smell them even before, clear to the corner, so that you'd be plenty hungry by the time you took your seat in Daddy's cafe, either at the counter or at one of the small tables along the wall. If few people came to the cafe—which he called Johnnie's, just as he did the old one—you couldn't blame the location, surely a favorable one. Through the plate glass windows on either side of the doorway you could look across the street to where Harvey Avenue became a fine boulevard, and just beyond to Lee School, where Johnnie and Cora Mae had gone to elementary school, and Sarah Jane after them. Little Brother would have gone there too, of course, would have been a big fifth grader by now, wasn't that a strange thing to imagine, or would it even be sixth grade. He would've been so smart, they would have skipped him a grade. Maybe he'd already be in the junior high now, hungry for algebra.

Daddy had the place all to himself, not another soul inside but him, sitting quietly beside the grill on a high stool, the grill clean as could be, as if spit-shined and waxed.

Well, he said, look who's here, and his eyes lit up and he grinned and stood and looked as though he might jump right over that counter. Two of my favorite daughters, he said. He had on his starched white shirt and little black bowtie.

Sit down, he said. Rest your feet. Can I get you anything—coffee, how about a bowl of chili.

We just ate dinner, Daddy.

We didn't come to eat.

Well, that's all right. You don't have to be hungry when you come see your old daddy.

I guess you see these suitcases.

I noticed.

We're going somewhere.

The thought had crossed my mind.

Don't you want to know where?

Sure, I do. If you want to tell me.

You tell him, Cora Mae. It was your idea.

We're going to Arkansas, Daddy. To see Little Brother's grave.

You don't say. Well—

Daddy, said Johnnie. I left Doyle Briggs. I got an annulment.

An annulment. Well. Tell me about Arkansas.

You don't want to hear about Doyle Briggs?

I've heard all I need to. What is this about Arkansas. Cora Mae, you're in no condition.

Oh, Daddy, I've got a long way to go yet.

You tell your mother?

No.

Arkansas. It's been a while since I was there.

You want to, come along.

I couldn't do that.

Well, we'll send you a postcard.

You bet we will.

Arkansas.

What I want to know, Cora Mae said, is will we have any trouble finding Little Brother.

You won't find him at all. He's dead. You'll have to travel a lot farther than Arkansas, honey, before you find Little Brother.

We're prepared to go all the way to Tennessee, if need be.

Cora Mae, said Johnnie, what a thing to say!

Daddy laughed, as she'd known he would.

Find Grover or Clement, he said. They'll show you the way. Your uncle George knows.

You're not going to worry about us, are you?

I wish I could go. Arkansas. Sounds like the end of the world. It's where I started out. Seems like I've been itching to get back ever since. You think I ever will? Not on your life. Not unless you haul me in a coffin.

Oh, Daddy.

Listen. I'm glad. You have got my blessing. Run along. Catch your streetcar. Get on your train. Send me a postcard.

We will.

You bet we will.

And they did. First thing. Bought the card in the drugstore at Danville, just after they got off the train. Here we are in Arkansas, cold but glad to be here. Johnnie wrote the message, but they both signed it. The card had a real nice picture of the Danville Main Street. Daddy'll recognize it, Johnnie said. He'll like this picture. They addressed it to him at the cafe. He could show it to Mama if he wanted to.

Was it cold! You wouldn't believe how cold, and barely December. Even on the train it had been cold, the wind whistling, making drafts ever which way. Oklahoma looked like a slab of ice, dark but slick, as it ran along past, a cold hard river lined by gray bare trees. When they crossed the river into Arkansas, the land seemed to tilt, dip, swirl, rise and fall, but still was gray.

A farmer took them out to Blue Mountain.

George Bagley, he said. Why, yes. I know the place.

Cora Mae was freezing. The farmer's car, a Model-T, had no heater. But she felt fine for all that. Wasn't she in Arkansas, headed for Blue Mountain. She couldn't say for sure when she'd been here last. Why was it so familiar, why did she feel so good being here, what business did she have in this place. Who could say and what did it matter. It was right, just as the swelling within her was right, it was something that had to happen. It was far from Don Temple, but her skin tingled the way it did when he touched her, the farmer's Model-T shaking on the deeply rutted road, the sky tough as whitleather, the hills humped like knuckles. Here I am, she said to herself, alive in myself, my blood my own, my body the world's body, this life within me the heart of kingdom come. Without me, nothing.

This is the place.

Watch your step, ladies. Look out for the ice.

The house sat back from the road, the unpainted clapboard siding almost bronze in color, shiny and smooth (she touched it, at the door, ran her hand across it, and it was lovely to touch). Starker than in memory, it rose up like the house of houses, with a porch that kept going on both sides, as if to hold or hug the house, make it stay put, resist the sky.

They probably won't even remember us, Johnnie said, but she was wrong. The stout woman who answered their knock—it was Aunt Billie, Uncle George's wife—spread her arms wide and said, Lord help us, if it isn't Jane's girls. Come in here out of the cold. Won't George be surprised.

It was like walking into a memory, going into that house, everything you saw at once recalled, but strange and new and perfect as you could imagine, from the row of gilt-framed photographs atop the mantel to the samplers on the walls, to the thick Bible on its own little table, whose legs curved sweetly, whose round top shone like glass, to the four chairs, two of them rockers and two of them stuffed, arranged in a square around the one footstool, such a proud footstool, upholstered in horsehair with gold fringe dangling.

Aunt Billie led them into the kitchen, where it was warm and light, with a linoleum floor and a big oval-shaped table made of oak. Above the broad white sink a window looked out on what had to be the barn, the very place where Cora Mae had been taken by Mildren, maybe it was the stable. She blushed, remembering it so suddenly and with such pleasure.

Take your coat off and stay a while, Aunt Billie said. Here, let me take them for you. Is it warm enough in here for you.

Aunt Billie folded their coats across her arm and took them out of the room, her thick heels loud in the hallway. Cora Mae looked across to Johnnie, sitting in one of the kitchen chairs pulled back from the table, her legs crossed, her eyes bright, why, she might have slept twelve hours in a feather bed instead of spending the night on the train, sleeping in her clothes, sitting up, the train shaking her awake every half hour or so. Cora Mae felt fine, she could go without much sleep at all, and it was strange and lovely to be in Arkansas, but she knew she didn't look a bit lovely. Strange, maybe. Crumpled, for sure, the big smock spread over her swollen body like a great wrinkled tent, her shoes (she had to wear oxfords now, ugly as men's shoes, that made her feet look big and blunt) scuffed up, dusty, whereas Johnnie's smart gray pumps looked so shiny and clean they might have just been purchased, taken that minute from the box.

Well, now, said Aunt Billie as she came back into the kitchen, it looks like some of us is in a family way. Land, and I didn't even know you was married, honey. News is a long time coming to us. Maybe we'd have heard a year or two from now, I don't know. How's your folks. Seems like forever since we saw them two. We used to come through Oklahoma City every year, you know, on our way out to the cotton, but we stopped that a while back. George, he don't much care to go nowhere no more.

Mama and Daddy are just fine, Johnnie said. Same as ever.

I'm sure they are. Good people, and devout. I was always partial to them two. Well, tell me about yourself. Such growed-up ladies, pretty as you can be. Can I fix you something to eat. You must be hungry. You have a long ride on the train? I know you did. It's nothing comes here but the milk run, stops at every wide spot in the road. Oh, nothing much changes around here. We're just the same. George in the fields, me here in the kitchen. Them boys, though—say, you wouldn't know them.

I'll bet we would, said Johnnie. We wouldn't forget our cousins.

Ain't that sweet of you to say so.

That Mildren, Johnnie said, he was such a tease.

We couldn't do nothing with that boy. Not a thing.

It was always a snake he had to show us. A dead snake, but he pretended it was alive.

Yes, that was his way. It don't surprise me one bit to hear it.

And Cousin Monroe, Johnnie said. I always liked Monroe so much.

So different—like a mule and a horse, them two. And borned just minutes apart.

Cora Mae could imagine Mildren coming in that door, tall and gangly, grinning, his auburn hair splashed across his forehead, parted way down on the side, his hands pushed deep in his pockets. What would he think of her now. Why, he'd laugh at her. Look at you, he'd say, look what you gone and done.

I am a married woman, she'd say. Mildren Bagley, you got no right to talk to me that way.

When is your time, Aunt Billie asked. Long about March?

Oh, yes. March. How'd you know.

I seen plenty. It's real nice, long about this time. You're over the first sickness. From now on it's just fine, it's real good.

Uncle George had walked in, quiet as a cat.

I can't believe my eyes, he said, two growed-up girls, the babies of my baby sister!

He was a big man, big-boned like Mama, with a broad, high

forehead and large ears set low. He walked slowly to each of them and gave them a hug. He smelled good, Cora Mae thought, like fresh hay, and was warm in his thick overalls.

You bet we think the world of you girls, he said, the world at least.

I knew you did, Aunt Billie said. You was always saying so. Girls, your mama is his favorite sister. He's always said that. She reminds him of his mama when she was young.

Yes, Uncle George said. Oh, yes. She has Mama's eyes. Jane even talks like Mama. Say, Mama will be so tickled to see you girls.

If it's one of her good days.

Oh, it will be, sure it will.

Uncle George took them to Blue Mountain, just as Cora Mae had imagined. She had slept and slept, dreaming of Daddy, who wanted to show her how a hog was slaughtered and what the choicest sections were. There was a lot more—Mama was in the dream too—but climbing the mountain she couldn't remember any of it. Up the deeply rutted road they walked. You can't miss it, Uncle George said, because of the gravestones. He would've gone all the way with them, glad to, but Cora Mae stood her ground. Her business this was hers and Johnnie's, and no one else's.

The sun shone now and then through the clouds. Yesterday's coldness had given way to a most peculiar warmth that put you in mind of summer, and all along the road pines and cedars and spruces that never lost their green needles rose up as if to fool you—they couldn't hide the stripped oaks, though, nor the bare maples with their weblike naked branches. Still, you sure didn't need a coat. We'll hang them here, Johnnie said, we'll just throw them across this low branch and they'll be here when we come back down. And not five minutes later, the road suddenly steepening, as if it meant to go straight up, switchbacks be damned, Johnnie rolled up her sleeves and Cora Mae followed suit, her breath short, her forearms beginning to perspire.

It can't be much farther, Johnnie said.

Yes, it can. It can be as far away as it wants. It can be beyond us, like death, a whole lot like death.

Clouds billowed up, silvery and tall above the pointy spruces. A hawk circled overhead, so quiet and calm, who would have thought he preyed on tiny things below, mice and rabbits and chipmunks, he looked as if he were meant for nothing at all, for the sake of wind, to show you how like liquid it was.

We must be getting close, Johnnie said.

We might be as close as we would ever get, we might be too far, already above the graveyard, a hideout you couldn't find to save your life.

Up ahead a groundhog went scurrying across the road. All the time the weeds rustled, something frightened, a squirrel, a chipmunk, a snake, something afraid.

This heat, Johnnie said. Who would have thought in December—

Listen, there goes another snake.

Quit it, Cora Mae.

Here come the buzzards.

That's a hawk.

See how they circle.

What's circling me is Doyle Briggs. I keep seeing Doyle Briggs, clear as day, behind every bush.

Well, see him then.

I see his eyes looking at me. You ain't no wife, he says to me. What kind of woman are you anyway. Is there something wrong with you.

Forget about him. You annulled him. He can't get at you.

He'll always be there. That's the way it feels. He'll never go away.

They go away. That's what they do best. Even when they come back, it is only to say, See you around, sweetheart.

Up and up they went, Cora Mae sturdy and swift in her blunt shoes, Johnnie teetering in her smart gray high heels, the red dirt glazing them. Lord, who wouldn't be tired. Beauty had its limits, Cora Mae figured, but still, she'd be beautiful, she'd take that grace, let the limits take care of theirself, she'd teeter on this road any day of the week.

Now and then she touched her swollen belly, a basket, a bucket, brimful of life, and you had to steady it even as it kept you so surely in place. She would carry it to the end of earth, this firm little basket steadily filling up.

And then there it was, the graveyard, no bigger than somebody's backyard, scarcely the size of Daddy's garden. You could have missed it if you weren't looking for it.

You aren't hurting, are you, Johnnie asked.

Just a little out of breath. Aren't you too?

A little.

It's a climb.

You think this is the place?

There's gravestones.

It could be somebody else's graveyard.

Look there at that white rock. See?

I think so.

It's the pumice. Daddy always talked about the pumice, the white rock all around.

Yes, I remember that.

The ground curved where the graves lay, as if it were in fact one big gravesite, the tomb of a giant, only a single marker visible at first, tall and shaped like a butter knife. This was Grandfather's tombstone, John Marshall Monroe, born 1853, died 1920. A cross in relief at the top of the stone.

Don't touch it, Cora Mae. And look out where you're standing. Bad luck!

It was a handsome stone, though leaning. Trees grew up tall all around, bare ones mainly, but a few pines shaded the sun and made it not as warm as it had been on the steep road. There was a little bit of a breeze now. You could get a chill, but it would pass as soon as you walked into the sun again. Through the trees the pumice deposits shone, great slabs of white almost too bright to look at. Weeds rose up, yellowed and bent.

There it is, Johnnie said. Why, it's no bigger than a candy box.

Little Brother's marker lay flat in the ground, a small gray rectangle: Theodore Charles Monroe, died August 6, 1923, age 3 mo., 12 days.

I had forgotten his name, Cora Mae said.

It was always just Little Brother.

He had a lot of hair for a baby.

And curly too. Red and curly.

A freckle-faced little boy, he'd have been.

Ten years old now. Older than Sarah Jane.

Maybe we'd have called him Charlie.

Oh, look. There's another Charles Monroe.

Cora Mae saw it. Flat on the ground too, like Little Brother's, for sure this one was meant to stand, its shape like John Marshall Monroe's, long, curved at the top, the yellow weeds across it like hair over a balding pate.

Who was he, Johnnie.

He's the one came out to Arkansas from Tennessee. Daddy's uncle. You remember. Daddy's told us about it. Aunt Esther must be here too.

Aunt Esther that sang so pretty.

That could have sung in the opera.

I remember. Something happened to her. What was it.

Daddy never said. He stopped when he came to that part. Come on. We'll find her grave.

Let go my hand. I want to sit here by Little Brother.

I'll find it. Look, I'll bet that's it.

Daddy just made her up, I'll bet.

It's here, Cora Mae. Look. Here she is. Esther Mae Monroe. You must have been named after her. I never knew that. Did you?

Of course she knew it. How could you not know a thing like

that. The Cora came from Mama's mother, who would be visited tomorrow. Uncle George said they must visit her, he would see to it they got there. Eighty years old and spry as she could be. She would want to see her granddaughters, you bet.

Your Aunt Esther—your great-aunt that is—was considered the most beautiful woman in Sullivan County, Tennessee, Daddy had said. I remember the stir she caused when she came to visit. Mother didn't care for her—that was plain as the nose on your face—Mother spoke to Aunt Esther in a tone of voice we never heard her use with anyone else, not a trace of music in it, dead level, but Father more than made up for it, he was talking with Aunt Esther every minute she was in the house, or else singing with her, for Papa had a fine voice, a clear baritone, oh he was a natural-born musician and she was another, and when she was in the house we had music, let me tell you.

Cora Mae had heard the story so many times that she seemed almost to remember Esther, hear that pure soprano voice that Daddy had imagined for her, as sweet as a thrush in the woods, a thrush, yes, she thought it would be like a thrush, something you would not hear except in the country, in the woods, in Arkansas. No common sparrow nor city robin.

Sometimes she thought Daddy had made up Little Brother too, even though she'd seen the coffin, the baby in his blue gown. That dead child bore little resemblance to the brother that Daddy had pictured for her, such a sterling boy, who would never feel the desire that washed over her like sweetness itself, but who would, as soon as he could walk, march ever-virtuous in a straight line to judgment, redemption guaranteed.

It wasn't Little Brother that she had inside her. Not Little Brother that was making room for himself deep inside her, taking what she ate into himself, sipping of what she drank. Flesh of her flesh, that's what it was. Don Temple's doing. Couldn't anyone doubt it. If she saw Little Brother when she touched her swollen self, saw him again snug in the whitewashed coffin that Daddy had made, his blue eyes closed and, you'd swear, a sweet smile on his face, this was only because she hadn't seen many babies, had she, and how else was she to imagine, how else conceive what she had conceived, you might say, wasn't that the way the mind worked, dreaming up what you couldn't otherwise dream of.

The ground was hard and cold, but that was all right, good just to take the load off your feet, as Daddy always says, Sit down, take the load off your feet. When Daddy came up here, he would have been plenty hot, he would have worked up a sweat climbing the mountain in the heat of the summer, August, she could see the sweat glistening on his hands, his cheeks flushed, forehead shiny. He would have set Little Brother in the shade, beneath that big tree, bare now but for sure thick and lush then, probably an oak, its shade cool, refreshing. The white coffin would look nice there, a comfort to see, with its little rim of quilt scraps all the colors of the rainbow. Daddy dug the grave. You bet he dug it, cutting back the weeds first, clearing a space next to his papa. He had a shovel, a long-necked shovel with a pointed and sharp tip that cut cleanly into the hot August earth, would take you as deep as you wanted to go, to the heart of Blue Mountain if need be. But Daddy didn't care to go that far. Didn't need to. He bore the heart of the mountain within him, he'd tell you so, just as Little Brother did, and you girls too, don't you never forget it.

What else are we supposed to do, Johnnie said. Now we're here and we've seen it, what else are we supposed to do.

Sit down. Rest.

I shouldn't have worn these high-heels. They were okay coming up, but going down they'll be murder.

Break the heels off of them, why don't you.

Cora Mae! What an idea. Shoes cost money. You're not serious.

Sit down.

Johnnie sat, stretched her legs out, crossed her ankles, pointed her toes, flexing her calves, shapely they were, always had been, her ankles slender and her feet small. Goodness, Aunt Billie said, you can't go chasing up the mountain dressed like that, it ain't Sunday, there's cockleburs, there's them jenny nettles all over the place. It's what I brought, Johnnie said. And wouldn't hear of borrowing any of her cousin's old overalls. Cora Mae had thought to bring along slacks. She wore them a lot anyway around the house and to the store, didn't you see them in the movies, and who paid any mind to what a pregnant woman wore. She showed, sure, you could tell easy enough without staring, anybody could see how it was with her, even Don noticed.

It was quiet up here, a nice place to be buried, certainly Daddy had been right about that. She thought she might just lie down alongside Little Brother and be done with it, let Johnnie throw a few shovelfuls of dirt on her, it would be enough. Tell Mama I've gone to California, tell Daddy I've stayed in Arkansas, I'm helping on the farm, I'm pressing seeds into the dark Arkansas dirt.

Some days were just fine and others hell to pay. Now it seemed she couldn't count on a minute's peace. The thought of that child within her, why, how could such things be. She hoped to God it would be a baby girl, a baby girl that could grow up and attend Mount St. Mary's Academy, smart in her blue blazer, taught by the nuns how to be good, how to know right from wrong. If it was a boy it would be too easy to confuse it with Little Brother, who was good all right but dead.

Johnnie leaned against Grandfather's tombstone, her eyes closed, her legs straight out in front of her. Probably dreaming of candy kisses, peppermint sticks—it was hard having such a good sister.

Something rustled in the bushes. Birds hunched in the tree-tops —why hadn't she noticed them before. They did not sing. High above, a hawk soared, easy as breathing. It was a nice breeze blowing, amazing this warmth in the month of December, you could imagine it June again, Don saying, Honey, I never heard tell of such skin, it beats everything, it is made to touch, you smell like a flower, you feel like heaven, I want to enter your gates, I want to stay and stay, there's no place else for me.

Wasn't that a nice time. Lasted about a minute.

That sun feels so good, Johnnie said. You'd think it was summer. I haven't felt so relaxed in I don't know when. I feel almost like a little girl again. Doyle Briggs is no more than an ant.

A fly. There he is, that fly there. Watch out.

Cora Mae!

Squash him. Swat him. Step on him.

That's not what I meant. Quit your laughing.

I'm sorry. It's just that—an ant.

Well, you know what I mean.

Yes. I think I do.

She didn't though. Not really. But it didn't matter. She loved her sister at that moment. Dear Johnnie, she didn't deserve the trouble that had taken her. Daddy was right to love her best— next to Little Brother, that is. As far as Cora Mae was concerned, Johnnie was ever so much better than Little Brother.

Soon they went down the mountain. They found their coats still hanging on the branches where they'd left them and slung them over their shoulders, walking at a brisk pace. Hand in hand, they walked along the rutted road to Uncle George's house, the trees rising above them, bare branches curving in the cooling air, a chirring starting up, like crickets but less raspy and deeper. Once from the brush came a loud rapid fluttering sound—you might have imagined a car motor revving up—and up flew a big brown bird right in front of them, across the road and quickly into the dense tufts of twisted, entwined dead branches.

I thought I'd die on the spot, Johnnie said later. I must have jumped out of my skin. I just knew it was a snake.

A flying snake. Well, this is Arkansas.

Monroe came to supper, but Mildren was in Fort Smith, seeing about a new flatbed truck.

He needs a new truck, Monroe said, like he needs a hole in the head.

He'll have it, for all that, Aunt Billie said.

Monroe was a big man, who had been so skinny his trousers hung on him like feed sacks. He had bulging forearms and broad shoulders and great black nostrils as prominent as eyes. Like Uncle George, he wore denim overalls, a collarless blue shirt with the sleeves rolled up just above the elbows, and dirt-coated hightop shoes, the leather cracking ever which way. Something about him reminded Cora Mae more of Aunt Billie than of Uncle George, though. It was funny how you noticed something like that. When he was a boy, staying overnight in Oklahoma City on the way to the cotton fields, he hadn't reminded her of anybody at all. He was just himself, as she was herself. But now there he sat, and the more you looked at him the more you saw his mama. It was partly the eyes, their breadth, the brows thick and protruding. But really it wasn't a matter of physical features. Rather, it was as though she had got inside him, her soul in his smile, in the way he touched his coffee cup to his lips, in his hushed laugh, as if it embarrassed him to be amused, in his hands when he took a crust of bread to his mouth—a slowness to it in marked contrast to Uncle George, who cleaned his plate before anyone else and wiped his mouth with his hands. She wondered if it was the same with her, if anybody troubled to look, if they would see how like Mama she was, how kin to Daddy.

I am eighty years old, Grandmother Bagley said, and deeply regret it.

She sat in a rocker, her frail shoulders wrapped in a blue woolen shawl, her cheek swollen with what Cora Mae figured had to be a plug of tobacco, though it was some time before she actually spat, hitting with ease the shiny brass pot beside the chair.

It's a great comfort, she said, to look death in the face. And who might you be.

They're Jane's girls, Mama Cora. Jane's girls from Oklahoma. Jane who.

Jane, your daughter, that married Marshall Monroe.

I never cared for them Monroes. A dancing and singing bunch. There's more to life than such carryings on.

You always said you like Marshall Monroe.

I liked plenty. That was long ago.

This one's named after you, Aunt Billie said. Jane give one of her daughters your name.

Welcome to it. Good riddance. I never liked it.

The room was hot, a coal stove right in the middle of it. The windows had no curtains, appeared to be nailed shut, and the glass was wavery and brownish. There was a smell, you couldn't say what it was, something burned, something sour. Grandmother Bagley's rocker creaked. She wore men's shoes, just like Uncle George's, dusty and cracked like his, like Monroe's, the big rounded toes sticking out from beneath the folds of her skirt like a pair of huge thumbs. Her hands lay still in her lap, white as the pumice rock up on the mountain, the veins thick and high, curving so gracefully and in so many directions that Cora Mae found it hard to take her eyes off them. A body so old needing all those veins—imagine that.

You girls want to see something, Grandma asked. Lean in here close.

She spat into the pot, and her cheek was smooth now.

Come closer, she said. I ain't going to bite you.

Oh, Mama Cora, you don't need to—

Her mouth looked funny, and Cora Mae remembered then. Here came the teeth, edging forward, and then she reached up, pulled them from her mouth.

Here, she said, extending the set of teeth in the palm of her hand. You can hold them yourself if you want. They won't bite you. See for yourself.

She ain't quite right in the head, Aunt Billie said later. Some days she's clear as a bell, but you just never know which way she'll be.

They went to catch the train back that evening. Uncle George flagged it down for them, just like he did when they were little girls, and Cousin Monroe grasped them by the elbow as they stepped up onto the car. The train didn't seem in any hurry to leave. Nobody else got on, and nothing seemed to be taken off or put on. They had the car almost all to themselves, just an elderly farmer towards the front, his bald head shiny and pink. Through the window they could see Uncle George and Cousin Monroe, standing there with hands in pockets, looking down at their shoes. It was getting dark fast, the days shorter and shorter, and across the field behind the two men the trees alongside the road looked like a black wall. But way back beyond them the hills rose up, and they were still a nice grayish blue color, curving into the pink sky. Now here came a dust cloud along the road, something big and black in front of it.

Is that a car, she asked Johnnie.

I don't know what else it could be, Johnnie said.

It followed the curve of the road and came right up to where Uncle George and Monroe stood. A truck, a flatbed truck, and out of it jumped Cousin Mildren. She would have known him anywhere, lanky as ever. He ran around to the other side of the cab and opened the door. A woman stepped down. She had on a white dress and white shoes. Mildren yanked her by the hand and together they came running for the train, which, wouldn't you know it, started just then to edge forward. He saw them looking though, and he and the woman walked alongside the train, waving and grinning, while Cora Mae tried to raise the window. She was sure he was shouting, I'm married. I went and got married. There was more, but she couldn't make it out, the train gathering speed, getting louder, black smoke puffing.

That beats all, Johnnie said. I believe that was Mildren.

It was. Our cousin Mildren, with his new flatbed truck.

I thought he was saying he got married.

I think you're right.

That beats all. Won't Aunt Billie be surprised.

The old farmer turned around then and said, I had one do that on me just t'other day. Run off to Little Rock, come back with a woman. His wife, he said. They don't have no respect no more. The girls is worse. A girl'll run off at the drop of a hat.

He turned around again, didn't require an answer.

The hills began to glide by, though slowly.

We didn't see any of Daddy's kinfolk, Johnnie said.

He didn't say we should.

Maybe he thought he shouldn't have to say.

Anyway we saw some of them.

We did not. Who'd we see, Cora Mae.

Our grandfather. Our aunt Esther. We saw Little Brother.

Dead and buried. Some visit.

All night they were on that train. Johnnie went right to sleep, her head on Cora Mae's shoulder. The train crept along, slowing sometimes to a crawl, stopping at every excuse for a town and sometimes for no reason at all that you could tell, in the middle of nowhere, pitch dark outside, it might have been Arkansas, it might have been Oklahoma. Cora Mae couldn't for the life of her go to sleep, though she felt tired and sore. She thought of Don Temple for a while, could easily call to mind his face, the little mustache neat as a pin and his dark sad eyes, or remember his sweet talk, his honeyed voice, his touch that made her warm all over. She imagined that they were riding in his Reo roadster, somewhere out of town, into the flat red clay land that was worn smooth by the constant wind. Dust made little twisters and tumbleweeds followed like big dogs. Don was telling her a story, a sad story, he warned her it was sad, told her she could listen or not but he had to tell it. His left eye twitched, and what a long thin neck he had, the Adam's apple big as a knuckle. He was talking about his daddy. It wasn't right, he said, I know it wasn't right. I was to blame, he said I was, but it wasn't right. The words were lost, she heard him talking but the words wasn't the thing he meant, she knew, they weren't the sadness, they didn't tell her the reason for it, just sounds, and so she wanted him to know that, and she touched his hand, the fingers curled around the steering wheel, hard and rough they were and part of his sadness, and she wanted to tell him that. You can't help nothing, she wanted to say to him, it's just the way we are. But that wasn't true either, that was only words and not at all like the roughness of his fingers. The tongue itself—my, wasn't it a miracle, didn't it beat all—put to such a use that surely it never was meant for, the saddest muscle.

Then they came to a river, the water red and slow-moving. We'll stop here, Don said.

Take off your clothes, he said.

Such a little thing to ask of her.

Follow me, he said.

Did she have any say.

Into the water he led her, his hand in hers. How warm the red water, how superior to the cold wind, the current soft, soothing. Trees leaned in along the banks, their bare branches like pitiful webs, nets to catch the light. Then she went under, not once closing her eyes though the water stung, so heavy with silt and sand, and there was really nothing to see. This way, he kept saying. It's only a little farther. His dark coat rose up behind him, flapped slowly in the deep current as if it were a strange fin. Now she wasn't so sure. It might not be Don at all, but Mildren. I'm not who I was, she wanted to tell him. I'm not a girl anymore, a grown woman big with child, and it ain't yours, Mildren Bagley.

'Tis too, he said.

'Tis not.

Ain't you my bride.

No man's bride. Never.

We'll see about that.

They weren't in the water now. The old farmer was looking around, grinning. Never knew no woman, he said, that was any count. Little Rock, that's where they usually end up.

Light was such a long time coming. Then it was everywhere. Johnnie leaned against the window, her mouth open wide, her hands folded away gently in her lap. The farmer's head tilted forward, slumped down. He might have been praying instead of sleeping. The light was gray, but it was light, the land outside the window solemn, still, dark, without trees, no houses nor roads. It went on and on towards the line where the light began. The train did not move. No wonder the strange stillness. The car neither shook nor swayed. You could rest easier now, if you were of a mind to. Close your eyes and see again the grave of Theodore Charles Monroe, the curving yellow weeds, the sky above as broad as time and ever so sweeter.

Johnnie stirred, looked up.

Where are we, she said.

Stopped.

The train jerked to a start again. The light was coming fast now, no stopping it.

Looks like we'd be there by now, Johnnie said, yawning.

Soon enough, they'd be there soon enough. And when they got there, the brightness, Cora Mae was certain, would be damn near unbearable. It wasn't love, no, sir, love had nothing to do with it. A winter sun, that's all, the glare off a windworn plain.

. . . .

IX

The World Faraway,
The Flame Near

Clara Temple never expected Cora Mae to pay her a visit. Cora Mae was the last person she would've thought might come calling.

Come in here, honey, she said. What a nice surprise.

It's no social call, Cora Mae said. It's no friendly visit.

Well, come in anyway. You're my daughter-in-law.

You don't have to remind me of that.

This was a Sunday afternoon in early December. She had stretched out for a little nap and had been dreaming of John Temple, whom she gave little thought to in her waking hours. In the dream he was swimming in a river that she had to get across. On the banks beyond him something was hiding in the weeds, and so she had to be careful, once across, to walk as swiftly and silently as possible towards the tall buildings and brightly lit stores that, inexplicably, stood clustered in a nearby field.

Now Cora Mae walked swiftly across the room to the window. She wore a gray cloth coat that was too tight, considering her condition, a good four, maybe five months advanced, and oxford shoes like a convent girl's, the white knobbed toes badly scuffed.

Clara was living in the Aberdeen Apartment Hotel at that time.

Her apartment was on the top floor, the sixth, and on the south side, so that she could look out her window and see all the way down Robinson Avenue, some dozen or more blocks, to where the two new skyscrapers rose up, thirty-two stories each of them, a sight she never dreamed she'd see without going to New York. Such progress. It was no wonder Captain Lovell and men like him were so hopeful. This place has a future, Captain said. Yes, she always said, but what kind of future, Captain.

She had no business in a place like the Aberdeen, with its plush-carpeted lobby and its silver-haired tenants wrapped in foxfur. Captain, she said, it's not my style.

It'll grow on you, he said.

Two weeks ago he'd moved her in here. After all, she wouldn't stay long, his fortunes such as they were, here today gone tomorrow, and hers used up.

This is a nice place, Cora Mae said.

Everybody loves a tall building.

It's all right, she told Cora Mae, if you like it. It's just a temporary arrangement. I won't be here long. Captain—that is my fiancé, you know—is looking for a suitable place for us. A little house such as you have would suit me just fine.

Cora Mae drew back from the window.

Mrs. Temple, she said, I didn't come here to make small talk.

I'm sure you didn't, honey—

And don't give me any of that honey business.

Goodness, child, it's just a way of talking.

I don't care what it is. I don't want it.

Listen here. Did I invite you over here?

No. I'm here of my own choice.

And not mine. Let's just understand that.

Okay. Just don't *honey* me. I had enough of that.

And you mind your manners, girl, or come another time when you're ready to.

I'm sorry. I want to talk to you.

Standing up, or sitting down?

Thank you. I'll sit. Where do you want me.

That easy chair will swallow you. Let's sit on the davenport. Throw your coat anywhere. Or do you want me to hang it up for you. I do have a closet or two in this place.

I'll just leave it on, Cora Mae said, taking the coat off and handing it to Clara.

I'll just hang this coat up right here in my hall closet.

Cora Mae sat stiffly on the davenport, clasping her hands at her lap. She had worn no hat, and her hair looked windblown, though not too messy, as if she'd run a brush through it before entering the apartment, but only in a few places. She had long bangs hanging in thick yellow-brown curls almost to her eyelids. Clara thought Cora Mae's hair had grown longer since she'd seen her, and darker, thicker. She'd only seen her a couple of times, of course, the last time almost a year ago. Right after Don had married her he brought her over, introduced her. Cora Mae had not seemed in a mood to talk. Clara figured Don had had to persuade her to come. Well, who could blame her, such a young thing she was, who wouldn't be a little nervous. She had a pale complexion, even had a few freckles on her nose, and a pouty lower lip. Her hair was about as light as it could be and still not be blond, with a tinge of red to it that gave it a sense of motion even though held firmly in place on both sides by big tortoise shell barrettes such as a little girl might wear. She wasn't no little girl though. No, ma'am. Her eyes told you that. Deep hazel and downright womanly, the brows nicely shaped and darkened, the lashes long and curled. She was prettier now, had come into her womanliness for sure. Even in those schoolgirl oxfords she didn't look like a little girl. Some women did in their first pregnancy, their cheeks getting plump and red, but Cora Mae looked like a grown-up woman. It was in the depth the eyes took you to.

What I want to know, Cora Mae said, is who the man is that I married.

What do you mean. I thought you was going to ask *where* he is.

I said who. I meant who, not where.

I heard you all right. But I still don't know what you mean.

Sometimes he's not there when he's there. What kind of man is that, Mrs. Temple.

Oh—please don't call me that. Call me Clara.

Clara. Can you answer my question, Clara.

No, I can't. He was a quiet boy. Well behaved. Not like his brother Leroy at all. Everybody liked Leroy, and Leroy had to have a crowd around him. Don kept to himself. He was good to me. Never talked back. With his daddy it was something else.

That doesn't tell me who he is.

It's what I can tell you. Does your mama know who you are? She might have an idea.

It's only an idea. You're no idea. You don't look like an idea.

I don't know what I want. I don't know why I'm here.

He was a good boy. Never gave me any trouble.

He's not here. He's nowhere.

He's got his peculiar ways, I suppose. He's a lot like me, I always fancied. He makes his own way.

He's gone. He's out there somewhere. Not here.

I often feel that way myself. He gets that from me, I guess. Once I dreamed I was in Tennessee. I knew it was Tennessee, even though I have never been to Tennessee. It was so familiar, it might have been where I grew up. My daddy was there, and my sister Celestine. I was a little girl and believed I never would die.

I don't know what you mean.

Mortality, child. I mean mortality. It took a long time for that to dawn on me.

The dream. You started to tell a dream.

Celestine rode atop my daddy's shoulders. She swatted him with a willow switch, but he didn't move. Behind him, mountains. The bluest sky. Tennessee, I told myself.

It was a dream.

You never know where you're supposed to be.

I dreamed of Don's granddaddy.

My father?

No, the other one. His daddy's daddy.

Elzick Temple.

That's the one. Lives in the country. Don was going to take me there. We stopped at a river, the Cimarron. We went swimming in that river, and never got to his granddaddy's house.

That man. He once came to Missouri. He stayed two weeks. This was before Don was born. I remember it well. Leroy was just starting school. Father's coming, John said. Lord, I didn't know he had a father. Never mentioned him, not once. Of course, John Temple never mentioned much at all. Sat and sulked. If it rained he took it personally. John Temple and I ran away and got married, you know, just like you and Don. Once I asked him. Where does your daddy live. My daddy, he said to me, my daddy burns in hell. I thought he meant his daddy was dead. You can imagine my surprise when I hear him say that his father's coming for a visit. Has he been set free from hell then, I asked. From Oklahoma, he said. He's coming from Oklahoma.

In my dream, Elzick Temple stood in a deep hole. He said, Come here, girlie. Look what I've got. I know you'll like it.

His other son had died. Elmer. That's why Elzick came to Missouri, as I recollect. He had a lot of children, but Elmer was the only one he ever cared for, John said.

Behind him in the dream was a mud house. It seemed to me I was supposed to go there. I could rest there. I was very tired. But first I had to climb down into that hole in the ground with Elzick Temple. Then I saw my sister Johnnie looking out at me through one of the windows of the mud house. She wasn't smiling or waving or anything. Just looking at me.

He said to John—I recollect this like it was yesterday—John, he said, I'm bereft. Elmer is dead. And John said, It had to happen. That's all he said. It had to happen. Ain't that a comforting thought now. But that was his way. You couldn't avoid nothing. If it was to happen it would happen. As for me, I believe you have to take hold of the stick, and swing it. I liked Elzick Temple. I admired his spirit. He was bereft, but far from dead himself. I couldn't make a connection between him and John to save my life. There was a flame in the old man, a coldness in the son. At last John sent him away. Told his own father to get out. He saw it too, I know. The presence of his father made him see into his own heart. He couldn't stand the sight of it. So he sent his father away and told him never to come back.

In my dream I saw a big fire and knew that I was to go there. There was a broad field to cross. On the other side stood Don Temple. He was waving to me. It was all right, he said. Nothing to it. Just walk on through. I couldn't move. I wanted to do as he told me. I believed him when he said it would be all right. But I couldn't move.

Sometimes, Clara said, I think a dream is the only way we're here and now—do you know what I mean? A dream is the present, and all the rest is . . . I don't know.

The past?

Yes, I guess so. And the future.

I don't think there is any future.

Look at yourself. Honey, look at yourself. You're big with the future.

It will kill me.

That's no way to think. Listen, that house you dreamed of, that house is yourself.

I don't understand.

What you dream of is what you are made of. It's the only now you can ever know. That baby inside of you, it's already got its own dreams.

Maybe I'm dreaming its dreams.

For a time, yes, for a time maybe you are.

What did you dream, when you dreamed Don Temple's dreams?

I didn't say I had his, did I?

I think you meant to say it.

Maybe I've forgotten.

How could you forget such a dream.

All right then. I was not myself. That was the first thing. I was not myself and the world was a long ways off. There was a fire and I was that fire. This fire was in an open space, in a kind of hollowed-out place in a prairie, like a saucer in shape. The world was faraway and the flame shot up to the sky and reached outwards in quick red bursts.

You were on fire? This is the dream that you were on fire?

Yes. But I wasn't myself and I was the fire, the heat and the danger and the beauty my own. Have you ever felt that way? Maybe not, no, not yet, but you will. Oh, it's a wonderful feeling, nothing to be afraid of at all, honey.

But this was a dream.

A kind of dream, yes. A special kind of dream, I'm telling you.

Where does Don come in. It was his dream too, remember.

Oh, it was. Yes, it was. But that doesn't mean he was in the dream. Honey, neither one of us was there—that's why it was his dream too.

You said you were there. In the fire. That's what you said.

But I wasn't myself. I was as much my son as myself. And I knew that. I was nowhere to be seen. Just that flame, and the world such a long ways away. When I woke—if it can be called waking—I had the sweetest feeling. Happiness, the sweetest happiest feeling. I didn't want to go back, understand. That was part of the happiness. I didn't feel sorry that it was over, didn't need to go back. The memory was as fine as the dream. And it has stayed with me all these years. I can call it up again at any time and believe me it is a great comfort.

You never dreamed it again.

No.

I thank you for telling it to me, Mrs. Temple.

I thought it had to be kept secret, that if I ever told anyone, then I'd lose the joy it brought me. I was mistaken. The joy is still there, strong as ever.

It didn't change when Don was born.

No, it did not.

A blessing, isn't it.

That's the truth, honest to God, Cora Mae.

Mercy, see what time it is!

Do you have some place you have to be?

I have to be going. Where's my coat?

I'll get it for you. But tell me, do you know any better who he is, now we've talked?

Oh, yes, Cora Mae said. He's your fire. He's burning you up.

When Cora Mae's time came, she called for him and he wasn't there. She knew it was time. How could you not know it. In between the contractions she thought: there isn't anything to this. I could do this with one hand. Then the contraction came— who would have thought. Nobody was made for this, and it was going to last forever.

She called Johnnie. Thank goodness she would be at work and not at home, where Mama would be as like to answer as not. She didn't care to have Mama with her. She wanted her sister.

There ain't nobody here by that name, the man said.

She had called Woolworth's. Johnnie hadn't worked there for months, had quit that job when they went to Arkansas. How could she have forgotten. She was at Kerr's Department Store, at the jewelry counter. By the time Cora Mae could find that number and get it dialed, here came another contraction. She slammed the phone down.

Don Temple, she shouted, where the hell are you!

She lived through it, and when it was over, there wasn't a thing sweeter ever happened to her. She just couldn't get enough air. Bring me that, she called out, bring it to me. They did. At last they said, Here she is, your baby girl, Mrs. Temple. And when that child, her dear daughter, took hold of her breast, tugged at her nipple, it was as if life itself took hold, drew her from herself, left her pure and shining in a beautiful place, a bright sun throbbing, the sky in that place pulled as taut as skin, and the body it composed as comely as all desire, the shape, the scent of sure-fire redemption.

Marshall couldn't believe his eyes: daughter of his daughter.

A miracle, Jane said.

And she wept, which amazed him and frightened him. He took her in his arms as much to comfort himself as her, and it was a long time before they could walk down the corridor and out the doors of the hospital, St. Anthony's, a fine and solid place made of bright red brick.

She'll come home now, won't she, Marshall said.

Home? Why, no, I don't expect she'll come home.

Not even for a while?

I don't expect so.

I'd think it would be easier for her. At first.

She won't come to me, Marshall. She'll go back to that empty house. Johnnie'll stay with her a while, I expect. I'll go to her if she wants me. I don't expect she'll come home.

Maybe Don'll be back.

She didn't have anything to say on that score. She looked away. It was not often that you could mention Don's name in her presence and get away with it. This birth had an effect on her all right. She looked as if she might cry again, and she did, twice on the bus ride back across town, and then on the porch of their house, before he could get the door open and let her inside. Once inside, she threw herself onto the sofa and sobbed mightily. He knelt beside her, stroking her shoulders. What is it, he asked,

but the truth was, he didn't feel so good himself. Seemed he'd
been feeling low ever so long, what was a fellow to do, the cafe
failed again, can't find work, depending on the paycheck of his
daughter to put food on the table, Jane taking in ironing, doing
housekeeping for Mrs. Perry, and Cora Mae, bless her heart, at
least the man sent her money, she didn't have to worry on that
account. He did not like to think where the money came from,
how it found its way to Don Temple's pockets. But she had a roof
over her head, food on the table. She'd take good care of that
baby girl all right, be a good little mother, raise her up sweet and
strong.

X

. . . .

Power in the Blood

Cora Mae saved her money for months, started putting back nickels and dimes, just like her mama, and then dollars, two and three at a time. She began to save for her wedding dress the day she came home from St. Anthony's Hospital with little Gloria Clara and found in the mailbox an envelope, ten dollars enclosed.

Well, she had said to the baby, your daddy is the strangest person. I believe we can live without him, don't you. The envelope had no return address, no postmark, no stamp, and so she knew he had delivered it himself, been right here in Oklahoma City while she lay up there on the fifth floor of St. Anthony's Hospital, encircled by nuns that talked of the holy miracle of giving birth and nurses that stuck needles in your arm, and he had not thought it convenient to call on her nor incumbent on him to take a look at his daughter. To hell with love and cherish, honor and obey. Don't you give your daddy the time of day, she told Gloria. That will fix him good. Take his money but not his love. The one is worth something and the other ain't.

This was the first time he had not delivered money to her in person.

All that long night Gloria cried, and if Johnnie hadn't been there to take turns at the rocking chair, to pace and pat and occasionally change the diaper, Cora Mae didn't know what she would have done. She would not have slept that night nor the three days and nights that followed, she knew that. Then Gloria calmed, slept hours at a time, cooed and grinned when she woke, sucked so sweetly and with such lovely abandon that Cora Mae did not mind the soreness that came to her nipples. She sent Johnnie away and believed that she and this beautiful child were after all meant for each other and could sustain each other until the end of time.

What do I need him for, she said, when I've got you, honey, Mama's little lamb.

Gloria Clara, Johnnie said. Where on earth did you get that name!

I thought it up, Cora Mae said. Isn't it pretty.

Oh, yes. I would never have thought up such a pretty name.

It just came to me.

In truth, only the first name had just come to her. The middle name, Clara, was Don's mother's name. Cora Mae used it deliberately, in spite of Don, who had never suggested such a thing, nor any name at all, the subject never coming up. She admired Clara Temple, who had been kind to her and who understood more than you would have thought about love and life and making do and doing without.

Think of a man as temporary, Clara had told her, and you won't be disappointed.

Cora Mae put aside two dollars of the ten she found in Don's envelope. When the next one came, this one postmarked Wichita, Kansas, she put aside two more. She had a good twenty dollars put back before she realized what she was saving for. Johnnie had come on her day off from Kerr's Department Store and said, You go on off, get out of this house. I'll take care of Gloria. You go out somewhere and have you a good time. And so Cora Mae had taken the streetcar downtown and walked from store to store looking at the goods in the windows. Johnnie had been right. It was surely a joy just to be out in the open world again, among people, with the sky above and the earth below. It was May, late May, she had not realized it was May at all. Had she thought it would always be April, the birthmonth of her daughter. But here it was, May, the leaves deep green and plump, the sky a hazy summery blue, the air warm. Why, you could live forever in a day like this, Don Temple be damned, as he most surely was, off in Texas somewhere no doubt.

She came to Kerr's and saw in the window the prettiest thing she'd ever seen. White—all white, like the best kind of summer cloud, wispy and frail, glimmering silver when the light touched it just right. A dress, a wedding dress, yes, and she at the end of a marriage, waiting for the final decree of divorce. But still. She never had one like that, she never had a thing close to the likes of that dress. She stood before Justice of the Peace Clyde Early in a pink jumper, a pink bow in her hair, her heart thumping, hoping to God the sorry soul standing before her wouldn't ask her flatout how old she really was, wanting nothing more than to be done with it, say I do, I do, sure, you bet, I do, and wouldn't he let them go then, let them kiss and fly and begin at last to live their lives, their sweet secret life. She never dreamed of this, never thought of what might come before, herself in a white dress, white shoes, white veil, the cloud itself, cloud of bliss, held in place by the blue sky of May.

She walked past the window, tried looking in other windows, the male mannequins (though of course they were not male, were not anything at all) in their jaunty sportcoats and perfectly pressed trousers, children mannequins in pinafores, their cheeks rouged—painted, actually painted, to look like rouge, or like the circle of blood that the rouge was meant to resemble. Not all the windows had mannequins. Some had cans of paint, rows of shoes, stacks of pear-shaped jars, crossed tennis rackets, matched towels, soap, socks, watches, hammers, diamond rings, hats on blocks. She got almost to Broadway, had passed Veazey's Drug-

store, Dean's Jewelry, Newbill's Clothing, and stopped in front
of T. E. Marquis Photography Studio. There she saw a large
framed photograph of a bride, the gown long, with a train, the
veil like a burst of mist.

What was she thinking of. She had been married and was a
mother. Her wedding had already taken place and her marriage
was over.

She turned around then, walked back to Kerr's, pushed open
the doors, went straight to the bridal department on the mezzanine, asked to try on the gown in the window. Seeing herself
reflected back from the mirror, the hemline not quite low enough
to hide the tips of her black pumps, her skinny hands extending
from the ruffled sleeves, her fingernails unpolished, bitten to the
quick, she wished that she might withdraw into the dress.

It's not right, she told the saleslady.

We would alter it, of course. When would you be wanting it?

I'm sorry. It's not right. I'm what needs altering, not the dress.

Oh, honey.

Outside again, the sun bearing down—much warmer now, as
if summer had caught hold while she had been in the store—she
felt weak, a little dizzy. Surely she was not young at all, an old
woman, older than her mother.

She returned to the window. So imperturbable, that bride, her
beauty as calm and composed as a potato. It was no use trying
to scorn such beauty. Johnnie had it. It came natural to Johnnie.
Maybe Mama had it once. Sometimes when Mama moved just
so, touching the dishrag to a plate that already shone, bending
to reach a speck of dust on a spotless floor, the light pushing
through the window as if towards home, she gave off a glimmery
loveliness and you saw her when she was young, when Daddy
fell in love with her. Mama probably never had a white wedding
dress. You couldn't imagine her as a bride. She wouldn't ever tell
about her courtship, her wedding. She spoke of hardship, depri-
vation, how as a little girl she had been grateful for the littlest

thing, scraps, hand-me-downs, kind words, approving glances. Once she said, Your daddy was mistaken when he begun to court me. He heard another woman's voice and thought it was mine. She wouldn't explain, wouldn't say a thing beyond that. It's the truth, she said. You can ask him.

But Cora Mae couldn't imagine asking Daddy such a question. Daddy seemed a living secret, hidden even to himself. Daddy had built a coffin for Little Brother with his own two hands and then had delivered that pretty box to its plot in Arkansas. Now, wasn't that a fine thing to have done. Someday she would tell that story to her daughter: the hammering of the nails, the sanding of the wood, the careful painting, the choosing of the quilt scraps. She could imagine herself doing that, saw herself sorting the scraps, white here, here blue, black throughout, and stitching them together, tacking them to the edge of the casket. She saw herself boarding the train for Arkansas, explaining to the porter what precious cargo she entrusted to his care. She felt the vibration of the train, the halts at each station, and saw the passing land, flat and vast. Then in Arkansas, she climbed the mountain with Little Brother, only now she was carrying Gloria Clara, and Johnnie walked by her side, and, remembering that trip they'd made together last fall, she saw that even in her imagination what began as Daddy ended in herself.

She went back in the store, again tried on the dress.

I wonder, she asked the saleslady, who was a small pale woman about Mama's age, nearer fifty than forty, wearing a pretty pink dress with a lace-edged collar, I wonder, ma'am, if I might put the dress on layaway.

She smoothed the bodice of the gown, turning, looking at herself in profile through the three-way mirror. She had a nice figure, had not gained so much weight while carrying Gloria Clara, and was almost as trim now as she'd ever been, her waist a slim twenty-four inches, her hips broader than before her pregnancy, but she had always been too slight in the hips anyway, and her breasts fuller, naturally, from the milk for Gloria Clara, but here too the difference was in her favor.

I'm glad you came back, honey, the saleslady said. I thought when you tried on the dress the first time it was lovely on you.

Then I can put it on layaway?

Sure can. And when you pay it off, we'll have you put it on again so that we can measure for alterations. When is the date?

June. I like a June wedding, don't you.

Oh, yes, but that doesn't give you a good deal of time.

Time. How much time do I need. What do you mean.

Why, to make the layaway payments. You did say layaway, didn't you.

Yes, ma'am, I did. But I'll pay it off in two weeks. How long do the alterations take.

Oh, we can do that for you real quick. In three days, guaranteed. And you'll be happy with our seamstress's work.

Two weeks, plus three days. That will still be June, won't it.

Oh, yes. Unless they've changed the calendar when I wasn't looking!

Then I've got time.

Cora Mae did like the looks of that dress. She wished she didn't have to take it off. Why hadn't she seen it the first time. What ever had made her think it wasn't right for her. It suited her to a T. She was born to wear just such a dress as this, her skin tingled, silken, alive.

It will look even nicer, the woman said, with white shoes. Our shoe salon has some real pretty ones. White satin. I'd get white satin if I was you. You can put them in the layaway too.

Cora Mae stood before the mirror. She clasped her hands in front of her, she smiled, she turned a little to the side, tried another smile.

I know just how you feel, the small saleslady said. It was the happiest moment of my life when Mr. Goldsby proposed to me. My mama made my dress. We didn't have much money in those days. Daddy was a poor dirt farmer out in Greer County. Mr. Goldsby was a schoolteacher. He passed away two years ago. October the second. What name should I put on the layaway slip and how much of a deposit did you have in mind. We usually like to have two dollars, if it's not inconvenient.

Five dollars, Cora Mae said. Make that seven-fifty.

That left her twelve-fifty from the twenty she'd put back, enough to buy the shoes outright, with some left over. Another ten dollar bill would await her in the afternoon mail, she was certain. She was divorcing Don Temple, but the money wouldn't stop.

The money didn't worry her.

Nor was the absence of a bridegroom a cause for concern. Wasn't there men aswarm everywhere? She knew where they went, what she had to do. In the mirror she saw a pretty woman. Any man would stop and look twice. It was a feeling that Don Temple always gave her, that she was pretty, desirable, a person any man would be proud to claim as his own.

Walking out of Kerr's, into the hot May sun, she felt the heat. It was men staring at her, that's what it was. Let them look. Let them think their thoughts. Did they imagine that she did not see them in their neat gray suits, smell the sourness in their breath and hear the jingle of their keys and coins as they strutted from bank to bank. From their newsstands they eyed her over their magazines, from their cafes they looked up at her from their coffee cups.

On the streetcar, halfway across the viaduct, pressed up against a large man who smelled like a cigar, she realized that she had forgotten to buy the white satin shoes. No matter. She would get them later in the week when she went back to pay the first installment on her wedding dress.

Back home, she found Johnnie walking in circles, Gloria Clara in her arms.

She sure missed her mama, Johnnie said. Yes, this is a mama's girl. Started crying the minute you walked out the door.

Cora Mae took the baby and sat down.

Missed your mama, did you.

Would've cried the whole time if I hadn't picked her up. I swear, I might have walked to Kingdom Come and back, keeping her quiet.

What a bad girl you've been to your aunt Johnnie. Naughty Gloria Clara! Aren't you ashamed of yourself.

Oh, Cora Mae, don't talk to that baby like that.

She doesn't know what I'm saying.

They know more than we think, I'll bet. No telling what they know.

Sweet thing. No heavier than a feather.

She put Gloria Clara in the crib. When she returned to the front room, Johnnie had stretched out on the sofa, kicked her shoes off. You would have thought she was sound asleep, and Cora Mae started for the kitchen to get herself some ice tea, but Johnnie said, What did you do.

Just laid her down.

No. I mean what'd you do this afternoon. Go shopping?

Yes. Shopping.

What'd you get.

Nothing. I just tried on some things. You want some ice tea?

Listen how quiet that baby is. Wouldn't do that for the world while you were gone.

I'm going to get me some ice tea. Do you want some or not.

The baby started crying.

Better see to her, Johnnie said. It's been like that all afternoon. I'll get the ice tea.

But no sooner did Cora Mae walk into the bedroom than that baby quietened down again. Didn't even have to pick her up this time. How sweet she looked, asleep on her tummy in the little crib that her own mama had slept in—and her aunts Johnnie and Sarah Jane, and Little Brother. Uncle Little Brother. Uncle Ted. She guessed Little Brother had died in it, but it wouldn't do to think about that.

I know, said Johnnie, bringing in two glasses of ice tea. She stopped crying as soon as she saw you, didn't she. She knows her mama's here.

The ice tea tasted good, cold and sweet.

What'd you shop for, Johnnie asked. Did you see anything you liked?

I went to Kerr's.

Oh, I'm sick to death of Kerr's. I had enough of Kerr's.

Well, I'm not there all the time like you. It's a nice store.

I'll tell you, if that Bill Haynes doesn't leave me alone, I'm going to lose my job. Oh, why couldn't every day be a day off.

There's plenty that would jump at the chance to have your job, Sister.

Would you?

I've got my hands full.

Yes. And a husband that sends you a paycheck.

He's not my husband.

The best kind of husband, if you ask me. An absent provider.

The money's for my baby.

Money's money. It's hard to come by.

He's not my husband. I don't have a husband anymore. I did once, but I don't anymore.

I had one once too. Wasn't that a fandango.

What ever become of that poor boy.

Doyle Briggs? Still working at Harbour-Longmire's. I see him now and then. He eats his lunch at Woolworth's. I used to too. Then one day he sat down next to me. Didn't say a word to me until he'd studied the menu and ordered. Blueplate special, he said, with a tall glass of milk. And then: Why, it's Johnnie, isn't it. How in the world are you, Johnnie. Can you imagine that— as if he hadn't realized where he had sat down!

Weren't there any other seats?

Sure, there were plenty of other seats. It was almost one o'clock. I was about finished with my pie. Everybody was going back to work. I was going to be late myself. Lord, it's hot in here. Where's your fan.

It's in the bedroom.

Never mind. You might wake that baby. Anyway, there I was. Finishing my cherry pie à la mode—

A la mode! Johnnie, how do you keep your figure, the way you eat.

I don't always have ice cream on my pie. If I hadn't on that day, maybe I'd have been finished and gone before Doyle Briggs came in. Just my luck. How in the world are you, Johnnie, he says. I had my mouth full. Well, he says, and how are your folks. I could have choked to death. The pie crust was like splinters in my throat.

Poor Doyle.

Poor Doyle my foot. Did I ask him to sit down there next to me?

Why shouldn't he. Would you rather he ignored you?

Yes. Yes, I would have preferred that. I surely would. I didn't have anything to say to him. What if it had been you, and Don Temple sat down next to you. Think of it that way.

It couldn't happen.

Oh, Cora Mae, it might too.

I wouldn't give him the time of day.

See there. That's just the way I felt. Doyle, I said to him, Doyle. I must have said his name half a dozen times while trying to chew up my pie, not knowing what on earth to say to him. You're looking good, I thought to say, but I saw in the briefest of glances that he didn't look good at all. He looked thicker, redder, his wiry hair bunched up on top of his head, and he smelled like mothballs. I told myself I mustn't be rude. I washed down my pie with a big swallow of water. I said to myself, you've got to look that man in the eye. He never did a thing wrong to you but fall in love with you and marry you. Then he said, Look here what I got, and I had to look then.

Johnnie stopped, took a sip of ice tea, then another. Cora Mae knew there was no hurrying her. Johnnie would tell her story in her own way and finish it in her own good time.

I tell you, she said, rattling the ice in her tea glass, men are a wonder. They are truly, as Mama would say, a caution.

Johnnie smiled, gazed out the window. The late afternoon sun flooded through the panes and through the dotted voile curtains. Wind kicked up dust in the street.

Bill Haynes said he wanted to draw a picture of me. Can you imagine that.

Who is Bill Haynes.

He's that jewelry salesman that hangs around my department. I've told you about him.

Can he draw?

Oh, yes, he certainly can.

I can imagine it then.

He brought some of his sketches for me to look at one day. This was just a week or so ago. He had them in a big manila envelope inside his sample case. He took the sketches out one at a time, holding each very carefully up to the light. I wasn't allowed to touch them, you see. He had to do the handling. Oh, they were works of art, all right. He really can draw, Cora Mae, and you know what he draws? You know what the subject of each and every one of those sketches was?

I'm sure I don't, Johnnie.

Why, drawings of women! Faces, pretty faces, some looking at you head-on and others in profile. I didn't know what to say. What could I have said? There were dozens of them. He kept pulling them from the big envelope, holding the picture up, looking at it and then at me. I thought you'd like them, he said. Who are they, I managed at last to ask. Did he know all these girls? Oh, yes, he said. Sure, he knew them. They were girls he had run around with at one time or another. Girlfriends, I said. Well, he guessed I might call them that, if I insisted. Bill Haynes, I said, there are dozens of pictures in that envelope. Oh, well, he says, some of them I drew twice.

Cora Mae laughed. Johnnie could always make her laugh. She got that from Daddy. It was a gift all right.

Some of them he drew twice, Johnnie continued. Doesn't that beat all. Yes, men are a caution, I tell you. Now, Doyle Briggs, that day he sat next to me at the Woolworth's lunch counter, he said he had something to show me.

They always have something to show you.

Don't they though. Their new knife. A rabbit's foot. A picture of their mama. An old penny. A Confederate dollar. Always something.

Well, what was it.

Oh. It was glasses.

Glasses?

You know, reading glasses. Not drinking glasses. He took the case out of his suitcase pocket, opened the case real slow, unfolded the glasses just as slow, breathed on the lenses and brushed them on his lapel, then eased them on, using both hands. I remembered then. He had needed glasses but couldn't afford them. And just as I was about to remember why he couldn't afford them, he said, Mama's got her teeth. That was the reason, you see. His mama's false teeth. He had to get her a new set of teeth before he could buy himself a pair of glasses. It was one of the first things he told me when I started going out with him. When I remembered that, and saw him grinning at me in those glasses, I said to myself, Why, I must look as different to him as he looks to me. And I laughed then. Couldn't help myself. He probably never even saw me clearly. All those times we were together I was only a blurry outline. I don't know why that should strike me as funny, but it did. I just started laughing.

Choking on your pie, I'll bet. Serves you right.

No, I'd swallowed the pie. Quit worrying about the pie, Cora Mae. I'm not talking about pie. I'm talking about Doyle Briggs. I'm talking about men. I'm talking about love. Okay?

Okay. What happened next.

Johnnie took a deep breath, then a big swallow of ice tea.

Charlene brought him his blueplate special, a steamy piece of chicken-fried steak, smothered in gravy, with a little dab of peas and a roll on the side. You forgot the milk, he said, and at first I thought he was talking to me instead of Charlene, who had already turned away and was headed for the grill. Ma'am, he said in a loud voice, I ordered a glass of milk. I was trying desperately hard to quit my giggling by coughing. I'm sorry, I managed to say. He began to cut up his meat into little bitty portions. It's all right, he said. I'm not a man to bear grudges. I forgive you.

He looked up at me then. The steam from his meat had fogged up his new glasses. He set down his knife and fork carefully on the edge of his plate and took off the glasses, folded them and put them back in their case—did all this slowly and deliberately, you understand, same way he'd taken them out, as if he had to concentrate or else he might forget something. The case snapped shut with a loud whack. He examined it. You would have thought the insult had come from it instead of from me. He looked at it a long time. It was just a plain old black case, but nice enough, I suppose, if you've never had glasses before and needed them the way he did.

I didn't know what to say. I told him I liked his glasses and was glad he finally got them. It must make it a lot easier to see, I said. But he wasn't going to say anything more. He looked down at his plate, the meat still steamy, and began to eat. Guess I'd better get back to work, I said. He didn't say a word. He was pushing the peas onto his fork with his finger. I left then.

And that's it? Cora Mae asked. Nothing else happened?

I felt bad about it. I went back to work and had the worst

case of heartburn I ever had. I was mad at him and rude to my customers. Once I thought I saw him looking down at me from the mezzanine, his glasses big and shiny like a couple of mirrors, but it wasn't him. I wanted to sit down and cry. Why can't they leave us alone, Cora Mae. Why do they have to keep on haunting you.

Don Temple doesn't haunt me. He's good at keeping his distance. But I don't hold that against all men. I mean to find me another one.

Oh, sure. Don't we all.

I want a June wedding.

You better get busy. You don't have much time.

All the time I need.

Have you got a groom in mind.

That's the least of my problems.

Cora Mae! Have you met somebody?

There are plenty of men. A dime a dozen. I never realized how many before now.

A man is one thing, a husband is another. Looks like you would have learned your lesson on that score.

Cora Mae laughed. Oh, it wasn't at what Johnnie said, which was true enough, she supposed, or at least fair. But she was suddenly remembering how she used to watch Johnnie on the sly, how she thought Johnnie had a secret power that made her attractive to boys.

What's so funny, Johnnie asked. I don't see anything funny. A husband is a serious proposition.

I just had this picture in my mind. It wasn't anything you were saying. I had this picture of you, the way I saw you a long time ago. And I remember how I used to spy on you.

Spy on me?

Oh, yes. I was so envious of you. What was it about you that the boys admired so. That's what I wanted to find out. I'd hang back and trail you, watching and listening. You had one boy after another hanging on your every word. I wanted to know what you said to them. I listened, I committed your words to memory, went home and recited them before the mirror so that I could get your expressions, your gestures right.

Cora Mae. You didn't.

I did. Remember this? *Don't you like the big thunderheads, the way they roll up and up, silvery domes rising in a blue, blue sky.*

What on earth are you talking about.

And then comes the distant thunder, stately and grand.

Cora Mae.

And the whoosh of wind with the smell of rain in it.

Have mercy.

They're your words, Sister, every last one of them.

I never said them. I know I didn't.

I heard them. I memorized them. Others too, but those were always my favorites.

I never said a thing like that. You made them up, Cora Mae.

I used them on Don Temple, but they didn't take.

Serves you right. Nobody in their right mind talks that way.

I heard you. You could take the commonest subject and make it sound beautiful. I would've given my eye teeth for that gift. Still would.

You always had the beauty, not me. That fair skin.

Skin deep. No more than that.

More than enough.

It won't do. Won't last.

What will.

They went on that way for some time. The baby slept and slept for such a long time and so soundlessly that at last they had to sneak into the room and be sure she was still breathing. A pretty thing she was. Nothing lovelier, her breath steady and calm, as if the room itself whispered the secret of beauty. Too soft, though, and wordless. You could never understand it.

As soon as Cora Mae pushed through the door, breathed in the perfumed air, she saw Johnnie, regal and elegant at her station behind the jewelry counter. Opposite her an elderly man in a fur-trimmed overcoat was holding her outstretched hand, bending down as if to examine the palm and wrist closely for defects. It was the bracelet Johnnie wore, of course—Cora Mae saw in an instant—and not the wrist that the man looked at. Johnnie held her wrist out indifferently, looking the other direction. She might have been stifling a yawn. Or looking at the other man who stood at her counter, at the end farthest from Cora Mae, a much younger man, dapper in a wide-lapeled tweed suit, his dark hair parted in the middle and slicked straight back, his full lips set off nicely by a mustache so thin it might have been penciled on, like Bette Davis's eyebrows. His wide, loosely knotted tie had crescent moons afloat in a shiny purple sea, and the handkerchief in his breast pocket rose in three matched sharply edged points. He caught your attention all right. For sure, he had Johnnie's attention, even in the presence of this fur-collared gentleman fingering the bracelet on her wrist. Cora Mae stood at the counter a full minute, she was certain, before Johnnie glanced in her direction. She started then, withdrawing her hand abruptly from the elderly gentleman—you would've thought she'd been caught doing something she was ashamed of, something Mama would say a nice girl never did.

Where on earth did you come from, she said.

Clean air.

You surprised me, sneaking up like that.

I didn't sneak, Johnnie. I walked in like everybody else.

That's right, the dapper young man said. I saw her coming.

I'll bet you did, Johnnie said. You don't miss a note.

The fur-collared man was standing up straight now, looking at Cora Mae. He had big blue sad eyes set close together atop pale, high-riding cheeks.

I beg your pardon, he said, and then, to Johnnie, Shall I come back later when you're not occupied.

It's my sister, Johnnie explained.

Sister! the other man said. You never told me you had a sister.

I don't know why I should have. What business is it of yours.

An interested bystander. Call me an interested bystander.

Bill Haynes! You can be so silly sometimes.

Natural-born charm, that's all.

Silliness. Such silliness. As charming as a worm.

Rudeness, the fur-collared man said, turning abruptly and walking away, down the aisle towards the shoe salon.

Now look at what you've done, Bill.

Johnnie was far from angry. Cora Mae knew her well enough to see the situation.

Aw, Bill was saying, there's more where that came from.

And he grinned at Cora Mae when he said it, winking at her. She grinned right back. Why shouldn't she. He had nice eyes, dark and flashing. Why, he was scarcely more than a boy. Who was he trying to fool by that mustache, that tweed suit, that silken tie with the crescent moons. No more than a boy.

Like a worm, am I, he said to Johnnie. Charming as a worm, eh.

Cora Mae, Johnnie said, are you all right, honey?

Sure. Sure, I'm fine. I just—

She saw a necklace in the glass case. It rested on black velvet. It had the tiniest rubies, set all in a golden row. The rubies shone so and had expression, like eyes, some sad, some happy. Some very sad. If you put that necklace around your throat, it would absorb all the sadness that came your way. But the happiness it drew from your own heart.

I never heard, Bill Haynes said, of a charming worm.

There's plenty you never heard of, buster.

That's for sure. I never heard of any sister of yours, for example.

There's another where that came from.

You don't say. What else don't I know about you.

The weight of my soul. The speed of my blood. How much my daddy loves me. How much I owe to my mama.

How's that again.

Johnnie, Cora Mae said, do you have a break coming soon?

She sure does, Bill said. Said she'd have a cup of coffee with me. Say, why don't you join us.

Why don't you let me take a rain check on that, Bill, Johnnie said.

Sure, sweetheart.

And he gave a little bow—a gentleman, this boy—and you could see that his black hair had already begun to thin at the top of his head.

I think he loves me, Johnnie said over her cup of coffee.

He's cute.

Oh, he's sweet enough. And he's no Doyle Briggs. Say—where's that baby?

With Mama.

I might have guessed.

You sure might've. Where else would she be.

On somebody's doorstep, I guess. In a basket.

Mama dotes on her. So does Sarah Jane.

Who would've thought.

Johnnie, I'm not right.

Not right. About what.

In myself. I'm not right.

She wasn't sure what she meant. Wouldn't Johnnie understand? When they were little girls they'd gone out in the garden where Daddy bent down between the rows of lettuce and okra, his hands scraping the dirt, stroking it almost, as if it were skin, his own or a lover's. She loved to watch him there, longed to kneel beside him, press her own fingers into that hard and cool ground. Daddy would understand. In a minute, he'd understand. It's who we are, he'd say, doomed to live on and on, one way or another. Some say No, some Yes. The rest of us say nothing. Our roots go on, deeper and deeper. Deepest of all is flame, a hot core consuming dust and rock alike. In the garden Johnnie skipped from row to row, singing brightly, as Mama had taught her to:

> Would you be free from the burden of sin?
> There's power in the blood,
> Power in the blood.
> Would you o'er evil a victory win?
> There's wonderful power in the blood.

Daddy knew something, you could be sure of that, but he would never tell. And what Johnnie knew, well, it couldn't be told. You heard it when she sang "Power in the Blood," but not in the words. The words were nothing but sounds, and those sounds said, This is who I am and will always be. Know me and know what you are not.

Cora Mae, Johnnie said, tell me what's happened.

Alone I'm not right.

Who is—ever. Alone or not.

With Don I was right—at least for a while.

Not long enough. Forget him, Cora Mae, the sooner the better. He's long gone.

But you're not rid of him, not in your heart.

Mama says marriage lasts, whether you want it to or not.

Oh, it lasts, all right. The question is, How long.

She said to me, Cora Mae, she said, do you think I never wanted to leave your father.

She didn't say that!

She said to me, Cora Mae, if I had a nickel for every time I thought to myself, This is the end, this is the last straw, this is as much as any woman can be expected to bear, if I had a nickel for every time I said, This is no way to live, this is as dead as any mortal was meant to be, why, I'd be the wealthiest woman in the world, I'd be richer than Mrs. Rockefeller, I'd be living on Easy Street, I'd be wearing golden bracelets, golden earrings, and nothing short of silk would ever touch my skin.

Mama said that. Who never spoke two words to me on the subject of matrimony.

Cora Mae, she said, Cora Mae, as often as I've loved your father I've hated him.

She didn't say that.

She did. She said, Daughter, the love in your heart is too much for mortal man. It overflows. It is God's love.

Now it's starting to sound like her.

If I had a nickel, she said to me, for every time—

Lord, if I had a nickel for every time she started a sentence with if I had a nickel—

For every time I lay in bed, listening to your father's steady breathing, that calm deep sleep he fell with such ease into, and I couldn't sleep a wink for the thought of what I had to do the next morning, minute by minute, when to wake up which one of you, how the milk would look, its whiteness, the cream on top, how the yolk drops through the cracked egg, how the skillet sizzles, grease popping, how your father sits there, looking at nothing, his eyes like holes, pits, deep as sin, what could he be seeing, what could he be wanting, the fork in his hand, food on the plate, biscuits and gravy, eggs over-easy, the way he likes them. Sitting there, fork in hand, as if to say, There's nothing to nourish a man here, nothing to stick to his bones. What is a woman to do? Can't sleep, that's for sure. And there he is, deep in his dreams, who knows what they dream of, maybe they don't even dream, maybe it's just pure sleep, sweet and simple and dark. I wouldn't be a bit surprised. I wouldn't put it past them. If I had a nickel for every time I lay there, awake and already busy in my mind while he sleeps the sleep of the dead, I'd be rich as the Queen of Sheba.

Oh, Cora Mae, you sound just like her. I closed my eyes and heard Mama.

I have her voice by heart.

You do, you do.

Stay with them, she says. They're not worth it, but you have to stay with them. It is God's will.

When I left Doyle Briggs, she wouldn't speak to me at first. She didn't want me to marry him, and she didn't want me to leave him. After a few days, she said to me, Johnnie, there's some things that happen in this world that just wasn't meant to be. There's some things we just wasn't meant to understand. There's some things too big—most things that matter, I sometimes think.

She knows some things, after all.

She meant to say she forgave me. She squeezed my hand. After that, all was as before.

She won't let me off that easy.

You've been married longer than I was. You've borne a child.

He's no father. He's no husband. Johnnie, I love him so much. Alone I'm not right.

You're alone with him or without him, sounds like to me.

I have to change my life.

More power to you.

I have to become more than I am.

With Doyle Briggs, I was less. I wonder if I'm even less now.

Mama says, Less is the rule. It might have been the Eleventh Commandment: Thou shalt settle for less and less.

And be grateful for it!

Praise God for paltry things.

Mercy.

Johnnie seemed suddenly to remember her coffee, took one sip and then another. She looked so pretty, Cora Mae thought.

There was some comfort in having so pretty a sister. You could imagine yourself, almost, with that perfect nose, those dreamy eyes, yourself but not yourself.

The month of June had come, entirely of its own accord. The air again seemed choked with leaves, the afternoon heat ready to descend. Our common difficulties, the new President had said, concern only material things. Maybe he was right. We can only be afraid, he said, of fear. Yes, but wasn't that quite a lot. And what could he know of common difficulties. In China, *The Daily Oklahoman* said, people ate one another to avoid starvation. Urshel was kidnapped, Machine Gun Kelly arrested, Wiley Post flew around the world. On storefront windows blue eagles began to appear, the Germans chopped off communists' heads, Governor Murray called out the National Guard to keep houses from being sold for delinquent taxes and used the Guard again to keep Negroes from celebrating Emancipation Day in Hassman Park. Oh, it was awful times. Daddy couldn't keep a cafe running, but he could swing a hammer and dig ditches for the WPA.

The heat came down, each day swifter, heavier. No bridegroom stepped forward.

XI

· ·

The Home of Dreams

All that summer, long past June, the money kept coming. Cora Mae went ahead and made the payments on her wedding gown. When she went to Kerr's, the envelope of cash in her purse, she asked to see the dress again. Then, satisfied that it was what she wanted, she stopped by the jewelry counter to say hello to Johnnie. These trips were a trial, since she carried Gloria Clara. A sweet baby, Gloria Clara nonetheless grew tired and irritable on these outings. She might sleep soundly, lulled by the rocking and shaking of the streetcar, and then, in the hot sun or the department store crowds, object loudly to the very idea.

Johnnie took a break and went with her to pick out the shoes.

It's the craziest thing I ever heard of, she said. You aren't engaged, you don't even have any prospects, do you?

Cora Mae had told her, she wasn't going to discuss the matter. She wanted Johnnie to give her advice concerning the shoes, she liked Johnnie's taste, but Johnnie mustn't question her on this. Trust me, she said. I know what I'm doing.

And after the first flush of excitement, after she'd come back to Gloria Clara with that layaway ticket, after she'd dreamed several nights running of the wedding, herself with the bridal bouquet, her skin the satin of the white gown, she thought it was true, she just might be crazy. What made her think. . . wasn't it presumptious to imagine . . . and why even imagine? With Gloria Clara at her breast she felt such a contentment that she'd never known. Why then this other craving.

But it did not go away. She told herself for a time that all she wanted was the dress. No more than that. There did not have to be a wedding. It was the dress, it was what she might have worn when she swore to honor and obey Don Temple. And she would feel again, in the dress, what she'd felt then, the adventure of it, the promise, the sense of arriving somewhere and of setting out.

Maybe it was just that she wanted Don Temple back. She couldn't have him back, it would never be as it was for a brief time with him, and so she settled on the dress. But that was a silly idea! She was the one who sent him away, she was the one sick of him.

The shoes fit fine. She liked them almost as well as the dress.

They are awfully pretty, Johnnie said. The heels aren't too high, but they're high enough.

You wouldn't see them, of course. It didn't make a bit of difference if they were pretty or ugly. The wedding gown was long, it brushed the floor. The shoes might peek from beneath the hem from time to time and be glimpsed by happenstance, but no more than that. A strictly secret beauty, all right.

Oh, there was nothing practical about it, nothing reasonable. But what was practical about wedding dresses anyway, even in the most reasonable circumstances. You wore it once and that was that. You had, so to speak, your day.

Johnnie held Gloria Clara while Cora Mae tried on the shoes.

Doesn't your mama look pretty, she told the baby, who tugged at a strand of Johnnie's hair.

The salesman, an elderly man with smooth white hands, smiled kindly, though he was confused. Pretty baby, pretty mama, he said. Someday she'll be a bride too. Before you know it, she'll have her own wedding gown and walk down the aisle in shoes like those.

She's the mama, Johnnie said, nodding towards Cora Mae. I'm the aunt.

Oh, he said. Then this is—

Her second marriage. Right.

No, that's not either right, Cora Mae said, turning from the mirror. I have no plans to get married. There's no fiancé, not even a boyfriend.

I beg your pardon, ma'am. I misunderstood. But ordinarily we sell those shoes for weddings, you see.

I understand that, said Cora Mae. I'll take them.

The man smiled again. He was very graceful slipping the shoes off her feet, wrapping them in tissue paper, returning them to their pink box, his smooth white hands as if made for just this purpose. Don's father had been a shoe salesman, Cora Mae remembered. Perhaps he still was. It was no life at all, Don always said. This salesman asked no more questions, humming to himself as he wrote up the bill. While Cora Mae took the cash from the envelope in her purse, he attended to the baby, still in Johnnie's arms, and cooed pleasantly at it. Gloria Clara was sucking hard on her little fist. She had a desperate look on her face, her cheeks reddening.

Here, Cora Mae said, handing the man the folded bills. And then: Johnnie, you better let me take her.

I think it's too late, Johnnie said.

The money came in the form of crisp new bills, usually fives. Seldom was there a note. The postmarks: Wichita, Kansas; Gainesville, Texas; Dallas; Kansas City; St. Louis; as far as Chicago, as close as Norman. Some without postmark, hand-delivered in the dead of night, in the mailbox at the break of day when, with Gloria Clara in her arms, Cora Mae stepped out onto the porch to breathe the cool fresh air before the sun beat it down and the dust wore it out.

She didn't like to read the notes that came sometimes with the cash and was glad they came so seldom. It wasn't what he said that bothered her. He seldom said anything, save to report on his whereabouts, his endless itinerary. *The Mississippi River is the widest thing you ever saw. Dallas is the place of the future. Next I am headed for Texarkana. Next, Memphis. I am doing fine. How are you.* He did not ask about Gloria Clara.

It wasn't the idea of the letters that bothered her either. She thought it was all right for him to write to her. They might not stay married, but they kept alive. No, what it was—well, it seemed that the handwriting itself was what got to her, the little loops and curves, the evenness of the line, the surprising daintiness of his *s*'s and *k*'s, the grace in his *o*'s and *a*'s and the neat tiny *e*'s and *r*'s. It was not easy handwriting to read, so small and fancy. It was as if the real message wasn't in the meanings of the words at all, but lay curled in the shapeliness of the letters, as secret and slick as the man himself. Reading the letters, she seemed to see the hand that made them, and she wanted to touch that hand, it felt so close to her. Such desire was painful. She wished he would not send anything but the money. At least then the notes would stop too.

The money wasn't just for Gloria Clara. She knew that. Divorcing him, she had insisted on no alimony, no settlement. It was to be over, their marriage was to end, and that would be that. Once they had agreed to share their lives, and now they would agree to stop that sharing.

I never meant, he had said, to be away from you. I never *felt* away.

But he did go away, didn't he. Went and went, until she couldn't say for sure where she was, with him or without. She could not even believe in the life that grew in her womb, could not imagine that her passion might spark anything but other passion, a want that led only to more wanting and took her therefore deeper into her own mysteries, neither here nor there.

Yet the life *was* there. It came and it went, and now was no more a part of her than the table she ate off of, the glass she drank water from. Heart of her heart, her daughter now saw with separate eyes, heard through her own ears, and the blood that kept her warm was her own blood. You could not deny that. In this respect, Gloria Clara was her daddy's girl for sure—which was to say, no one's, her own hidden self, entire and no more knowable than the sky, the dirt, the butcher knife.

Don Temple sent the money to her, to Cora Mae. What did he know of his daughter, after all. He sent it to Cora Mae, she knew, not because he wished to remind her that she must depend upon him, that he would remain the source of her sustenance even in his absence, but because the money for him was a part of himself. He wanted to give himself away, would pick clean his own bones if he could, let his lifeblood flow where it might, and become the vacancy he constantly looked out on and confused himself with.

This much became clear to her: she was not going to be any-body's June bride. Not this June anyway. By the end of the month she had four payments to make on the dress, although she had bought the shoes, the matching satin handbag with pearls inlaid. She had bought silk stockings—the real thing—and a full-length silk slip. But she didn't have the gown and no groom had been forthcoming.

You'll have a new daddy soon, she told Gloria Clara, who cooed and giggled as if she approved.

However, Cora Mae began to think that a groom would not be necessary, that the dress would be enough. Didn't she have the idea of Don Temple, the gist of him, delivered to her by the U. S. Mail. Could any husband be better than that, wouldn't they all reduce to the same blessed spirit: regular cash. Money in the bank.

In the newspapers she saw photographs of the smiling Franklin D. Roosevelt, she read of bank failures, farm foreclosures, bread lines. Her own father had no work. Wasn't she fortunate, who did not need to work, who knew that the essence of her former husband would arrive in the mail when she needed it, would pay the rent and put food on the table.

An absent provider, Johnnie said, was the best kind. Johnnie got nothing from Doyle Briggs. She did not stay married to him long enough to know what he might amount to.

July came. August. Gloria Clara slept all night now. In the daytime she played happily with whatever you put before her, a spool, a spoon, a cup, a paper sack. The dress was paid for and brought home. What folly it seemed. Cora Mae left it in the wardrobe for a long time, still in the cardboard box. Whole days passed and she did not give the dress a thought. Her soul seemed to have escaped her—or, rather, it seemed to reside in Gloria Clara, all her energy compressed and transported into that small figure of demand and delight, duty and wonder.

In September the girls returned to Mount St. Mary's, fresh and pretty in their blazers and checked skirts, saddle shoes and white socks carefully rolled. Once again the nuns appeared in the schoolyard. Like dark, thickly plumed birds they strutted in the yellow grass, silent, their heads cocked as if listening for danger.

She was almost happy. She had the dress, the shoes, the silk stockings, the lacy silk slip. She knew she had them, but did not need to put them on. From time to time—not often, perhaps every other Sunday or so—she took Gloria Clara to Mama and Daddy's. Sometimes Johnnie was there, talking of what had happened at Kerr's that week, the strange customers, the odd retorts, the boss's endless complaints. I wish you didn't have to work that way, Mama said. Mama didn't mean to make Daddy feel bad about accepting the money Johnnie gave them. At least Cora Mae didn't think so. But Daddy certainly paled when he heard a remark like that.

Oh, I don't mind it, Johnnie said. What else would I do.

I wish I worked in a store, Sarah Jane said. I'd like to work in a store like Kerr's someday.

I'll bet you would, Johnnie said. I'll bet you your feet wouldn't like it so much though.

It's them shoes you wear, Mama said. I can't understand how you walk in them, let alone stand in them all day.

You stand on your feet all day, Daddy said, and your feet are going to hurt. I don't care what kind of shoes you have on.

I know that. Some hurting is worse than others though.

Maybe so.

You know it's so, Marshall. Don't be so ornery at the supper table. It's bad for your digestion.

Pass Johnnie some more of that cornbread.

It's delicious, Johnnie said. Did you make this cornbread, Daddy?

No, it's your mama's.

He won't make it anymore. Won't cook hardly a thing.

Oh, I'll bet, Johnnie said. I can't imagine Daddy not cooking. That would be like you not canning, Mama.

All the same, he don't do it.

Nobody cares to eat my cooking.

You make the best chili, Johnnie said. Nobody makes chili like you do, Daddy. And peach cobbler. Cora Mae and I used to snitch bites of your peach cobbler, didn't we, Cora Mae.

Yes, Cora Mae said. Oh, yes. At the restaurant, you mean.

At the restaurant, sure. It was your idea, not mine.

Yes, I remember that. Peach cobbler. Blackberry too.

You girls thought you were getting away with something, Daddy said, but I'll tell you what. I always knew about your snitching. Didn't matter to me. There was always plenty. I made plenty extra.

Yes, Mama said, and gave it away to any stranger that asked. But he won't cook anymore, won't even fry a egg.

Times like this, Cora Mae had to excuse herself. The baby,

she said, I'd better see to the baby. And she went into Mama and Daddy's bedroom, where Gloria Clara lay sound asleep on the big bed, the late afternoon sunlight slashing her in two, her tiny legs lit up and the rest of her body in shadow. Oh, honey, she said in her thoughts, it'll be different for you and me, won't it. We'll look out for ourselves, won't we. We'll be as happy in twenty years as we are right now. You and me, sweetheart. This old world had just better watch out. You won't have to worry over me either. No, ma'am. I'll have my own, and you'll have yours. I promise you that, baby. You won't have to work in any Kerr's Department Store in order to put a roof over my head and food on my table, I promise you that. We're going to take care of ourselves, aren't we, darling.

She began to be careful with the money Don sent her. She put back as much of it as she could. She took some of it and gave it to Johnnie. It's for Mama and Daddy, she said. You shouldn't have to bear the burden all by yourself. They're as much my responsibility as yours.

Johnnie said, Well, why don't you give it to them yourself.

They wouldn't take it. You know they wouldn't take it. It comes from Don Temple.

So Cora Mae paid her rent, bought what few groceries she needed, and split the rest with Johnnie. Her own half she put in an envelope marked Future. And she stuck the envelope beneath her mattress—not because she imagined that spot a good hiding place, but because she liked the idea of sleeping above it every night. What a pleasure when she could add a few bills to that envelope, feel it grow thicker and heavier.

Still, it was not enough. It could never grow fast enough. Don Temple must not be depended upon. He would not send her money forever. There would come a time when she would begin to spend what was in the envelope. The money would go quickly then, and she would be left hopeless. She must find a way to

take care of herself and her baby. But she would not work like
Johnnie, not as long as Gloria Clara depended so upon her. In
four or five years maybe, but not now. She felt very strongly about
that.

She remembered the wedding dress, took it out, examined it.

One night she sat Gloria Clara on a pallet in the living room,
and then she brought in the dress. Gloria Clara was sitting up
easily now, her back strong, her neck muscles hardening fast.
Isn't Mama's dress pretty, Cora Mae said, holding the dress close
to her body.

It *was* pretty. She had forgotten how pretty it was.

Mama's going to put on her wedding dress, she said.

She pulled the shades and undressed right there in the living
room. What difference did it make, wasn't it her house, each
room hers to do what she pleased in it?

Gloria Clara stayed busy with her pots and pans, putting one
on top of the other, then shaking spools in them. Her hair was
growing in thicker now, and darkening. It had been so wispy
and blond at first, but now it had a reddish cast to it and fell
in springy curls at her forehead and ears. Her eyes, too, had
changed color, just as they were supposed to, from the blue of
her birth to a greenish gray. You've got your grandmother's eyes,
she told the baby, the Bagley eyes, same as your mama. It would
have been nice if you had your granddaddy's dark eyes, but it's
all right, you're just fine.

She saw neither Don Temple nor herself in the baby, though
Johnnie said when Gloria Clara grinned she reminded her of
Don. Cora Mae didn't see it though. And she would never tell
Gloria Clara that she had the Bagley eyes. You are nobody but
yourself, she would say. You aren't your daddy and you aren't
your mama. You aren't your grandparents nor none of their people and don't you forget it. You are yourself, the sweetest baby
on earth.

And for sure, she thought as she pulled the wedding gown over her head, for sure you have been afflicted with the silliest mama in the world.

Oh, but didn't the gown feel icy cold at first against her skin, her arms sliding through the long sleeves as if through ice. Made you shiver. Then a warmth came, a pleasant heat, a snug release when the dress fit itself to her body. Nothing silly at all about this. The shoes, what had she done with the shoes. She saw one, on its side, by the sofa, almost under it, how had it gotten there, and where was its mate. Then she heard the new noise Gloria Clara was making and, instantly, realized its source: the shoe, its high narrow heel swung against the lid of a pan.

Oh, honey, she said, bending down quickly in the long trailing gown, you mustn't hammer with Mama's shoe.

When Cora Mae took the shoe away from her, Gloria Clara looked startled, then grinned. It was *her* grin, not Don Temple's at all.

You think I'm playing a game, don't you, Cora Mae said. You think this is just for your own amusement.

Gloria Clara reached for the shoe.

No, Cora Mae said. This is Mama's shoe. Mama's very special shoe. Her wedding shoes. Not for Baby to play with. Mama's not playing a game with you now, sweetheart.

She stood up, felt a little dizzy, sat down on the sofa. Gloria Clara began to cry. Shown that the pan was still available, and a spoon to hit it with, she forgot about the shoe long enough for Cora Mae to slip into them and stand. She wasn't dizzy now, except a little with the excitement she felt when she walked across the room and back. Gloria Clara banged on the pot with the spoon while Cora Mae went to the bedroom for the hat and veil, the satin purse that matched the shoes, the white silk gloves. She sat at her dresser and adjusted the pillbox hat, seeing that it stayed firmly in place with a pearl hatpin. The veil came down over her face, extending to the level of her shoulders in front and back. It had tiny lace flowers appliqued in delicately slanting lines from top to bottom and a border of shiny silk. A lovely haze enveloped her, softening and soothing, working, it seemed, from the veil inwards to where the flame beat and shook in her blood.

In the other room Gloria Clara chattered merrily, making the sounds that had no words to hold them in, weigh them down. I speak that language, Cora Mae said to herself. I'm speaking it now.

She stood in the white dress. The image in the mirror had nothing to do with her. She had never felt happier. When she reentered the room where her daughter played, she might have been walking towards the sky. She was not alone. A man walked beside her—not Don Temple—this was a man she'd never met, never even dreamed of. It didn't matter who he was. His hand brushed hers, his solid footsteps echoed hers, his breathing paced her own. He wanted to pull her back into the dark hallway. She felt his desire as sure as she knew the smooth heat of the gown, the height the heels gave her, the net that meant her face. My sweetheart, he whispered. My darling bride.

There was a secret place he wanted to take her to.

On the pallet Gloria Clara waved her arms in the air and laughed.

Sweet baby, Cora Mae said. Oh, my sweet baby. The happiest baby in the world and the happiest mama. What in the world could be the matter with us. I feel so strong, honey, I could cry. You feel it too, don't you. I know you do. Where do we get this strength, I wonder. Oh, it doesn't matter, does it. We've got it, that's what counts, and it's wonderful. Nothing can touch us, not when we're happy and strong like this, nothing at all.

The checks kept coming. One night Cora Mae had the strongest feeling. She was certain that this was one of the nights Don would deliver the check himself. Putting Gloria Clara to bed, she could feel his presence, believed that if she looked out the front window just then, she would see him walking past. She imagined him walking past the house several times, circling the block. He waited until he saw the front bedroom light go out. He would know then that she had put Gloria Clara down. Then he circled the block again, waiting for the last light, the light in her bedroom, to go off. He would walk past again. The house would have to settle well into its darkness before he would consider stepping onto the porch, opening the mailbox, slipping the plain white envelope inside it. Several nights ago, she had awakened, hearing Gloria Clara stir, and then couldn't get back to sleep, certain she heard his footsteps, ever so soft, on the porch steps. She had not gotten up, had at last gone back to sleep, and when she checked the mailbox first thing in the morning, Gloria Clara in her arms, nothing was there. The check came with the mail, postmarked Baxter Springs, Kansas.

On this night she turned out the lights but did not go to bed. Gloria Clara slept soundly. It had been a cool early autumn day, and tonight there was a sharp edge to the chilly air. For the baby's sake she had earlier lit the gas heater in the living room— otherwise she could have found pleasure in the evening's gathering coldness. After she turned the lights out, she shut the heater off. Her eyes adjusted quickly to the dark. After all, nothing was unfamiliar in this small house that in so many ways resembled the house of her parents, the rooms bearing the same simple relation to each other, two bedrooms along one side joined by a short hallway, the bathroom in between. Front room connected to dining room by a broad, arched doorway. Her dining room served also as kitchen, whereas Mama had her kitchen separate, with its little closed-in back porch for the storing of each year's canned beans and peas and tomatoes. Mama and Daddy's house was only ten blocks away, but it seemed much farther.

Oh, he was out there. He stalked this house, he breathed the cool night air, taking it in as if he stole it. He had the check in his suitcoat pocket, snug alongside his warm chest, sealed in its white unaddressed envelope.

She took off her clothes, but did not put on her nightgown. Undressing in the dark, as she always did, she did not feel like going to bed. Why couldn't you stay up, undressed, as late as you wanted to. Where was the harm. The lights were out, nobody could see inside. And what if she decided to go outside. Where was the harm in that. It was dark as pitch outside, dark as far as you could see. The night air would be cold, soothing, cleansing. How else wash the daylight from you.

But Don Temple was out there. He would see her. She did not want that. She would have to stay in the house because he was out there stalking her in the darkness, stealing all the night air for himself. He would not set foot in the house, but he would claim her if he found her outside. You know he would. She did not for one minute confuse Don Temple with that other man whose bride she was. Don Temple had no secret place to take her to. He was everywhere, he had no place to hide, poor man, he was out there right now, no secret room to hide in. So she had to stay put, didn't she.

She sat very still in the chair next to her bed and felt safe for a while. But what was to keep him from coming into the house after all. She could not lock him out. He had a key of his own. He could come in any time he wanted to, touch her any way he pleased, pulling her close to his hardness. See what a state you've got me in, he would say, as if that gave him the right, as if that gave any man the right, to bury himself in her.

Honey, he said to her once, I become you.

And she had thought at first that he meant the way a dress might become her, a pretty hat, a new pair of shoes.

Are you a necklace, Don Temple, she had laughed, are you a shade of lipstick, a permanent wave.

I lose myself, he said. In you I'm lost. I become you.

She understood what he meant. Hadn't she felt it, his presence in her, his blood, his bones, his muscled skin, his tongue, his quick and lovely death. Who could possibly bear the beauty of it. Not her, not any woman, surely, who has her own precious blood to live up to, more skin than she knows what to do with, nerve and ligament to spare.

He must bear his own death, die in himself, not in her. She was becoming enough without him. New life, for example, for God's sake, quickened in her womb, and she must bear that.

She *had* borne it, brought a daughter into the world as if in spite of herself, in spite of him. And now she became something else. The birth of Gloria Clara seemed only another conception. Don Temple didn't have a thing in the world to do with this one, a seed she'd swear her own soul set in motion.

Now moonlight was shining through her window. It leant its pale pretty light to her dresser top, with its row of tiny jars and bottles, the satin-covered jewelry box (a gift from Don Temple), the velvet pincushion Mama gave her, the brass letter opener, barrettes, hair ribbons, hairbrush and comb—it was comforting to see that each object, though stiller and more remote, remained itself.

She went to the living room, where the moonlight was even brighter, and opened the front door. She would keep the screen door latched, but she would stand here as long as she wished, letting the chilly air wash over her naked body. If Don Temple passed by, he would see that she was here, in the rented house his checks paid for. She was not afraid of him. He would see that too. He would pass on by. The next check would be delivered by the mailman, postmarked a town in Texas or Kansas or Missouri that she had never heard of except to know he had been there, he had traveled through them, perhaps on a night such as this one, and he would be there again. When she tried to imagine what those places were like, she remembered riding with him across Oklahoma, the drive that was their wedding trip. She saw again the flat empty land, felt the wind shake the car, the dryness settling into her throat, dust in her mouth.

It has its own beauty, Don had said. A tree ain't everything.

She had made him turn around, marry her closer to Oklahoma City. She knew he was right about the beauty though. She acknowledged the beauty, she recognized it. It was as far from Daddy's green hilly woods of Arkansas as you could get, and the vastness of it sickened her with its cloudless endless sky, its hard cruel horizons. All the same, the fright she felt came from the beauty she saw, a beauty borne of vacancy, of absence. Don had misunderstood her and she had not tried to explain. After all, she couldn't have explained it, did not understand it herself at the time, it didn't dawn on her until later, after he'd turned the car around and they were leaving that land behind for good. The towns, even the few with a wide brick Main Street and a two-story bank building made of sandstone, couldn't fool a soul: they would not last, they were not even made to last. Don left the road and took her to an empty house, an abandoned farmhouse, the dust around it drifted into dunes, blown in curves that softened the hard edges of the house, made it look as though it had risen from beneath the ground and still had a ways yet to go. He had begun to make love to her there, and they might have spent the night in that house of dust, but the air was too thick to breathe and she had choked on it, could not breathe easily again until they were back in the car, the air as if purified by the speed with which you drove through it.

So he was out there, speeding through the heavy air, lightening it with his constant motion. His home was that house made for dust to live in.

It was beautiful, she said through the screen door to Don Temple, your treeless flat land was beautiful. Your house of dust might have been the home of my dreams. It's what we come to again and again, my lost husband. I knew that then and I believe you've always known it. It's what you wanted me to see, isn't it, when you took me out there, a starkness that underlies all things, the beautiful barren land that nurtures us, makes us what we are to become.

She stood there at the door, composing her thoughts, until she noticed that she was shivering. Then she stepped back, closed the door. It was cold. Even in the house it was cold. How long had she held the door open? Long enough to let the chill in, long enough for Don Temple to pass by many a time. Still shivering, she looked in on Gloria Clara and, although the baby slept soundly, spread a second blanket over her.

The room was darker now, the moon no longer shining directly through the window. She found her flannel nightgown, put it on, added another blanket to her bed, and climbed into it. She kept shivering and couldn't sleep, couldn't get warm until at last she brought the baby to her bed. Gloria Clara woke up, but only briefly, and then was asleep and cozy and warm in her mother's arms, her body's heat going straight to Cora Mae's blood, it seemed. It was lovely, she told the baby the next morning, with you cuddled up against me I slept the sleep of the dead.

Several days later, on an evening when she had no feeling at all of Don Temple in the neighborhood, his check having come in the mail that very day with a Liberal, Kansas, postmark, he showed up at her door, a sheepish grin on his face and his hat in his hand.

Is that baby walking yet, he said. I thought maybe she'd be walking by now.

Gloria Clara was in fact struggling to crawl off her pallet on the floor when not sufficiently entertained by pots and pans and spools, and was at that moment pulling herself toward the arm of the sofa, desirous of her mother's coffee cup. But no, she hadn't walked yet. They don't usually walk at six and a half months, she told Don as she lifted Gloria Clara from the floor, distracting her attention from the coffee cup.

Look here who's come to see you, she told the baby, who had begun to cry when removed from range of the cup.

And he came in, walked into the living room as if he did it

every day. Gloria Clara wouldn't calm down, the whole visit, Daddy or no Daddy. It was close to her bedtime and she wanted her milk. But Cora Mae didn't want to nurse the baby with Don there. So she had to try to keep Gloria Clara amused the whole time of the visit, which, fortunately, wasn't long. It seemed long, but couldn't have been more than fifteen or twenty minutes.

He said about as little as could be said and still use words.

He hoped she was doing fine.

He wondered when Gloria Clara might begin to walk. "The little girl," he called Gloria Clara, and she wondered if he might have forgotten his own daughter's name.

His business was brisk. He didn't expect repeal of prohibition to take hold in Oklahoma, and people with a taste for whiskey wasn't going to find legalized 3.2 percent beer to their liking.

His mama was okay. And how was hers.

Was her daddy working? A shame, but maybe this so-called New Deal would change some things.

He hoped she was doing fine.

Was the checks sufficient? She mustn't worry. He'd see to it she was taken care of.

He certainly hoped she was doing okay.

She hadn't seen him since Gloria Clara had been born. It was the first time, to her knowledge, he'd laid eyes on his daughter. If she hadn't had to mind the baby, she believed she would have shaken him until he said, Okay, I know, I'm not supposed to be here, you told me never to darken your doorstep, I got no claim to be here and yet here I am and what in the world are you going to do about it, I am here just like you knew I would be here, any time I pleased, whenever it struck my fancy.

He didn't say any of that. In the end he said he hoped she might go out sometime. She was a young woman, he said, and she ought to get out of this house from time to time.

Where, she asked him, should I go. What should I do.

There's places, he said. It's a big world. There's plenty of places.

Then he was gone. He had not asked if he might come again, and so she had not had to tell him that she hoped against hope he would not.

A day later a package came. She hadn't heard the delivery truck drive up, and the knock on the door, three heavy thumps, scared her. But Don wouldn't come back, she was sure.

It was a package from Kerr's.

I didn't order anything, she told the delivery boy.

I reckon somebody did it for you, he said. It's paid for.

He was a tall boy with a flattened-out nose and hollowed-out cheeks. He almost had to lean down to see her through the door.

I see you got a little one in there, he said.

Gloria Clara had pulled herself up at the arm of the sofa so that she could stare at this latest stranger.

Don't you worry, she told the baby when the boy had gone, no more daddies are going to come calling to see you.

It was a dress in the package, a black dress, high-cut and long-sleeved, with rows of red and silver and blue sequins extending in a downward-swooping arch from shoulder to shoulder. She looked for a card. Couldn't find a thing.

She called Johnnie.

Well, yes, Johnnie said, I guess I know something about it, but I didn't buy it.

What do you know, Johnnie.

Maybe I'm not supposed to tell you.

Did Don Temple buy this dress.

I wouldn't say no and I wouldn't say yes.

Did you pick it out for him.

Yes, I did. Yes, I can tell you that. Oh, Cora Mae, I didn't see the harm in it. Is it all right? It's faille. It's a good dress. He said he wanted you to have something nice. Said maybe you'd go somewhere if you had something nice to wear. Is it all right?

The dress?

Well, yes, of course, the dress. Do you like it? Does it fit?

I haven't tried it on.

I thought it would look so good on you. Cora Mae, it's an *expensive* dress. If you don't want it—

Oh, I'll keep it.

Well, go try it on, right now, okay?

Sure. I'll go try it on.

You can exchange it if it doesn't fit.

I'll give it a try. Good old Don.

It was a nice thought.

Yes. He always did have some nice thoughts.

It's a pretty dress, isn't it.

Johnnie, I'll try it on.

She did try it on. And she did like the dress. It was tight-fitting, but that was the way it was supposed to be, you could tell, and the sequins glittered in the sunlight.

Your mama's not such a bad looker, she told Gloria Clara. Plenty of men would be glad to be your daddy. We can take care of ourselves just fine, can't we.

XII

. . . .

The Cooling Dark

There goes a woman of the world, Leon Udell said to himself
when he first saw Cora Mae. I sure could love a woman like
that. She looked older than nineteen, sitting alone at that little
table in the shadows at the Arcadia Ballroom. She wasn't paying
attention to the music. That cowboy fiddler wasn't her style.
Cigarette smoke drifted past her, and dancers waltzed by.

He knew she had noticed him as soon as he walked in the
door, his brass belt-buckle shining, his khaki slacks pressed to
perfection, shoes spit-polished to a glassy sheen. Right there, he
said to himself, sits a lady that loves a man in uniform. He had
not come across one of that kind yet, though he had been assured
(*warned* was his mama's word) that plenty of them lay in wait.
Until she told him that, he hadn't been so sure that the CCC was
for him. A life of ease might suit him better. These days it was
no disgrace not to have a job.

The CCC ain't soldiering, his papa said. It ain't a thing like
soldiering, far as I can make out. There's no enemy. Nothing to
attack, nothing to defend.

But Mama said that Roosevelt had the right idea after all. Leon
would get a fair shake in the CCC, without no one shooting at
him.

Plenty of boys was joining the Civilian Conservation Corps. Up to now, nobody would pay him for doing a thing. Unlike his mama, who took in ironing and twice a week polished the floors and shined the spoons of rich folks in Fort Smith, he had no special call to work.

Mama's people came from Texas. Her papa's granddaddy, she said, had his throat slit at the Alamo. After that, the family's fortunes declined.

In the CCC he got a dollar a day, three square meals, a roof over his head, and snappy khakis to wear, belt with brass buckle included. The camp he was sent to was not even in Arkansas; it was in Oklahoma City—just a few miles outside it anyway, close enough so that you could easily get in on a Saturday night. Often he was taken for a soldier. How's it going, Sarge, a bus driver said. Don't take any wooden nickels, soldier, a drugstore clerk said. Sometimes small boys followed him, studying his stride.

They had to get up at dawn in the CCC camp and go kill prairie dogs and jackrabbits. Ask any farmer what was the greater threat these days, Germans or jackrabbits.

It was a good day's work. Before supper you had a recreation period—basketball goals had been put up at one end of the campgrounds and a football field marked off at the other. There was snooker, which Leon liked a good deal, and table tennis. After recreation you put on your dress uniform for supper. Only the trained eye could discern the difference between a CCC uniform and a regulation Army uniform.

He could go home every month or so if he wanted to, but he didn't much want to. Oklahoma was finer than Arkansas. When he got a ride from camp into Oklahoma City, he watched for the bank buildings. You could see them from a long ways and it gave you a funny feeling when you did. There were two of them, brand new, and taller than anything in Little Rock.

One Saturday—the same day he saw his bride-to-be in the Arcadia Ballroom—an Oklahoma City boy named Darrold Peters told him that one of those tall buildings had a slide that ran right down the middle of it, all thirty-two stories.

You want you a slide, Darrold Peters said, why, I'll show you the slide of your life.

And he led Leon into the lobby of one of the buildings, a fine lobby, the elevator doors trimmed in gold. Just to ride in one of those elevators would have been fine, but Darrold said they mustn't do that. Only one was operating, this being a Saturday, and you didn't want the attendant to notice you. So you watched to be sure the arrow above the doors showed that the elevator was way up there somewhere, and then you crossed the lobby quickly and entered the door that led to the stairs.

Up and up they went, every landing the same except for the yellow-painted number, the grayness hurting your eyes after a while, not a single window along the way to look out of.

This sure better be good, Leon said.

At last they came to the number 31. The stairs ended. Darrold opened the door slowly, stuck his head out and looked both ways.

All clear, he said.

As soon as the door was cracked, Leon felt a sweet breeze, and once he stepped through that heavy gray door and into the hallway he saw the open window first thing. What a sight. All sky. And the city—there it lay, stretching as far as the eye could see, the streets like little ribbons, tapering and then overlaid by dark knobby trees.

Long way down, ain't it, Darrold said.

Pretty far, yes.

Can you imagine falling that distance.

Lord help.

Truth was, he could imagine it, had seemed to feel the sensation of falling as soon as he'd seen through the open window that clear space. The air struck him clean and sweet, and he opened his mouth to it, as if to receive food from the sky—angel food, and not his mama's cake but the honest-to-God real thing. A slight dizziness came, and a shivery thrill, as if he had already jumped from the window, and he seemed to feel the wind in his blood, speeding his heartbeat, his brain become a cloud, his head full of sun and moon. Didn't last a second, that feeling, no longer than it took to grab hold of the window ledge to stop the shaking of his hands.

You wouldn't live long, Darrold said. You'd die before you hit the concrete. The fear would kill you. That's what they say. That's what they mean, scared to death.

Himself again, Leon admired the view, caught his breath, wondered about that slide. It'd better be worth the climb.

Oh, it is, Darrold said. Damn right. You ready?

It was an inside slide. Leon had never seen the likes. Darrold led him through another door, and at first it was only grayness, just like the endless staircase, and he thought this might be some kind of trick. Then he saw what looked like a long sewer pipe, headed downwards through the core of the building, dark and curving, big enough to stand up in. You could never stand, though, once you entered it, not at that angle.

It's a fire escape, Darrold said.

I'll be. How'd you ever find out about it.

Fellow told me. Lots of boys come up here. Don't nobody care as long as it's on the weekend. What's the harm.

Why didn't we ride the elevator up then.

I said they don't care. I didn't say they make it easy for you. What I mean is, they look the other way. Ready?

What do you do?

Sit down and push off.

It's dark.

What do you need to see for? It's no place but down.

Yeah.

Just follow me. Don't yell or nothing.

And he was gone without another word. Leon listened for a

minute before he heard a slight whooshing sound, and then he sat down and pushed off, same as Darrold had done. Well, he thought, they got strange ways in the city, but I am not one to be left behind. I can keep up with the best of them. The metal he slid on was cool, and the air that hit his face, though also cool, had a heavy stale feel to it. If only Berta could see me now, he thought, remembering the girl he'd once loved for a while, from afar, watching her with her widowed mother at church, kissing her once before she knew better at a Sunday school outing on Magazine Mountain. Why, Leon Udell, she'd said, whatever did you mean by that! Nothing, he said, laughing. She didn't think it was a laughing matter. Then she took up with Delbert Dawes, the preacher's son, and never looked him in the eye again. Where was Delbert Dawes now, he wondered as he plunged down the dark tunnel in the tallest building in Oklahoma City. Still back in Arkansas, he'd bet, and look here at where Leon Udell was. Who would have thought.

That was the last thing he remembered thinking. He was certain he didn't faint. Thoughts stopped, that was all, and maybe a little dizziness, he supposed he must have gotten a little dizzy in that spiraling tube, anybody would have gotten a little dizzy. Whatever, it was not so bad, it felt pretty good, and he didn't much want to ever talk about it.

Afterwards, they rode the trolley out to the State Capitol Building and admired the oil derricks that stood in front. From there they went into the Historical Society Building and looked at tomahawks, arrowheads, warbonnets, and other souvenirs of the time when the Indians roamed.

Then they went back downtown. They bought Coney Islands at the Union Bus Depot on Grand and Walker, heaped with mustard and chili and very satisfying, and then watched people file into the buses. By and by it was dark and getting a little cold.

Let's get us a cup of coffee, Darrold said. I know a place.

They had been standing alongside the doorway, facing the

buses, in that way able to see the buses and people coming and going.

So long, Mac, Darrold said to one of the drivers that was collecting tickets, but the man didn't even look up.

They walked over to the next block, which was Main Street. The stores were closed, but still a few people walked around, looking at the dummies in the windows. The coffee shop that Darrold had in mind was closed, and so they went back to the dinette counter in the bus depot.

In a little while a couple of fellows from the camp came in, smoking cigarettes and talking loud. They wore their dress uniforms, just like Leon and Darrold, brass buttons shining, and it pleased Leon to see how greatly they resembled soldiers on leave. If they did, then he must look the same.

One of these new fellows, a tall gangly boy from West Texas with a chipped front tooth and rosy cheeks, said, This is the deadest town I ever been in. I reckon we're going to have to get on one of these buses and go clear to Amarillo if we want us a good time.

Hell fire, Darrold said. You all just don't know where to go. This is one hell of a fine city.

We're your men, Okie, said the other new fellow, a fat boy from Kansas. Lead the way.

Does anybody know what time it is? Darrold asked.

Clock's right there on the wall, the West Texas boy said. Can't you tell time, Okie?

I guess I can, Darrold said. Can you remember a fellow's name?

Leon liked the way Darrold came back with that. Leon wasn't no Okie, but he didn't like the way some of the boys from neighboring states used that word. His mama had raised him up to have better manners. Not everybody could be from Arkansas.

Come on, Darrold said, pushing his saucer across the counter. In fifteen minutes the hottest place in the city'll be open.

Fifteen minutes, the Kansas boy said. What's the rush then.

You got to get in line, Kansas, that's what. You're in the big city now, not out in the cornfields.

It was the Arcadia Ballroom that Darrold led them to, right across the street from the bus depot. There wasn't no line. They went right into the bright hall, and the first thing Leon saw was this woman walking across the broad dance floor, a woman of the world, he said to himself, a woman he might could love, in black shiny leather high-heel shoes and a black dress with red and blue jewels sewn onto the top part, right above where her chest came forward in two of the sweetest little points you could ever hope to see, Arkansas *or* Oklahoma. In one hand she carried a tiny black purse that was speckled with jewels—diamonds and rubies and rhinestones—and in the other a bottle of beer. Even the beer bottle looked special, and it sure was, 3.2 beer legal only a couple of months. That dark brown bottle tapered upwards like a—well, it was just a beer bottle, but in her hand it made you think crazy thoughts. It might have been a oil derrick such as they'd seen that afternoon in front of the Capitol, or it might have been the bank building that they slid down the center of. No mortal bottle. And on the wrist of the hand that held the bottle, a bracelet caught whatever light the jeweled purse didn't need and shot out sparks from it.

Standing with Darrold and the others, he watched her. She sat by herself off in the corner. The fiddles started up and the dancers swayed and dipped in the smoky air. The Kansas boy said that if you went to Wichita there was a lot of places like this, and Liberal had a notable establishment or two. The Texas boy said, See that woman over in the corner? I'm going to dance with her.

The hell you say, Leon said, and next thing he knew, much to his surprise, he had hold of the Texan's arm and was squeezing it hard. The hell you say, he said again. That one's mine, you hear, Texas! That one belongs to Leon Udell.

Say, the Texan said. Say.

Before the Texan could say more, Leon was striding across the dance floor. He pushed through the circling couples toward that dark corner, aiming himself for the woman of the world in her black dress with the shimmering jewels. Then, at her table, he thought he was at the top of that slide again. He opened his mouth to speak, but no words were there.

Better sit down, soldier, she said. You look like you had a hard day patroling.

He sat down. He remembered his mission.

Well, Marshall thought, love never knew no rules. It could come and go, and it certainly did, taking its own precious time and yours too. He was in the garden when Cora Mae came to him, the earth warm and moist, for it had been a rainy spell, unusual this time of the summer. On every hand weeds sprouted forth, lovely and lush, but you had to pull them before they could flower or send roots down deep and begin to suck away the food dirt meant for beans and corn, cabbage and okra. He laid them out neatly in the smooth rows, not rising from his knees until he reached the path that made a perfect square border all around the garden. Then he went back and scooped up the clusters of weeds, depositing them in the wheelbarrow awaiting at the other end of the row.

He hadn't heard Cora Mae coming up on him. Out here like this of warm summer evenings in the long light, he seemed neither to hear nothing nor even to think a thought. Sometimes he imagined he might hear the reaching of the roots, the outstretching of leaf and blossom, the steady thickening of branch and stem. It would be a sweet whisper, that sound, a little like wind in the trees. Sometimes he heard sparrows, gathering in the elms, and that sound sang in his head with the silence of the sky.

Daddy, she said. Daddy.

She touched his shoulder. He looked up then, saw her standing behind him, her face edged by the dusky sky. It was his little girl he heard, whether Johnnie or Cora Mae he couldn't have said.

Hello, stranger, he said, rising.

She coughed, a deep raspy cough.

Sorry, she said.

Was she all right?

Yes, she said. I'm fine. I'm going to get married.

Get what?

Married, Daddy.

But I thought—

That I'd never get married again, I know. That Don Temple would've been enough for anyone.

Something like that, yes. Hadn't it been only a few weeks since the divorce was final?

But he's been gone longer than that, Cora Mae said.

He was standing alongside her, and when she began to cough again he put his arm around her and drew her to him. She seemed to him so thin, surely as frail as a child, but in her high heels she was taller than he was.

Oh, Daddy, she said. I just want—

It's all right. I know. Daddy knows.

But he felt just then the weight of what he did not know, and tears came to his eyes, his daughter warm and trembling in his arms. It's all right, he kept saying, and it seemed that it was himself in need of comfort, here in this moment when he'd thought himself at peace with the world, his fingers in the dark moist soil, the garden green and good. She had grown away from him, his Cora Mae, a wife and a mother. What had become of the daughter, and where was the father she had known.

I'm not going to run away this time, she said. I want a nice wedding—

Well, sure.

Not in a church, she said, taking him by the hand and leading him towards the back porch.

Watch out, he almost said. Don't step on the weeds. For he was struck with how the clusters looked like bouquets, pretty enough to take in and put in a vase.

I thought, she said, I'd get married right here.

Here?

If it's all right with you. I already asked Mama.

What did she say?

To ask you.

Here?

He pictured Cora Mae in a white dress, standing in the middle of his garden, circled by thick-leaved lettuce and bush beans, the groom beside her like a straight up and down shadow, a fancy scarecrow.

In the front room, she said. Just a simple ceremony.

She stopped at the porch steps, took his other hand and looked him in the eye.

It'd just be family, but—why, Daddy, are you all right?

I'm fine.

Well. You're crying, Daddy. It's nothing to be sad about.

I'm not—it's just—my baby girl.

Oh, Daddy, I'm not your baby girl. There's Sarah Jane. You've still got Sarah Jane.

Oh, yes, I know that.

I haven't been a baby for the longest time.

Yes, oh, yes. You never was a baby, I believe.

Daddy. Now you sound like you're mad at me.

I'm all right. I don't know what come over me. Let's go on in. She said you was to ask me, huh.

She pulled him to her, took him in her arms, held him tight.

Daddy, Daddy, she said. It's all right, Daddy. It's all right.

He was ashamed. What kind of father required the comfort of his child.

You'll have your wedding where you want to, he said, pulling away from her. If it's in my power to help you have what you want, you'll have it.

I know that, she said.

It's the truth.

She smiled, facing him, her hand on the porch door. She had a dark blue bow clipped at the side of her head, and her hair curved beneath the bow and around it, everywhere ending in downturning curls. A great beauty shone forth from her. Why had he never noticed. It was her own beauty, for sure had nothing to do with him, and that was as it should be. Love made her, love gave her beauty, and, Lord help her, love would take her again.

They walked into the back porch, dark and musty, the kitchen light casting a beam across the shelves that lined the walls, lighting the rows of empty Mason jars ready for the canning of this year's crop of string beans, tomatoes, navy beans and pinto, beets, spinach, turnip greens. In the lighted kitchen Jane sat at the table as if waiting to be served. The table was clean and reflected back the light from above. It wasn't much count, that table, so small that only two could eat off it. When the girls had all been home, they took their meals at the dining room table, which had six good chairs. There would be plenty more room in the kitchen, take out that little table, but it had come from Jane's Grandmother Meachum's house back in Arkansas, and she wasn't about to part with it.

Mama, Cora Mae said, what are you sitting in here for!

I sit in here sometimes.

That's news to me.

It was news to Marshall too. When she sat, she generally took the divan in the front room, where she could spread the quilt she was working on. He couldn't remember a time when he'd seen her sitting so still, her hands unoccupied. In the glare of the light her face looked pale.

What did you do with Gloria, Cora Mae asked.

Why, I put her to bed.

With Sarah Jane?

No, I put her on my bed. Sarah Jane would keep her awake with all her tossing and turning.

And she didn't cry.

Not a lick. Went right to sleep. You can check on her if you want to.

In a minute.

Sit down then. Can't you sit down a while.

Yes, I want to, sure, I will—but what about Daddy? There's only the one other chair.

Jane looked at him as if she hadn't seen him until that moment.

I don't need to sit, he said.

Come on, Mama. Let's all go in the front room where we can all sit down. We need to talk.

Jane didn't move.

Go on, she said. You don't need to talk to me.

Mama.

I'll sit here. I'm comfortable right here. You all go on.

You sit down, honey, Marshall said to Cora Mae. You sit down and talk to your mother.

Where are you going, Daddy.

Garden. I got some things I didn't finish.

It's getting dark.

That's all right. You go on. Talk to your mother. I told you everything I have to say.

And it was the truth, he thought, back in his furrows, his hands in that sweet soil again. He'd do anything in his power to give her what she wanted. He'd told her that, he'd given her his solemn promise. He was her daddy, wasn't he. Damn right.

In the garden who could say how much time passed. He didn't keep track of the moon, the ground held his attention. But he was out there a long time, he knew, before he returned in his mind to Cora Mae's wedding, again saw her in a white dress, standing in the center of the garden where the furrows crossed.

But who, Marshall now wondered, was the groom, who was that tall figure in the shade by her side. It shamed him that he'd not thought to ask.

. . .

Get on to bed now. It's way past your bedtime, young lady.

Sarah Jane knew exactly what time it was. She was nine years old, had learned to tell time when she was five—Johnnie had taught her—and she did not like being treated like such a baby.

I'm going, Mama, she said. I'm going.

And she did, though it was only eight o'clock and just about everybody she knew got to stay up at least until nine-thirty during the summer. It wasn't even dark at eight o'clock. There was no arguing with Mama though.

What Mama couldn't tell her was when to go to sleep. She would go to sleep when it pleased her to, and not a minute before. Sometimes it pleased her to stay awake long after she heard Mama and Daddy go to bed. She liked it to be very dark and quiet before considering sleep. And sometimes, when she could be certain that the two of them were asleep, she got up and sat in the chair next to her bed. It wasn't at all scary. Your eyes got used to the dark.

Once she had even gone outside. After sitting in the chair the longest time and not feeling the least bit sleepy, she had gone to the window, seen how lovely Daddy's garden looked in the moonlight, and raised that window in a minute, soundlessly, so that she might climb through it and drop easily to the grass, a captive princess free at last. At first she did not move, stood there beneath the window and took in the lovely stillness, the darkness everywhere, the brilliant stars, leaves silvery in the moonlight. It was as if she did not need to go anywhere, that standing just in that place, shaded from the moon by the eaves of the house, was enough. Daddy's garden lay a few steps away to her left, the lettuce gleaming like jewels, the cornstalks like spears wildly ribboned. To her right, a greater distance but close enough to reach in a few seconds, the sidewalk, humped by the roots of the elm but thereafter stretching straight and true to the end of the earth, looked golden. She could walk right out there and never come back. It was enough, just to know that. She did not have to do it, not yet. But someday she would walk and walk, all alone. She wasn't going to be like her sisters and get herself moony-eyed over some man. What was a man anyway. Just a boy, grown up, and when she thought of the boys she knew—Davey Sheperd, Joe Dean Medford, Jimmy Shields, Bobby Elmore, even sad Paul John Cochran the Pentecostal preacher's son—she saw clearly the way it would be.

All the same, she had liked Don Temple all right. You didn't dare mention his name in this house, but she remembered how his eyes shone and how he never tried to pick you up and say what a big girl you were getting to be. Instead, he brought presents. Every time he came back from some place, he brought her some-thing, a comb with Welcome to Wichita, Kan., stamped in gold on it, a pink bandanna, a hand-carved whistle, a turtle with a decal on its shell that said I'm Itching to Get Back to Mineral Wells, Texas. Oh, she had a lot of nice things that he had given her, kept in a special place in the back of a drawer. Best of all, a scarf he'd brought all the way from Los Angeles, California, with palm trees on it, and the slogan The Golden State. Some day she meant to go to California. It had no winter and movies were made there.

Sometimes Johnnie took her to the movies. They went to the Saturday matinee at the Criterion or the Warner. Not often, be-cause Johnnie had to work. The women in the movies did not have to work. They wore flowing gowns and long gloves, they powdered their faces, rouged their cheeks, they danced and sang all night. Sometimes they ended up married and sometimes they didn't.

Johnnie had been married once, but it hadn't counted because it was only for a day. Sarah Jane couldn't even remember who the man was, what he looked like. It wasn't meant to be, Mama said. Daddy said nothing. Johnnie said, I made a mistake, a stupid mistake. There's a lesson for you, young lady. But what was the lesson. Not to make stupid mistakes? Sure, okay.

Cora Mae had been married a long time. It was hard to remember Cora Mae without Don Temple. It was almost like trying to imagine Mama without Daddy. But now she was without him for sure. That was called a divorce.

What ever was she to make of her sisters. Mama told her she must love them because they were her sisters, and she supposed that she did—though that was no reason—but, still, she couldn't really understand them. You don't have to understand them, Mama said. There's plenty you won't ever understand, child. Don't waste your time trying. Do your schoolwork and say your prayers.

Tonight something was going on. She heard Cora Mae come in, heard the baby Gloria cry and then whimper, knew that meant Mama had taken her, probably was rocking her. Cora Mae never came over this time of the evening. Nobody else did, for that matter. Cora Mae seldom came, period. Mama often noted it, complained of it. Johnnie didn't come often either, but then she had been living here until just a few months ago, sharing this very room, spreading out all over the bed too.

Oh, Sarah Jane, Johnnie said, you don't know how lucky you are. Enjoy yourself while you can. It'll all be over before you know it.

And she went right to sleep, usually snoring, her knee pressed up against Sarah Jane's back.

Still, she missed Johnnie a little. She had liked watching Johnnie get ready for work. Johnnie had pretty dresses, silk stockings, lacy underwear. On Saturday mornings when Johnnie had gone to work and Sarah Jane didn't have to hurry to get ready for school (though Mama would never let her sleep *real* late), she opened Johnnie's drawer quietly and took out a slip to try on, listening to be sure that Mama was in the kitchen. The slip was too big, and when she pulled the silk stockings on they were baggy, not tight and shimmery like when Johnnie wore them, but still she liked the feeling, as if she were pretty and grownup and California-bound.

You have such pretty hair, Johnnie said to her. I wish I had hair like yours. You and Cora Mae, you two got the hair in this family. I swear. The sun makes it light up and glow.

Johnnie had gone, months ago. When she came back, on Sunday afternoons, she always brushed Sarah Jane's hair and then put it up in braids. Once she took her to her apartment, clear over on the north side of town and then up two flights of stairs. The apartment was only a room really, with a bed that doubled as a sofa. It had a space off to one side that Johnnie called the kitchenette, and a single window that looked out on an alley. But Sarah Jane loved it. Short of going to California, this was surely the finest way to live, frilly curtains, a hot plate, a big easy chair, nobody to tell you when to go to bed, where to put your clothes, how to wash the dishes. If you wanted to stay up all night, who was to say you couldn't.

She was seeing herself in just such a cozy apartment, though with a better view than Johnnie's, perhaps of a busy street, when she heard Cora Mae come in. She heard Cora Mae talking to Mama, but they talked so softly, she couldn't make out what they were saying. Was it something about Don Temple? Must've been. Nothing else got Cora Mae upset.

Then she heard the back door slam, and the house was quiet again. She slipped out of bed, tiptoed across the hall to Mama and Daddy's bedroom, where, sure enough, Gloria lay on the middle of the bed, a quilt thrown over her. The room was almost dark, even though there was plenty of light left outside. You could have mistaken Gloria for a bundle of clothes. But Sarah Jane knew what to look for, and saw it, heard Gloria's steady breathing, smelled the soiled diaper. Once past the bed, she stood before the door, pausing only a second until she turned the knob and then peeked through the crack in the door. The lamp was on, but nobody there, just as she had figured. The front door was open, and the warm evening air smelled good.

The floor creaked just as she stepped into the front room. She kept going—clearly no one was in the house but Gloria and herself—boldly stepped into the dining room and then she crossed the doorway into the kitchen. She like to had a heart attack. Mama sat there, silent at the little table, her head bowed, eyes closed. Had Mama ever sat so still! You had to step back, and quick. What if Mama looked up. Oh, she would be in trouble then.

Sarah Jane backed away. At the edge of the sideboard she turned slowly.

Sarah Jane!

She walked faster. She ran.

Sarah Jane, you get in that bed.

Yes, ma'am.

Don't you wake that baby. Get in that bed right now, you hear me.

Yes, ma'am.

Oh, she was breathing so fast. Seemed like she couldn't get enough air. She pulled the sheet up over her, listening for Mama's footsteps. The baby whimpered, but only a little bit. Gloria's crying would certainly attract Mama's attention for a while, and Sarah Jane almost wished for that to happen, even though she knew Mama would remember seeing her in the kitchen and like as not blame her for waking Gloria and probably take a switch to her. By the time Mama could get Gloria back to sleep, though, Sarah Jane might could be asleep herself—for sure she could pretend to—and Mama wouldn't wake her up. That was her hope, for Mama never ever to wake her up.

But for the longest time she lay awake, listening for footsteps, voices, hearing nothing but crickets busy in the trees. Once she thought she might have heard voices—was it Mama and Cora Mae talking—and then she heard the baby cry out and she realized she had been asleep, dreaming of crossing a river, walking through fields of soft clay, sinking into that clay, deeper and deeper.

. . .

Who is he, Marshall asked first thing the next morning.

Jane honestly didn't know who he meant, and then, when it occurred to her that he was asking the name of the man Cora Mae was engaged to, she couldn't believe it. What had they talked about out there in the garden. Hadn't he been curious enough to ask about the man his daughter was going to marry?

I don't want a sermon, he said. I just want information.

Leon Udell, she said, handing him his coffee. His name is Leon Udell. He's in the CCC, at the camp out near Mustang. He's from Arkansas and she met him at a dance hall last November. She means to marry him, the sooner the better. What's the rush, I said to her. No rush, she said. I'm tired of waiting, she said. I want my life to begin, she said.

Arkansas, Marshall said. What part of Arkansas.

Why, Greenwood.

Greenwood? Almost to Fort Smith, if I remember correctly.

Said she wanted to start all over, and this time in a white dress.

I was through Greenwood often.

A white dress and white shoes.

Well, I'll be. A Greenwood boy. Udell, you say?

Leon Udell.

She watched Marshall tip his coffee cup so as to pour a goodly amount into the saucer, then begin to sip, loudly, from that saucer. Her daddy had done the same thing, bless his heart. But Marshall was nothing like her daddy, who once had said to her, Daughter, the men of this world are no count. Lord help the women to keep their menfolk trained towards the strait gate. Otherwise it's no telling where they might end up. Pray for them, Daughter, pray for your old daddy!

She prayed for Marshall, prayed for him often, and as often prayed for herself. Johnnie required prayer, and Cora Mae. In little Sarah Jane she saw abundant cause to beseech pardon, pray for generous intercession. Soon enough—who could doubt it— Cora Mae's baby would give reason aplenty for prayerful con-

cern. Thus rose up a world of sinners, as if each generation improved on the degeneracy of the last, flew ever higher into the
blue reaches of sin.

Used to be some Udells over by Belleville, Marshall said. You
suppose it's his Udells?

Marshall, I've never met the man. I only just last night heard
about him. What I heard, you would've heard if you hadn't
chased off to the garden.

Chased off is right. I was chased off from my own daughter.

Nobody chased you. I won't hear that talk from you.

You may not hear it, but I'll say it.

He sipped loudly from his saucer, shifted in his chair, looked
off towards the window. Oh, he was a handsome man, and mean,
sometimes, as the devil. Then in the next minute he turned as
tender and loving as a woman, as sweet as a girl. These times
in the early morning, Sarah Jane still asleep, was good times
generally. She liked the way the soft light touched on his clean-
shaven cheeks, making them look so smooth and white, putting
a kind of glow in his dark eyes. His hands never shook, holding
that saucer to his lips, and sometimes he gave her such a sideways
glance—she knew what he meant by it all right. She guessed
she knew his ways, his moods. And why shouldn't she, living
with him these twenty-two years. She was scarcely more than a
girl when he came along, complimenting her singing at that tent
meeting when it hadn't been her at all that he'd heard, but Lavon
Belle Ennis that had been taking singing lessons in Fort Smith all
her life.

He must have known it was Lavon Belle Ennis singing up a
storm. He'd just said that. He'd wanted to flatter her. Well, he
had done it. After that, he went off and she didn't see him for
the longest time, but she remembered him. She'd known him
pretty much all her life, of course, him and his family. She had
especially admired Mina, who married Brother Ted. Mina was a
year older than Jane, and was the prettiest, smartest girl in the

whole school. She had dark deep-set eyes just like Marshall—all the Monroes had those dark, dark eyes—and she had never cut her hair.

Marshall wasn't her first beau. She hadn't been the sort to attract a lot of attention to herself, and so there wasn't many boys paid her any mind, but there was a few.

I'll be gone, he said now, rising with his cup and saucer in hand. Where's my dinner pail?

Where it always is. On the supper table.

An Arkansas boy, you say. A Udell from Belleville.

No, I never said Belleville. It's Greenwood.

And she wants to marry him here.

That's what she said.

People do things different anymore.

Yes, they do.

Is she all right, do you think.

Why, I think so.

She was coughing something terrible out in the garden.

That night air, I suppose.

I suppose.

He was gone then, off to his WPA job, making a outdoor theater, of all things. It beat all, what they dreamed up for jobless men to do. There was this Leon Udell working for the CCC. Who knows what they had those boys doing. She wasn't one to complain. Marshall had been in an awful state, not working. He'd never stand in a soup line either, not even if he was starving. He'd give his own share of any food to her or Sarah Jane, she knew that, and swear up and down that he wasn't hungry. But a soup line? Never. They'd all starve to death first and he'd keep his pride.

Cora Mae was just like him.

She sat down. When Sarah Jane got up, she'd do the breakfast dishes, get Sarah Jane to dry them. It would be a few more minutes before that happened though. Always such a nice time of the day, the sun slanting through the window and across the table. Soon enough it'd be hot, but this time of the morning you still had some of the coolness of dawn, and had it all to yourself.

Clara Temple had wanted to come to Cora Mae's wedding. Why shouldn't she. Hadn't she known Cora Mae, hadn't she grown to like the girl, to think of her, almost, as a daughter. You got to know a person, feelings sprung up, you felt a connection, and then, just because of a severance of another connection, you had to cut yourself loose. She had not, for sure, chosen to like the poor child, had made no conscious decision, felt no obligation to love her, daughter-in-law or not. She loved her sons, prided herself on not favoring one over the other, loved Leroy and loved Don, and there was no way you could measure that love, divide it, weigh it. It was one love.

This did not mean she had to approve in the same measure of her sons' actions. What they did had nothing to do with how she loved them. Leroy could be a blustering fool, Don a stony-hearted shyster. Both boys sometimes seemed as slippery and impenetrable as a couple of toads.

But love, oh, it just kept on, went its merry way. Sometimes it seemed to her that all you had to do was get to know somebody, and once you knew someone you had them with you, they were in your blood, and wasn't that a kind of love. She felt that way about Cora Mae. It was a concern, an interest. When she compared this love to the other kind, what she had endured with John Temple, what she enjoyed with Cap Lovell, she wondered how it was that passion, romantic love, whatever name it went by, enjoyed such high esteem. It might make you flare up and fancy yourself as shameless as a summer sunset, brazen before the cooling dark, but the cooling dark always came.

So she would have gone, and brought a wedding gift, a china plate or a piece of flatware, and it would have seemed to her the most natural thing in the world. But she knew she would not be welcome.

As for Don Temple, he was a day late and a dollar short in

every department, showing up breathless at her door, as if, too impatient to wait for the elevator, he'd run the entire six flights. She regretted sending him the wedding announcement, never dreamed he'd take it as an invitation to come storming back, his eyes wild with desire or hurt. That look made her love him all the more, bless his ornery heart, her baby boy and every bit as grown up in his confusion and impossible longing as the best of them.

Mama, he said, is it done.

Baby, she said, come in here and sit down. I don't know what on earth you're talking about.

Damn you! Didn't you send me the damn newspaper clipping. You know exactly what I'm talking about.

Well, maybe she did. Of course she did. Thought it would be of interest, that's all—

Of interest! Of interest! Mama, do you know who you're talking to?

You are familiar to me, yes.

Well, then, for God's sake, tell me is it done, is it over, is she married.

If you can believe what you read in the papers. You saw the clipping, same as I did.

You sent it to me.

Well, then.

He sat down in the same place Cora Mae had sat, on the davenport, when she had paid her that unexpected visit. When had that been? Over a year ago, the poor child swelling up, her young body already making room for another life, a new ghost. Sat there in her schoolgirl oxfords, the white socks rolled, and asked who Don Temple was. Not where he was, mind you, but who he was. A much better question.

Don's cheeks were flushed and his forehead slick with sweat. He sat on the edge of the davenport, his hands squeezing his thighs.

She's mine, he said. She'll always be mine.

Son. She never knew who you were. She sat there, in that same place you're sitting, and asked would I please tell her who you were. What was I supposed to tell her.

He kicked off his shoes, stretched out on the davenport, rubbed his eyes, then mumbled something that she couldn't understand. She turned off the floor lamp by the side of the davenport. My baby boy, she thought, and a father himself. She wanted to tell him what a good boy he had always been, but that wasn't exactly true. Leroy had been the good one, destined to be as dull as his good father. Don had been trouble, though he could be the sweetest boy, coming to her with tears in his eyes, so frail, a sickly child, missing weeks of school at a time, shivering and pale in his narrow bed. She read him stories, brought him soft-boiled eggs, placed cool damp washrags on his forehead. Was she the one to blame after all? Was it something she had done, a sin she'd forgotten. Again and again she had had this truth borne in upon her: she was not meant to be a mother, she was not a good mother, she could never give her sons what they needed. Others knew what to do, instinctively, and did it, whereas she had had to consider first, learn as she went. She was smart. Luckily she was smart. She learned fast, all the simple things. And she could give her sons something like what they needed, something close to the real thing. Maybe they never even knew the difference themselves, God help them.

He was breathing deeply, stretched out on his back with his long feet propped on the arm of the davenport. He reminded her of Leroy, that time he'd come to Oklahoma, so helpless, exhausted. She took a blanket from the cedar chest and pulled it over him. Sound asleep. She sat in the easy chair across from the davenport, watched him for a while. What marvelous steady breathing! Surely we breathed our finest, were most alive, when we slept. We belonged to no one then and everyone was exactly what they appeared to be.

She was not sleepy herself. It was past her bedtime, almost midnight, but she felt wide awake. Earlier she had thought Cap Lovell might come. He had been in Dallas for three days and said that he might return by this evening. It was not his way to call her. If I'm not there, he said, then my business will not have been concluded. I will be there when I'm there and not a moment before. And I will be here, she told him, unless I'm somewhere else.

Wide awake, she went to bed. She was not thinking of Cap Lovell, but of John Temple, could see so clearly his fierce eyes, his large fists. I'm not myself, he'd said to her once, his passion flaring up like a house afire. How she'd loved him then, how she'd believed for a time that the fire would last and last. God put it out, doused it good. God said to John Temple, I am love. Serve me. God lied, she believed, as He surely must often do when troubled by human matters—by sorrow, for example, and love and guilt. He lied to suit his own purposes. And why not? Who else knew better what He was up to?

When she had left John Temple, he had said he would never look at her again. She must not imagine that she might return.

A return, she had said, was unimaginable.

She had raised up her sons as best she knew how. She must look to herself next. She had no regrets, though of course she had returned many times in her mind, imagined it thoroughly with an ease that amazed her, even when she knew that he had married again. She could forget that, forget the pain that had come between them, and yet remember the moments, rare as they had been, in which by virtue of his sin she was taken from herself. Remembering that theft—herself culprit and thief—she could conceive anything. It was a matter, she would almost say, of belief, something to be taken on faith. Well, but she supposed that was the way of all loving. John Temple she would have with her always. And Cap Lovell too, poor driven man, chasing his fortune as if it were a hat that kept getting blown off his head.

Her son would leave in the morning, if not before. He would grieve a long time. That was his gift, she suspected, a talent for knowing loss. It was what he carried of her in his blood. He hadn't lost Cora Mae though. She wished she could explain that to him. What you lost, what you kept grieving for, had little to do with your loving. You grieved for nothing but yourself, for the life you lost staying alive—a losing battle, yes, though neither battle nor, in the long run, loss. There was no enemy, no war. And how could you lose what never belonged to you.

This line of thought was making her sleepy. After all, it was time. She could hear Don snoring loudly in the other room, and the mantel clock ticking that once marked time above the fireplace in the home of her daddy's daddy. She would not think of her daddy tonight, would not call to mind a single phrase from one of his hymns, nor think of her poor mama starting a new life (oh so long ago now) at the age of sixty with a Baptist deacon on the verge of his last death. Well, she might think a little of her mother, of that honeymoon to the Holy Land and then the new husband, ten years her younger, a rich man, a banker, well-respected in Joplin and known in Springfield, dying without warning, friendless in New York, his storied fortune willed to the use of Baptist missionaries. She imagined the coins that would have made her mother's old age comfortable jingling in the deep pockets of lanky, hollow-eyed preachers who taught plumed black chieftains how to sing "The Old Rugged Cross." I am beyond you, she had said to her mother, who in the end seemed comfortable enough moneyed or not, sleek in her silk-lined box.

But who was beyond whom, she now wondered, wide awake again. Hadn't she heard, many a time, her mother's voice in dream after dream calling after her, as if to tell her what she'd neglected to say while alive, or what she'd not known to say because unenlightened. You could never hear the voice though, only know that it was aimed at you, that it was out there somewhere, headed in your direction, soaring for your heart, but taking its own sweet time getting there. *Beyond you.* And yet close as the devil.

Cora Mae, she supposed, slept soundly at the side of her new husband. Don must accept that, and must not trouble Cora Mae nor himself further. The trouble was in his own heart, along with the love, and he must live with it to the end of his days.

Such thoughts—would she never go to sleep. But she must have. It was daylight, birds chirping, and she was remembering a trip of some kind, a long journey—could it have been to the Holy Land—during which she had lost her way. The sun shone bright and warm through her bedroom window. It would be a hot day. She lay there in her bed for the longest time before she recollected that Don had come last night. But he wasn't here now. She did not have to move an inch from her bed to confirm his absence, which she could feel so surely in that apartment it might have had a strong smell—it did not, of course. Probably it was just the stillness, easily recognizable as her own.

XIII

· ·

The Gift of Caruso

A year after she had imagined it, Cora Mae had her June wedding. But something went wrong. She couldn't understand it. Standing in the living room of her childhood home, the Reverend Wiley before her and her daddy on one side, her bridegroom on the other, she felt already outside of herself, a memory. Her body had begun its betrayal, she knew that. She had recognized the gesture immediately, as bold and certain as the heat of this day, Reverend Wiley profusely sweating, Mama fanning herself with a bamboo fan marked Capitol Hill Ice Cream Co., Keep Cool With Us!

She went back. In her mind—somewhere—for sure not in her body—she sat at the Arcadia Ballroom in the black dress Don had given her.

Go out, he said. There's plenty of places.

She went into the room. Told to stay out, she went in. Little Brother looked pretty, all laid out, his eyes shut. The best baby, Mama said. No one could have asked for a sweeter baby.

Daddy's son, his little boy in a pretty ruffled box. She saw the dress she'd worn a year ago, a snatch of it, Johnnie's dress before it was hers, a piece of it—but this was later. First he lay on the bed. No, not on the bed. In Mama's lap. Mama might have been dead too. Only the air was alive, the dust set in motion by the sunlight.

Before that had come a great flood. There was not any danger though. Daddy said not to worry, the water would never reach them. You could smell it even if you couldn't see it, a smell like nothing else she had ever smelled, not bitter, not sweet, sly and ugly and thick in the warm gray air. Daddy showed them pictures in the papers, the boats in the streets, people waving, the water flowing through windows, pushing open doors, lifting furniture from the floor, shoes and hats and dresses washed away, and the chests of drawers themselves, chairs and beds. Then the mud, the red glaze left behind. She had seen that. Just down the block from Daddy's restaurant she had seen it halfway up the sides of houses.

Daddy sent her and Johnnie to Mrs. Perry's when Little Brother was born. Mrs. Perry had a big radio. Maybe it just seemed big. Mama and Daddy didn't have a radio yet. When had they gotten one? Sometime after Sarah Jane was born, she thought. A small table model. Daddy listened to "National Barn Dance" on Saturday nights. Mrs. Perry also had a Victrola. She turned it on once for her and Johnnie and it played the prettiest music, an opera singer, Mrs. Perry said, name of Caruso. Cora Mae had never heard the likes of it. Wouldn't it be nice to have such music for your wedding.

A man sang "My Blue Heaven" at the Arcadia Ballroom. She wore the black dress. Johnnie had picked it out of course, not Don. He'd only supplied the money for it. The wedding dress he paid for too, though he did not know this. He was a good provider. Whatever else you said about him, he was a good provider. His heart was in the right place.

You two are the best little girls, Mrs. Perry said. Why don't you just come over here and live with me and Mr. Perry, huh? Wouldn't you like that?

Mr. Perry came in. He was a small man like Daddy, but he had no hair. He smelled bad and had a lump on his cheek that moved around when he talked.

Come sit on my lap, he said. I don't have any little girls of my own. Can you imagine that—a man that ain't a daddy! Don't you feel sorry for me?

Johnnie sat on his lap, but Cora Mae didn't want to.

I've got a surprise for you, he said. Johnnie's such a good girl, she's already earned her reward. Now what about you, young lady.

Go on ahead, honey, Mrs. Perry said. He's just crazy about little girls.

He had the surprise in his fist, she could tell, a stick of gum, no more than that, not worth it, but she went, didn't want to hurt his feelings, and pretended to be happy to have his present.

What big girls you're getting to be, he said when he had the two of them on his knees. Next thing we know, you two girls'll be young ladies with babies of your own. Mrs. Perry never give me a baby, but you two look like fine little mamas all right.

The whole house smelled like Mr. Perry. It was like a basket of dirty clothes. When Mr. Perry put them down, they were allowed to look at Mrs. Perry's *Saturday Evening Post* magazines. The big radio wasn't turned on, not once. Cora Mae wanted to ask, but Johnnie said they mustn't, it wouldn't be polite. Next to the radio stood the Victrola, its horn pointing toward the window.

They were in that house such a long time, it seemed. Mr. Perry sat in a big rocker and had a brass bowl on the floor next to him that he spit into from time to time. He read the newspaper, but held it so that you could still see his small head and know that he was watching you. The world in the magazines was faraway and bright. Mrs. Perry called them to the kitchen to help with the supper. They husked the corn and snapped the stringbeans, then fetched whatever Mrs. Perry asked them to get for her. She had a footstool they could stand on to reach up in the cabinet. Through the kitchen window Cora Mae could see her own house, but couldn't see anything in the windows. The yard in between made the house too far away. Wouldn't it be funny if you saw yourself looking out one of the windows. She would've liked to sneak over and peek in the windows, see what was happening. A baby was coming, she knew that, but how. Anyway, Mrs. Perry wouldn't let them out of her sight. It was hot and steamy in the kitchen, just like at home. Mrs. Perry had a calendar tacked up on the cabinet. It had a picture of a snow-capped mountain on it and the words: Courtesy of . . . she couldn't remember who it was courtesy of.

Cora Mae had thought she would never see a mountain. Daddy referred to the mountains of Arkansas, but when he showed them to her she didn't think they looked like real mountains such as she had seen in pictures like this one on Mrs. Perry's calendar and in schoolbooks. A real mountain was covered with snow, not trees. Mountains rose straight up and you had to climb them with spikes that you hammered into the rocks and tied ropes onto. You couldn't drive up to the top of them or ride up in a wagon. There was no road to the top.

Oh, but now it seemed to her that the mountain in Arkansas where Little Brother lay buried was as grand as any mountain you could ever hope to see or climb. She carried Gloria Clara in her, of course, which made the climb more arduous than it might have been. But the road was steep and winding and deeply rutted, and when she looked behind her the ground they'd started from was farther and farther away, it sank lower and lower and was lovely to see.

It was Mildren come running after their train. Had he run off to get married, or was he trying to tell her something else. In the stable he tickled her feet with the straw, then began to kiss her. He pulled her hair back and kissed her neck, her ears. Does that tickle, he asked. No? How about this.

Mr. Perry moved his knees up and down.

Ride the horsey, he said. Giddy up, horsey.

She felt silly on his knee. She was too big for that kind of thing. She didn't see why she couldn't stay and watch Little Brother being born. Did they think she was a baby? They must have drawn the shades in the windows so that nobody could see in. Now it was almost too dark anyway. Supper was over, the dishes done. Mr. Perry slept in his chair beside the silent radio while Mrs. Perry worked her knitting needles back and forth and the tightly gathered yarn spread longer and longer on her lap. She hummed something as she knit, and now and then sang out the words: There's a great day coming, a great day coming, there's a great day coming by and by. Mr. Perry didn't stir. Cora Mae and Johnnie had looked at all the *Saturday Evening Post*s. Mrs. Perry gave them a pair of scissors and said they might cut out pictures if they wished.

If Don Temple wanted to come in, he would. She couldn't stop him. He had a key. Standing in the doorway, looking for him, she didn't mind the cold night air. Now and then her nipples, sensitive from nursing Gloria Clara, brushed against the screen door. Nobody could see her. She would not go out, did not need to go farther than the door. He would see that she was not afraid.

Go out, he said, you should go out sometime.

Before they went to bed, Mrs. Perry took them to her bedroom to show them something. She had something special to show them because they were such good girls. She knew their mother was proud of them, and, oh, she thought the world of their mother, a God-fearing Christian lady.

She led them through a dark hallway. Her bedroom had a dresser with an oval-shaped mirror. The bed, a big one like Mama and Daddy's, was pushed up against the side of the wall opposite the dresser, its headboard curving high with tall thick posts at each side, the posts rounded into two globes at the top and carved with deep straight lines all along the length of them. Mrs. Perry had a white bedspread and white frilly curtains. From a chifferobe in the far corner of the room Mrs. Perry took out a thick book with a black cover. It's my scrapbook, she said. Let's just sit here on the bed and I'll show it to you. Do you girls keep a scrapbook? Oh, you must start you one. You'll enjoy it so much when you get to be an old woman like me.

Mrs. Perry wasn't really so old. Though perhaps a little older than Mama, she was far from the frail, white-haired ladies that Mama called elderly. She had only a few gray strands in her auburn hair and could not by any stretch of the imagination be thought of as frail. Cora Mae bet she weighed more than Mama. She had thick ankles and wore white lace-up shoes with gracefully curving eyelets in the toe.

Cora Mae couldn't imagine being grown up. She never seemed to grow at all, and yet she knew she was taller this year than last. How would it be when you were as tall as Mama or Daddy? Why couldn't you see yourself growing?

I was a little girl once, Mrs. Perry said, just like you all. I know it's hard to believe, but I was, all the same, skinny as a rail.

Cora Mae sat on one side of her, Johnnie on the other, as Mrs. Perry began to turn the pages of the big scrapbook. It *was* hard to believe that Mrs. Perry had once been their size, but she had the pictures to prove it.

My uncle Norbert was a professional photographer, she said. He always told me I was such a pleasure to photograph—a natural subject, he said. It was the eyes. He went to St. Louis later and made quite a name for himself, but when I was a girl in Joplin he said if I'd just stay the same as I was then, he'd be happy to photograph me the rest of his life. Wasn't that a nice thing to say!

Cora Mae heard that voice so clearly, smelled that house, saw the lump in Mr. Perry's cheek, the light reflecting from the brass bowl he spit in, the big silent radio, the Victrola with its horn, the stack of *Saturday Evening Posts*, heard Mrs. Perry's laugh when she said *Wasn't that a nice thing to say,* the bedsprings squeaking. She seemed as much there, looking across the yard into the blank windows of her parents' house, as anywhere in the world. She drew the sheet up to her chin. Who had put these blankets on her? Too many. Couldn't they see that she was sweating. It was summer. She was certain it was summer. In June she had been married to Leon Udell. How had that happened. How did anything happen. It just did. God knew why. We were put here for a purpose, Mama said.

And my purpose? To shake in the cold wind. To bear the weight of these heavy blankets. To burn, then freeze. Burn again.

Bring my baby to me. I'm dying. I'm going to see Little Brother. *Is she walking yet?*

Like a house afire. Such strong legs. Such delight when she throws herself into your arms. Nothing like it. Nothing like it in the world. My baby daughter! My darling Gloria Clara. Not me, no, you're not me, not Don Temple, yourself, Gloria Clara, like no one else that ever walked the earth. You bear me in you, your death, but you aren't me, no, ma'am. Lord, honey, let me live a quiet life in you, let me ride back and forth in your heavenly little veins and never cause a stir. Oh, I won't cause a commotion, I promise I won't. I'll keep still and ride with you and then someday when you need me you'll know I'm there, your secret, the love that bore you and the death that takes you.

The baby slept. When she woke again, Mama would be all right, Mama would be strong, Mama would take care of her.

It was quiet in the house and dark. Leon was not there. Thank God Leon was not here.

Something's the matter with you, he had said. You want me to take you to the doctor. I'll go get you a doctor, Cora Mae. You hadn't ought to be shaking like that in the summertime. It must be a hundred degrees.

When she put on the dress she felt so warm. Not hot, no, just warm, just right. Then the satin shoes. Then it was time. They were waiting for her. A recording was playing. Daddy had borrowed Mr. and Mrs. Perry's phonograph, carrying it over here all by himself, though it was heavy and big. You could hardly see him behind it when he carried it across the yard. It had a crank on the side and that big horn. Mrs. Perry had brought it with her from Joplin, Missouri. She had saved her money ever so long to buy it so that she could hear the music she enjoyed when it pleased her to. Oh, it was old-fashioned, but it worked. It wasn't even new when she bought it. Mr. Perry had said he'd buy her a new one, and while she didn't doubt his word she wasn't going to hold her breath until he bought it.

Once, Cora Mae said, I heard the most beautiful music on your Victrola. It was Caruso, you said. I never knew music could be like that.

Enrico Caruso! Lord, yes. He's dead now. Isn't he dead, Mr. Perry?

Who's dead.

Caruso. Isn't Caruso dead.

Why, I reckon so. I never knew the man. Caruso, did you say?

Caruso. Enrico Caruso, the opera singer.

I'll tell you who's a singer. Grace Moore. Sings like a bird. A songbird. If the stars in the sky could sing, they couldn't do no better than Grace Moore. She's my idea of a singer.

Hush up about Grace Moore. Cora Mae is interested in Enrico Caruso.

If you want to hear good singing, listen to Grace Moore. That's what I say.

Mr. Perry had the same rocking chair, same brass bowl, but he looked smaller. He didn't seem to have shaved and the radio sat silent as ever in its big cabinet, next to the old Victrola.

I still have that recording of Caruso, if you'd like to listen to that.

Cora Mae had forgotten why she had come. Not to talk about music. She was going to be married. And the baby, well, the baby, what did a baby care for weddings.

Don't you worry, Mrs. Perry said. I'll take care of that baby while you're getting married. Now sit down. I'm going to play this Caruso record for you.

Mr. Perry spit into the bowl. I've got a Grace Moore too, he said.

It's an old record, Mrs. Perry said as she cranked the phonograph. It came with the Victrola. I haven't played it in I don't know how long.

The recording was scratchy and the voice sounded as if it came from another world.

He's singing in Italian, Mrs. Perry said. Or maybe French.

For sure it ain't English, Mr. Perry said.

Something came through. Caruso's voice rose above the sound of the orchestra and Cora Mae had to catch her breath. It wasn't the words. Italian, French, whatever, didn't seem to make a difference in the world. She understood. It might have been her own name he called out, her secret name. She had thought no one knew it, not even Don Temple. She felt weak, a little dizzy, but it was a sweet sensation. It must be that she was dying.

There, Mrs. Perry said when it was over. That's your Enrico Caruso.

It's just like I remembered it, Cora Mae said. Even better.

Well, you can have it if you want it. I never play it.

Oh, I couldn't do that.

Go on and take it. A wedding gift. Oh, I forgot. You don't have a Victrola, do you. Well, it's not much of a gift then, is it.

There's a story about Caruso, Mr. Perry said. You ever hear that story?

What story are you talking about. Oh, Cora Mae, Mr. Perry is such a caution.

Just that he sung such a bunch of sad songs that his tear ducts got plugged up. All that water had no place else to go and so it just turned around and went back inside him, filled up his lungs, and drowned him. That's what killed him, so I heard. Sorrow flooded his innards.

Mr. Perry!

That's the way I heard it. A fellow in the barbershop told it one day. I forgot it until just now.

Well, Mrs. Perry said, I'll tell you what, Cora Mae. You tell your daddy to come over and get this Victrola. You want that music for your wedding, don't you. I know you do, I can tell. I'd carry it over myself except for my back being so painful, and Mr. Perry's is worse.

Lord, yes, he said. I can hardly get out of this chair once I set in it.

You tell your daddy come get it. Borrow it long as you like and play that Caruso music at your wedding.

It was what she wanted. She knew it as soon as she heard the voice. The music came from within her, but the grieving in it was the world's grief, the deep sorrow of the sky.

Daddy'll come get it, she told Mrs. Perry. I don't think he'll mind.

She heard the music, the sadness of Caruso, who sang though dead, who sang that way because he was dead. She walked into the room while Caruso sang. Leon stood next to Daddy. Don Temple was somewhere else, she didn't know where, of course he would not be here. Johnnie walked by her side. Whatever would she do without Johnnie!

It's just fine, Johnnie told her. You look beautiful, Cora Mae. Makes me want to get married myself, almost.

But who is he, she asked Johnnie. I can't remember his name. I did a minute ago, but now I've forgotten.

Honey, oh, Cora Mae. What on earth has happened. What is the matter, Sister.

Reverend Wiley had on the same dark blue suit he always wore, but he had a rose in his lapel, a white rose, and clasped a big black Bible in his hands. When Little Brother died, he handed Cora Mae his hat and said, Where is your bereaved mama. He stayed for supper, eating a lot of cornbread, crumbling some of it into his buttermilk.

When she stepped up to him in her wedding dress and white satin shoes, the bouquet of daisies and forget-me-nots and babies' breath in her hands, the veil holding her firmly in place, so neatly tucked away inside herself, the Reverend took a deep breath, seemed to shiver a little in his tight suit, and dropped the Bible. Her groom, her husband—Leon Udell, that was his name— leaned down ever so quickly and picked the Bible up. The record was playing, Caruso singing from his other world, from the center of his death, a long ways off, you could barely hear it, he would never stop singing that song, he was singing it even when the record stopped, she could hear him.

You can keep that record, Mrs. Perry said.

But bring back the Victrola, Mr. Perry said.

You'll have one of your own someday, Mrs. Perry said.

The record went back, along with the Victrola. She did not need to have the recording. She did not care to have a Victrola of her own someday. Someday was a lie. You had the death of yourself in your blood. It was where the heat came from, and the chill that followed. All the rest was chance, accident.

Here's Mr. Perry and me, Mrs. Perry said. Our wedding picture. Look at us, solemn like we was going to a funeral. See what a thin thing I was!

In addition to her wedding ring, a thin gold band like Mama's, Mrs. Perry wore three other rings, a delicate gold one with a black stone, and two large ones encrusted with red, green, and white stones. The small ring she wore on her left hand, the little finger puffing out around it. How did she ever get it off. The others were on the right hand, first finger and middle. After the scrapbook, Mrs. Perry showed them her jewelry box.

I have a lot of my mama's things, she said. They had some lovely things in those old days. Oh, but I wouldn't never want to live like they did back then, no, sir, not for one minute. Just imagine getting into those long dark dresses, those hot crinolines and whalebone stays. A woman nowadays can breathe, praise the Lord.

Her room smelled like Mr. Perry too. There was a sharp perfume in the air, but breathe deep enough and you had Mr. Perry again.

They stayed all night in that house. Mrs. Perry made them a pallet on the living room floor. Then it was very dark and quiet. Cora Mae listened for floor boards giving or bedsprings squeaking, sounds she would have heard at home, but Mr. and Mrs. Perry went silently to their beds.

What do you think's happening, Johnnie whispered.

They were sleeping, Cora Mae guessed.

Sleeping?

They're sure quiet. What else would they be doing?

That's what I'm wondering. We couldn't hear them from here anyway, could we. No telling what's going on.

Cora Mae realized then that Johnnie meant Mama and Daddy, not Mr. and Mrs. Perry.

I wish I knew, Johnnie said. I wish—oh, I don't know.

We could maybe sneak over there, peek in the windows.

Cora Mae!

Then you'd know, wouldn't you.

They rose and went to the window. Cora Mae pulled back one side of the curtains, Johnnie the other. It was a fine darkness, a sweet breeze, and now the crickets started up, shrieking like mad. You could smell the dewy grass and across the way see the light in their house, faint, a pale orange.

Where's the light coming from, Johnnie whispered.

A light bulb, Cora Mae supposed.

But where? It'd be brighter if it was in Mama and Daddy's bedroom.

Maybe it's the living room lamp.

Uh-huh. But why are they in that room. Mama went to her bed to have the baby.

Cora Mae wanted to sneak out of Mr. and Mrs. Perry's house, walk across the wet grass in her bare feet, stand on tiptoe at Mama's window. How would it be, and why weren't they allowed to stay in their own house when it happened.

I'll bet the door's not locked, she said.

You wouldn't go inside, would you!

If there was nobody to see me I would.

Daddy would see you. Mama might too.

Not if—

Girls!

Lord, Mrs. Perry was right there in the room, the biggest thing you ever saw, in a white nightgown. In the dark her head looked like a basket of yarn. You girls hush up now, she said, and go to sleep. When you're wanted over there, you'll know it. You mustn't keep Mr. Perry awake with this whispering. It'll be morning soon enough. Then you'll know. Then you'll go home.

Oh, but it was so hard to go to sleep. The crickets had never been so loud, and then the moon shining its white light through the window. Cora Mae wasn't afraid. Mr. Perry's radio looked like itself, the horn of the Victrola like a big flower. Mr. Perry's rocker and brass bowl had been pushed back against the wall to make room for the pallet. Was Johnnie asleep? She didn't think so. Mustn't ask though. So nice, her sister lying beside her, that warmth, the steady breathing. What did they care about anyone else in the world. Mama would be all right, Mama would be just fine, Mama would call them to her, her little girls, and hug them and kiss them and promise never to leave them. But I'm not scared, Mama, not a bit. I know where you are, and Johnnie too, and the baby you've brought us.

She could not close her eyes. Wide awake, she would be this way forever, how does anybody ever go to sleep.

Oh, Cora Mae. Oh, my poor baby, my sister. Don't leave us.

Hush, Johnnie. I'm not going anywhere.

The breeze from the window played out. The crickets fell silent. Johnnie's breath came smooth and steady, she was probably asleep now. Then something cried out. Was it the baby being

born? She touched Johnnie's arm. Did you hear that, Johnnie?
Johnnie didn't answer. Cora Mae didn't dare speak louder. Did
you hear it, she wanted to ask, but dust caught in her throat. The
sound came again, a high flat moan. It came from their house.
Why didn't it wake Johnnie up, why didn't it wake everybody
up. It was no baby making such a sound. A baby wouldn't ever
sound like that. Then it stopped. Couldn't have lasted long at all.
She took a deep breath. It started up again. Still, Johnnie didn't
stir.

This time Cora Mae knew. It was Mama. Over there in the
house Mama cried out. It wasn't really loud, after all. Wouldn't
wake anybody that was sleeping soundly like Johnnie and Mr.
and Mrs. Perry. Cora Mae must have been the only one in the
world that heard it, unless maybe Daddy. It stopped, and then
it started again, the same high, flat-pitched cry. Mama cried out
for love and pain.

It was the last thing Cora Mae remembered.

XIV

. . . .

Mourners

It's no trip to Arkansas, Jane said. Not this time. Marshall, you're not going to take this child to Arkansas. I won't have it, do you hear me. This one's going to the funeral parlor, and the grave's paid for, right here in Oklahoma City.

Who ever said anything about Arkansas, Marshall said. I never said I'd take Cora Mae to Arkansas. You put her where you want her.

In the Sunnylane Cemetery, that's where she's going. In a regular coffin—it's already picked out and paid for. The hearse is coming. Now that's the way it's going to be, Marshall. Reconcile yourself to it.

I'm reconciled.

She had paid for it out of her grocery money, a little at a time kept back in an envelope for just such an occasion. Who knows what might happen or when. Ever since the death of Little Brother she had known they were not safe, not ever. You could only pray for grace and put back a little at a time to pay for what was bound to happen, grace or not.

Marshall knew all that. She may have thought him ignorant on the subject, but he knew what she had been doing, knew exactly where she kept the envelope beneath the tablecloth in the bureau, same place she kept the locket with the swatch of Little Brother's hair in it. And, yes, he had taken Little Brother to Arkansas, laid that coffin in the ground next to the grave of his own father, but that was a long time ago and what good had it done. *He* would not be buried there. They'd stick him where they damn well pleased, somewhere close and easy right here in Oklahoma City, one of those treeless places where the grass don't ever grow, the dust sweeping it clean, sloping onto the tombstones.

Too late, the doctor said. I'm afraid it's too late, Mr. Monroe. In his blousy checkered pants, his yellow bow tie and saddle shoes, the doctor looked like he'd expected a party. Wasn't he surprised.

Daddy, she had said, oh, Daddy, falling into his arms. What was he to do, her dress soaked through with sweat, his dear daughter Cora Mae, sobbing and shivering and frail as a leaf, who was the most robust of his girls, solid like her mother and with spirit.

Johnnie came running in afterwards, in her polka dot dress and white high heels, her pillbox hat cocked to one side, all out of breath and tears in her eyes, that baby of Cora Mae's in her arms.

Put that one down, he told her, and help me carry your sister to the bedroom.

He had been sitting with her on the sofa. August again, same month as Little Brother was taken, and just as hot. Two months ago, he'd stood alongside her in this living room and give her away to a stranger. And where was that stranger now, where was Leon Udell her husband?

Honey, he said, do you want me to call Leon.

He's in Arkansas, she said, visiting his mother.

Her voice was low, scarcely a whisper.

Can't talk, she said. My throat.

You don't have to say a word. Your daddy understands.

She was not sobbing as at first, though still shivery. Wouldn't let go of him, wouldn't let him get her so much as a drink of water. How long had she been here—seemed a long time, quiet in the house, Jane at church, his daughter shaking in his arms. Now and then she said something, just what he couldn't say, her voice unholy low, maybe she said Mama, maybe not, maybe no word at all, a word she couldn't say, bless her heart, her treacherous throat.

It seemed he'd never been any place else but here, in this room, in this heat, this hug, and then Johnnie was there with the little one, Gloria Clara, who just last week had walked across the room to him, laughing and clapping, while her stepfather Leon Udell sat in Jane's rocker and stared out the window.

Where's that husband of hers, Johnnie said. Where's that Leon Udell. I swear. First Don Temple and now this one. Have mercy.

The sun shone through the front window and the radio sat on its table, the sagging easy chair next to it, the *Sunday Oklahoman* on the chair, you could see the photograph of Roosevelt, waving.

With Little Brother he had boarded the train for Arkansas. Checked his baggage, that coffin with its precious cargo, assured of special care, that it would not be tossed about with the cases of clothing, this case containing the soul's garments, hand and elbow, amazing thigh and wondrous knee. He sat among the passengers. Little Brother rode below. Daddy's here, wherever that might be, here, yes, in this room, the train always rocking, the flat land in motion, passengers yawning, stretching their long legs.

We'll lay her out here, on the bed. Child, you're in your daddy and mama's room. Rest easy.

You go on, Daddy. I'll see to her. You go on. Watch Gloria Clara.

Then Mama came back from church with Sarah Jane.

What's happened, Marshall. What's happened.

He was sitting in the rocker with the baby.

Sarah Jane, Mama said, you take that baby and watch it.

Sarah Jane did as Mama said, took Gloria Clara from his lap, and Sarah Jane scarcely more than a baby herself, nine years old. They grew up fast or else were taken from you. When he had got off the train in Danville, George said, Marshall, our heart aches. Where is the child?

Little Brother was with the other cargo, though surely in a special place, a hidden compartment.

Let's find him, George said. We must claim him.

Nobody else will, George. Where's Mina. Where's Edgar. Where's Charlie and Clement and Grover.

Mina's on the way. Edgar's coming. The others I can't speak for. Did you send them a telegram?

Word was sent.

They'll be here then, Marshall. Don't worry. Your brothers will be here.

Little Brother was brought to them on a cart.

I'll be, George said. I never saw such a—

I can handle it myself, George. It's light, very light. Thanks all the same.

The graveyard was set into a rise, high on the mountain, near the house where Johnnie was born. He found the old road. You could still get a wagon through on it, used by the logging companies no doubt, and there were some houses beyond the clearing almost to the top of the mountain.

The road took a sharp turn about halfway up, then rose steeper, with cutbacks through hickory and oak and, the higher you went, sweet-smelling loblolly pine. The wagon, his brother Edgar's, creaked and swayed, the springs rusted and without much muscle to them, but the mule, his dark haunches shiny and ripply, climbed steadily, pulling the wagon as if he had nothing better to do. Through the flickering leaves the sky seemed almost white, and dust puffed up beneath the hoofs of the mule. A dry summer it had been, hate to think of this climb in mud, though it would mean hard ground to dig in. He had brought along pick as well as shovel—Edgar's idea, and a good one. A nice breeze rustled the leaves and kept him pleasantly cool, even in the sun —cooler in Arkansas than in Oklahoma, though certainly times came when you felt the heat. Cooler up on the mountain than in the valley below. He remembered some nights as early as August when Jane had to take out the blankets from the cedar chest. Fine sleeping weather, those times, windows open to a breeze with fall in it and the voices of crickets, tree frogs. Jane pressed soft and warm against him, Johnnie already quickening inside of her by then. That blood, where did it come from, such a miracle when you stopped to think about it.

Here came the turn where you saw the valley open up below and hills beyond, all tufted and knobby. Next a steep grade, up into a stand of sycamore and sweet gum, then the clearing, the white rock, the persimmon trees.

Esther Mary Monroe. Charles Thomas Monroe. John Marshall Monroe.

He had no stone cut for Little Brother. That would have to be taken care of later. He'd see to it. Now he took out pick and shovel, set to work, the ground hard as the devil all right. Such sweet air, though, as if meant for breath.

When he had brought Father up here, Edgar rode along. The rest said their farewell at the base of the mountain. It's a great trouble you're taking, Clement said. Father wasn't rightly thinking. The coffin, made of pine and varnished, looked made for a bigger man, its lid bowed upwards like the belly of a fiddle. Took two to lift it down from the wagon bed. The gravediggers, hired by Clement and Grover, came out of the shade and looked on with interest.

All set, one of them said. We'd best help you lift it down.

Tall lanky men in overalls, they took hold of the coffin and lifted it so easily it might have been made of cotton, then with good thick rope hoisted it down into the earth.

This is a mistake, Edgar said. I hope you know it, Marshall.

It's what Father wanted.

Who's ever going to come up here to see him. Who's going to tend the grave. It'll be overrun with blackberries.

He wanted to be here.

Little Brother, having no speech, did not express a preference. The choice was his, Marshall's. He felt the rightness of it so strongly he could not even begin to ask why. This coffin he made with his own two hands, with the wood he'd saved from the old commode when the city said put in plumbing, the city sewers had to be used. He knew that wood had to have its use in its time. No storebought coffin for Little Brother! No hired gravediggers either. This was his business.

When the sawing, hammering, sanding, and painting was done, he saw that it was not enough. What he had was a white box. It resembled a flower planter, a well-made one, yes, but something you might attach to a window, fill with dirt, plant roses in. And as he stared at the box, dissatisfied, the surface of it seemed to reflect back a rainbow, an encircling rainbow. So he would have to make a rainbow for it. He went to Jane's carton of quilt scraps, took out the worn shirts, the outgrown dresses of Cora Mae and Johnnie, and cut them into rectangles about the size of a folded handkerchief, laying each piece alongside the other across the floor of the back porch, right in front of the box, so that he might compare the colors that emerged to the ones he still could see in the whiteness of the box. When he had it right, he began to tack each piece in its proper order all along the upper edge of the box. The rainbow went all the way around. Now it would do. Now it was Little Brother's coffin, ready to go to Arkansas.

Here, Daddy, Johnnie said, let me take care of Gloria Clara. You go in there to Cora Mae. She's calling for you.

They had stretched her out in the bed, the spread tucked

beneath her chin. In this heat, a blanket lay across her feet. Her forehead shone and her cheeks too—why, the child would smother.

She's hot, he said. You've got too much covers on her.

She's gone, Jane said.

She's hot. See how she sweats.

She's dead, that's what she is, Marshall. Our baby Cora Mae is dead.

Johnnie said she was calling for me.

She didn't say a word. She just stopped breathing.

Sarah Jane stood at the door, but then was gone so fast you couldn't be sure you'd seen her. Jane sat in the straight chair by the side of the bed. The doctor was explaining that it was a mystery, such cases always a mystery, and a tragedy when not gotten to soon enough. Some you could save, but never at this late a stage.

You can go now, Marshall told him.

Who had called a doctor, he wondered, and when.

She's not leaving Oklahoma City, Marshall, Jane said. Don't you even think of taking her to Arkansas.

It was Wednesday, he realized, not Sunday at all. Cora Mae had come on Sunday, and had come to stay. Now it was Wednesday. Leon Udell sat on the sofa, his head in his hands. She'll have a decent Christian burial, Leon said to Marshall, the best money can buy. I don't have a cent to my name, but I'll find the money.

The arrangements are already made, Jane said. The plot is paid for. Reverend Wiley will conduct the services.

Don knew the time. It was a feeling he had. A quick coldness. The place he couldn't say. He was the only place, and now that world was gray and dim and cold. Trees, there was still trees, tall ones lush with leaves, but a long way off, back at the end of a broad plain. It was as if Cora Mae was there, in a kind of house, a gray clapboard house that you could not get into. He seemed to see it so true before him, could feel how it was with her in that house, locked in a room, looking into a mirror, unable to look away from it, in a house at the edge of the plain, where the trees begun, as much in the trees as on the plain, and the wildness was in the house instead of in the forest, in the dust that coated the table and mirror, in the rainbow the light made when it shone through her hair. I'm here, he wanted to say. I'll never leave this place without you, Cora Mae, I'm with you in this room, our hearts, our hands forever joined, ain't it so, say it's so.

Time always came when he went away. Otherwise trouble rose up like the devil, left him no place to be, tongue-tied and blood-short, lost in the hidden light.

He was aware of the wind shivering the trees, of dust in the air and the smell of rain. When the cloud came up, purple and tall, he saw that it didn't hold rain, but dust. In his Reo on a straight flat highway, he drove into the dust cloud. He had the windows down and the foot pedal flush to the floor, the sky darkening fast and the wind commencing to howl. He turned on the headlamps—mid-day and dark as night—and then the dust was everywhere, aswirl in the car, choking and stinging, and he thought at last he might get somewhere, the motor of the Reo whining but his heart singing.

He got to a ravine in the middle of a field. The car had not turned over, had kept its course, but the highway had curved. He could see it, straight again after a bend about a half mile back. Dust had blown up in dunes as high as the hood of the car. In the south the sky still was dark, but in the north had cleared to a pale clean blue with a few wisps of clouds, white ones edged with reddish gold. The wind had stilled to a breeze, and birds—you could see them hunched on the telephone poles—begun to sing, crows to caw. Dust lay thick on the floor of the car and on the seats.

He got out of the car, walked across the field towards a house
—it must have been a good mile away, shimmery in the afternoon
sun. Walking was rough going in that red dust, shifty beneath his
feet. Now the sky was blue everywhere, the dust storm blown to
kingdom come. He was thirsty and hoped he might find water
at the house, which was much farther from the car than he had
imagined. Of course he was not used to walking, and the sun
beat down on him.

This was flat country, the ground hard and almost without
grass, but the dust made it look strange, almost soft, with low
places here, high there, and in some places smooth as water.
Around the trunks of the few trees the dust had washed up high
as the branches.

The front door hung open and the windows was busted out.
He sat down on the porch steps, looked out on the red fields, the
hood of the Reo just visible at the edge of the ravine. The buried
blackjack trees looked almost pretty. Wind and light made the
leaves flicker and gave a white edge to the unshapely branches.

He walked back to the Reo. It started right up, and he edged
it forward slowly out of the ravine, for a while drove along on
the open fields, the Reo swerving from time to time as it struck a
slope of dust. Once these fields had been planted with no telling
what—corn, wheat, cotton, rye—but the dust storms had put an
end to that. What did folks have in mind, placing their hope in
country such as Oklahoma. It baffled him, for sure. He remembered his granddaddy's talk of the great opening, the rush for
land in 1889. Everybody wanted their 160 acres, even if it meant
living in a dirt house for years. Then this dust that came from
the air.

He drove a long time across barren land, then came to the
highway. The sky had darkened considerable, but off in the west
flamed up something awful, bands of slender clouds athrobbing
with fiery light. Such sunsets in Oklahoma: it is the dust lingering

in the air, the play of long-gone light on risen topsoil, the best
sunsets busting loose in the wake of the worst dust storms like
rainbows of drought and blight.

Oklahoma City lay in the east, aglow with its own lights,
above it the harvest moon rising. Time came back to him. It was
September First, 1934. Cora Mae slept forever, laid to rest a week
earlier. Ask him where he had been, and he'd say West Texas, I
been out in West Texas.

. . . .

White Shoes

Leon did not like to say it, but to him Cora Mae was even more beautiful dead than alive. They had put her wedding dress on her, according to his wishes, and used a brighter shade of lipstick than she ever put on.

Everything was already paid for. He wouldn't have had to pay a cent out of his pocket except he wanted her buried in the wedding dress and that cost extra. She wore a blue dress at the viewing and her wedding dress at the funeral. Changing her was what cost extra. Her mama wouldn't hear of paying for that, and so he was stuck with the tab. He didn't know where the money would come from. In the two months he'd been married to Cora Mae she had spent every dime he earned. He had resolved to say something to her about this.

None of his kinfolks was there. His mother had come for the wedding and could not afford another trip in the same summer.

To tell the truth, Cora Mae had not been the bride he had expected. The best part was seeing her in that white dress. It had been a hot day and he was sweating something fierce in his CCC dress uniform, but she looked cool as a cucumber when she walked out of that front bedroom and into the living room. The preacher, a fat man with big pink hands, dropped the Bible, and when Leon bent down to pick it up for him, the man touched him on the shoulder and said, Bless you, boy. The hand felt hot and heavy, as if the day itself had got ahold of him.

Now, sitting on a folding chair in the front row of the Street and Draper Funeral Parlor chapel, it was even hotter. He wore his CCC uniform even though he hadn't been in the CCC since he was married. Husbands wasn't allowed. Now he was in the WPA and they didn't give him a uniform.

The same preacher that married him and Cora Mae stood before him, just back of the open casket, his big pink hands raised up in the air. *Lord, bless us in our frailty. Lord, guide us safe through our earthly tribulation.* He had been preaching a long time. It was easy to lose track of the words.

Leon had come to Street and Draper's early that morning. At the viewing the night before, they had told him he could if he wanted to. They understood, the man said, that he might desire a last moment alone with the deceased, and it could be easily arranged. The man, who had the whitest teeth you ever saw, seemed to expect him to want to, and so Leon thanked him and said yes, he'd certainly be much obliged.

He realized when he left that he hadn't really wanted to. What he wished was that he could go back to the CCC camp and forget the whole thing. In the morning he would rise to the bugle call like before, jump into his khakis, and go out into the broad, hot fields to club rabbits. Late in the afternoon, he would return for a game of snookers in the camp rec room, and in the evening he and Darrold Peters would take in a movie downtown, then go to the dance pavilion at Springlake or Blossom Heath. They wouldn't go to the Arcadia because that would remind him of Cora Mae.

He was only eighteen years old and believed that life had treated him unfairly. It had started out okay. Even school hadn't been so bad, when he thought about it now. Not much had been expected of him and he knew it wasn't going to last forever.

When he joined the CCC and was sent to Oklahoma City, he began to think that the fun he deserved was at last headed his way. Then, right off the bat, he had met Cora Mae.

Before that, he hadn't given much thought to the opposite sex. He had some pictures on loan from his cousin Fred that he kept in the bottom of a drawer and took out once in a while to look at. These ladies didn't have much on in the way of clothes, just scanty little things strapped here and there, but they all wore shoes. The shoes had real high heels on them. The ladies had the littlest feet. He never saw a woman in Greenwood, or even in Fort Smith, with feet that little, though some of them wore high heels. His mama, a big-boned woman with a high forehead and long neck, wore black lace-up shoes that had a thick heel not more than a inch and a half high.

For the most part, he never thought of the girls in school as women. Mary Jean Hicks, who wore lipstick and painted her cheeks, looked like she was trying too hard, and Sophie Gatewood, though built like the ladies in the photographs, had a chin like a football player and buck teeth. The prettiest one, May Rose Townley, was too tall and had long skinny feet. For a while he fancied himself in love with Berta Wells. He didn't know why. It was just a feeling she gave him when he saw her. When he looked at the ladies in the photographs he began to see her face on top of their bodies. Then when he next saw her he imagined the body of one of the ladies with its tiny undergarments underneath Berta's plain, shapeless clothes. This excited him. He watched her during geography class and it made the time go faster. She smiled back at him once or twice and, whenever she said hello, pronounced his name as if it had special meaning. Then when he made his move, tried to kiss her at a Sunday school picnic on Magazine Mountain, she looked shocked. He thought she might hit him, but she only asked him what he thought he was doing. He didn't know what to say. He laughed, which just made her madder. Anyway, it hadn't been him she smiled at during geography, but Delbert Dawes, the Methodist preacher's boy, who sat right behind Leon, carving initials on his desk. Leon figured those initials must have been D. D. plus B. W. He saw the two of them sneak off together into the trees during the evening hymn sing. Since his only reason for coming had been to attend to Berta and impress her with his fine singing voice, he cussed himself out and didn't sing another hymn.

None of that prepared him for Cora Mae.

Nipped in the bud, the preacher was saying. *Taken in the honeyed blossom of youth.*

He guessed so, but even though she had been only a year older than him she seemed older, not young at all. That had appealed to him at first. The ladies in the photographs were older too, women of the world. He thought it would take a woman of the world to get at him, and Cora Mae, sitting all alone at that little table in the Arcadia Ballroom, cigarette smoke swirling around her, rhinestones sparkling, rubies and diamonds too, looked every bit the woman of the world, and he didn't mind telling her so.

She laughed, but it wasn't a laugh like Berta Wells's.

After that he met her every week at the Arcadia. They danced and listened to comedy routines in between. They drank beer out of long-neck brown bottles and smoked cigarettes. He had never done any of these things before meeting her, though he had drunk rotgut and smoked cornsilk. His dancing might could've been a little smoother, but even when he came down on one of her toes she never complained. He told her what it was like growing up in Greenwood, Arkansas, and even when he stretched the truth now and then to make the story more lively she never disbelieved a word.

He should have known better. A woman her age with a little infant. The infant hadn't been any trouble. Slept like a log. It was what the baby meant. It kept reminding Cora Mae of the man that was its father. She never said so, but Leon was sure it did.

She wouldn't put that man out of her mind, that was the trouble. When he saw her only on Saturday nights, Leon couldn't see this, but when he was married to her, when he took her on a week-long honeymoon to Hot Springs in his home state of Arkansas, when he introduced her to his mama and papa in Greenwood and showed her the sights of Fort Smith, when he showed her the photographs he'd never returned to his cousin Fred, when he had done all these things for her and she still wouldn't say a word about her former husband, he concluded that she never stopped loving the man.

You don't look happy, he said to her. You don't ever smile anymore.

She gave him a smile then that made him shiver. She guessed she just was missing her baby girl.

What can we hope to know, flawed vessels that we are. We can't even fathom the depths of our imperfections.

He kept thinking of when he was much younger—nine or ten—and he and some of his friends, led by an older boy, Preston Dalton, went off together after school. Preston lived up on the mountain, farther back than any of the other boys. He was a head taller than Leon—he might have been twelve or thirteen, though in the same grade as the rest of them—and was missing a front tooth. You didn't dare tease him about the missing tooth. He was known to be mean, a rough character. Also, because of his age and his backwoods home (no one had ever been there), he seemed mysterious, a walking dark secret. Leon felt privileged when Preston Dalton asked if he and Elvin Beasley and Joe Mack Givens would like to do something different after school. All had chores awaiting them at home, but they wasn't about to make excuses to Preston Dalton. Maybe they would get to see Preston's home way up on the mountain.

But Preston only led them a little ways into the woods, not far off the road at all, to a spot where a bunch of shrubs grew up high enough to hide behind. The shrubs were thick and smelled faintly sweet. Pine needles made the ground soft. It was shady and cool.

Tell you what, Preston said. Let's set down right here.

They sat.

Preston talked for a while. He said school was a waste of time. He meant to quit when he turned sixteen and do something to make money. He wasn't sure what exactly, but he had some ideas. Also he meant to have him a woman. He knew what a woman liked, he said. Then he was quiet for a minute. Joe Mack asked him if he'd ever had a woman. Leon wasn't sure what having a woman meant, but he understood from Preston's grin that the question was a good one.

Wouldn't you like to know, Preston said. I'll just bet you'd like to know, wouldn't you. You all want me to tell you what it's like, don't you. Sure you do. I was just like you when I was your age. It's a natural curiosity.

To Leon, Preston was never their age. Ever since he could remember, Preston had been bigger than anybody. And he always knew things—not things they learned you in school, but things you wanted to know about. Girls, for example. Women. How to catch a frog, how to skin a rabbit.

Preston's face grew serious. He sat with his legs stretched out in front of him, not crossed like the rest of them. He had been leaning back on his hands, but now he sat up straight and spread his legs wide, moving his hands to his hips, then, to Leon's astonishment, to his crotch. He was unbuttoning his pants. Next thing you knew, he had reached in and pulled out his ding-dong.

You all got you one of these too, I'll bet you, don't you, Preston said. Less you're a bunch of girls. You ain't a bunch of girls, are you? Naw, I didn't think so. How about you, Elvin. Are you a girl? No? Joe Mack? Naw, I didn't think so. Leon? No? Well, then you got one of these just like mine, don't you.

Joe Mack was the first to begin unbuttoning his pants. Leon was next. Elvin hesitated.

What's the matter, Elvin, Preston said. You leave yours at home this morning?

Elvin turned red as a beet, but he unbuttoned his pants then, like the rest of them.

Leon tried not to look at Preston's ding-dong, which, he believed, was bigger and longer even than his daddy's. Why, it looked like a fish. His own was small, and he worried that it might never grow any bigger. It seemed scarcely bigger than a worm, or your little finger. He felt somewhat better when he saw that Joe Mack's wasn't any bigger than his, and Elvin's was actually smaller. No wonder poor Elvin had been so embarrassed.

This here is what a woman likes, Preston said.

He began to touch himself. It looked a little like he was petting that thing. It might have been a pup he held in his lap. Then it began to grow before your very eyes. Leon couldn't help looking.

You can do it too, Preston said. You got the same equipment. Just touch it real soft at first. That's the way a woman does it. Ain't you never done this before? Why, you're big old boys. I bet you done this lots of times already.

Leon looked at Joe Mack. Joe Mack looked back at him. Should they be doing this, Leon wanted to know from Joe Mack. Joe Mack looked away and began to touch himself the way Preston showed them. So Leon did the same. Elvin was doing it too.

Feels good, don't it, Preston said.

It did. It was a little like the feeling you got shinnying up the flag pole. Leon had noticed that just a little while ago, purely by accident, and hadn't told no one about it, shinnying every chance he got. It sure beat playing baseball.

Joe Mack had a pained expression on his face. He wasn't getting a bit bigger. Leon was though. He didn't need to look, he could feel it, he could feel that nice aching. He was touching harder, squeezing it between his thumb and first two fingers, up and down, up and down. He heard Preston breathing heavily. He saw Elvin smile and close his eyes. Joe Mack was working hard but seemed to have no luck. His forehead was shiny with sweat. Birds sang. Had they been singing all along? The sky appeared to turn sideways. Then he didn't seem to be anywhere at all. The aching felt so good, he could climb and climb and never stop, go right up through the sky, that's where he was headed all right, climbing higher and higher. Lord help!

When he opened his eyes, he saw that Preston had stopped. Elvin said, Oh, shit, God damn, and then he stopped too. Preston laughed, and buttoned up his pants. Joe Mack had his eyes closed and was still going at it, gritting his teeth. At last he gave a big sigh and stopped. There might have been tears in his eyes.

Did you feel it, Preston asked.

Sure, Joe Mack said. It was swell. God damn.

Elvin just grinned and his face was red. He turned away from them to button up his pants. Joe Mack did the same. Leon had to stand, and when he did, so did the others, even Preston Dalton. They made their way quickly through the underbrush and to the road. Preston began to whistle. He had the prettiest and fanciest way of whistling you ever heard.

Blessed are they that mourn: for they shall be comforted. Blessed are the pure in heart: for they shall see God.

He had not wanted to come here this morning. It seemed to him enough that he was staying in her house, the house her other husband still paid the rent for. It never felt right, and he wished he might now and then go back to the barracks. In the dark of her bedroom she reached for him as if in a hurry. It wasn't how he thought it would be. He wanted to turn the light on and look at her, but was too embarrassed to ask. Oh, she got him going all right, but afterwards turned right around and went to sleep without so much as a how-do-you-do, just when he felt like having a cigarette and talking about all the things that had happened to him that week on the WPA, some of the jokes he had heard and the clever remarks he'd thought to make on different occasions. He wasn't such a dull fellow, if she'd only give him a chance to show her.

On Sundays he lay around the house—her house and that other man's—and read the funny papers in the *Sunday Oklahoman* while she occupied herself with the baby, which was walking real good now and quite capable of snatching his funnies right out of his hand. Sometimes her sister Johnnie came over, the two women sitting in canvas chairs out in the tiny backyard, talking a steady stream at each other while the baby banged on pots and pans.

The night before the funeral, the baby wasn't there. She had been taken to Mr. and Mrs. Monroe's house. He stayed in Cora Mae's house all by himself. He sat on the porch until it got dark, then walked around the block. Really, he didn't want to go in that house. He wasn't afraid or anything. She certainly wasn't there, and she hadn't even died in this house. Still, it just didn't feel right to go in it.

He would've liked to go downtown. He wouldn't go to the Arcadia Ballroom or anything though. It wasn't a good time he was after. No, what he'd really like would be to go up in that tall bank building, the one Darrold Peters had showed him, with the slide that dropped right down the center of it, an inside fire escape, thirty stories or more. He would climb the thirty flights, no complaint, and then go look out the window, just as they'd done that Saturday when, later, he'd first seen Cora Mae at the Arcadia Ballroom. The view would be different at night, the air cooler. He could look as long as he wanted to, and then go find the door to the slide. That slide hadn't frightened him a bit, and it wouldn't at night either. In fact it would be just the same at night, no windows anywhere along the way, dark and cool as you go down, turning and turning, your heart thumping faster and harder all the time.

The bank building was surely locked up at night anyway. When he had walked around the block three or four times, pausing only to look across to the few lighted windows of Mount St. Mary's (couldn't see any of the nuns), he went into the house. Cora Mae wasn't here. He would see her in the morning, he had a appointment at Street and Draper's, she would have on her wedding dress. Why did it feel like she was here then. He turned on every light in the house. Alone, he was surely alone. It wasn't a big house, just four rooms. She had a radio, but he didn't care to turn it on.

He went to her bedroom. Supposed to be *their* bedroom, his and hers, but he never thought of it as anything but hers. The bed she'd shared with her other husband, the dressing table with its row of little jars and bottles, the mirror she had seen herself in, her jewelry box with the diamonds and rubies and rhinestones he'd so admired when he first saw her in the Arcadia Ballroom. He wouldn't open that box. Wouldn't her soul come jumping out at him if he did?

Naw, it wouldn't. Get a hold of yourself, Leon Udell.

He lay down on the bed, rolled to her side of it, got up, opened the wardrobe. Now he decided he wanted a memento. Tomorrow or the next day Johnnie and Mrs. Monroe would come over here and take everything away. He could just see Johnnie wearing Cora Mae's pretty black dress, her rhinestones, her little hats, her white gloves. Mrs. Monroe would take table and chair, the throw rug, the curtains. Didn't he deserve something for his trouble.

The radio came to mind, but he couldn't imagine carrying that thing around.

On her dresser she had a framed photograph of her sister, another of her mama and daddy standing in their front yard. Those wasn't any use to him.

The baby's bed looked soiled, a rubber ball in one corner, a bottle with a nipple on it in the other, some milk still in it.

In the kitchen he examined the coffee cups—there were four

of them—trying to decide which she was accustomed to drinking out of. All four were in the sink, hadn't been washed. Also two plates with egg yolk hardened on them. He guessed he had eaten off one of those. The plates had a blue circle around the edge. They came from her daddy's old cafe, she had told him. The cafe had gone out of business a long time ago. One of them plates might make a suitable memento, but he didn't feel like washing it.

He went back to her bedroom. He took the black dress from the wardrobe, laid it on the bed. The silvery flowers around the top, just above where her breasts would be, flashed as brightly as when he'd first seen her. It made him nervous to look at it, and he put it back on its hanger in the wardrobe. In her chest of drawers, everything lay folded and fresh and spicy-smelling. He began to take out her underthings, the silky slips, the stockings. Every last item in its place. Underpants he'd do last of all.

Then he came to the envelope. It wasn't even sealed. A fat brown envelope with a bunch of photographs and some letters. Not as many photographs as it had seemed at first, maybe a dozen or so, and just two letters. A couple of the pictures was her sister, one with a man he never saw before, the other a studio picture marked H. C. Green on back, with the date March 10, 1931. Johnnie was younger in this picture than in the one Cora Mae had on her dresser. She wore her hair shorter then and had on a pearl necklace and pearl earrings. There was a picture of her little sister Sarah Jane, unless it was Cora Mae when she was just a girl. It might have been Cora Mae, that peculiar smile, like she was about to ask you a question. There was some more of her mama and daddy, and another that he knew was Sarah Jane, in her Sunday school dress and with a big bow in her hair. None of these was any interest to him.

Here was the one, though. Here was the one he knew he'd find. The man with the thin mustache, the sly grin. He stood out in the open, no building of any kind in sight, no trees or bushes, grass growing in clumps. Squinting, the man looked away from the camera, as if trying to see something off to his right somewhere. He wore a double-breasted sportcoat, unbuttoned, and no tie. He had his hands in his pockets. Leon looked for a name on the back, but there wasn't anything written there. It had to be the husband. He knew it was the husband. So she had saved a photograph of the man. Probably took it out and looked at it often.

One of the letters was dated November 7, 1924, Cromwell, Oklahoma, and began: My Dear Darling Daughters. Something her daddy had written when he was away on a trip. But the other had nothing at the top except Hello Sweethart. Leon read this one straight through, though the handwriting was hard to read. Honey, I sure am missing you. I am not so far off really, just in Texas, but it seems like the end of the earth because you are not anywheres near. The car runs just fine, no troubles, just a big dust storm forced me off of the road for a spell. Ate at a little cafe called Johnny's, just like your daddy's use to be, but the food was not as good, though the coffee okay (strong, how I like it). They all say this country is going under fast account of the dust, people leaving in droves. Same in W. Okla., a crying shame. Some say it is the dust, some say the bankers. I wouldn't know, but I see them going, I pass them on the roads all the time, you have to wonder how far they'll get and if it will ever be any better. You take good care of yourself I am sending you a big hug and a kiss and hope you are thinking of me now and then and are not too lonesome. Your loving husband Don Temple.

She never stopped loving him. Why else would she save such a letter as that. Leon put her clothes back in the drawers, just the way they was, and the envelope with the pictures too, only he kept out the letter and the photograph of her former husband Don Temple. She didn't need them. He might put them back before tomorrow or he might just keep them for a memento.

In the meantime he'd set them on the nightstand, there, the

photograph propped against the base of the lamp, the unfolded letter next to it.

Then he took off his clothes and climbed into her bed.

And there shall be no more death, neither sorrow, nor crying, neither shall there be any more pain: for the former things have passed away.

Awake, Leon saw the man's face first thing and didn't know where he was. He looked around. Her dressing table, the rows of jars, the hairbrush and comb. Her mama and daddy's picture, just visible on the edge of the dresser, as if they peered down at him. This is how she would feel, he thought, waking, surrounded by herself. She would look at the man's picture first thing, just as he had done. Maybe she would take it in her hands, bring it close to her. Then reread the letter. Hello Sweethart. Honey I sure am missing you.

He remembered what day it was, what he had to do. He had told the funeral man he would be there to see her. Why had he agreed to such a idea!

He dressed hurriedly. Might as well get it over with. And, after all, he didn't need any more time in this house. He'd never spend another night at this place. He gathered up the smattering of clothes that he owned, a couple of shirts in the wardrobe, some undershirts and socks tucked away in the bottom drawer of her chest of drawers. His shaving gear in the bathroom. It all fit in a brown grocery sack. Should he shave? Naw, no need to, such light whiskers. He could get away with twice a week if he had to, and he had just shaved yesterday. He looked sternly at himself in the mirror. The CCC dress uniform with its brass buttons, green tie, shiny lapel insignias, suited him to a *T*, he had to admit. They told him he could keep it as long as he wanted. You could easily take him for a soldier in the regular army. Hadn't Cora Mae done that very thing when he first introduced himself. He told her, eventually, that he was in the Civilian Conservation Corps and not the real army. It was like the army, he explained.

Only difference was in the CCC, instead of huns you fought a terrible destructive animal that the farmers couldn't handle by themselves.

He wished she hadn't asked him what the destructive animal was.

How, she asked, could you hit a bunny rabbit over the head.

You did what you had to do. And they were *jack*rabbits, not bunny rabbits. Desperate hordes of them. She never saw the like!

Some day he'd be in the regular army.

He went back to her bedroom where he saw that he had left the photograph and letter on the nightstand, the bed unmade. Let the bed stay messed up. Mrs. Monroe would take the sheets anyway. He folded the letter and put it in his pocket, along with the photograph.

Then he left for the funeral parlor.

Snatched away in the full bloom of life, carried off to meet her maker!

Mr. Udell. Won't you come right in.

It was the man with the real white teeth. He wore a dark blue suit with a flower in the buttonhole. He was half a head taller than Leon, maybe close to six feet, and he leaned his head to one side when he talked. His suitcoat fit him tight and his tie was bunched up, though held in place by a silver clasp with a pearly cross on it.

This way, Mr. Udell. Or should I say Private Udell?

Mister. I been discharged. Honorable.

Yes, well, Mr. Udell, she's ready, just as you've requested. Right through here, sir.

Leon knew the way. He had been here all during the viewing last night. The room was just around the corner, down the hallway and on the left. A cardboard plaque sat on a little table outside the door. Cora Mae Udell, the plaque said. May She Rest in Peace. Her mama had picked out the slogan. It was good as any.

The door was open.

You may go right in, the man said.

I will, Leon said. When I'm good and ready, he wanted to add, but he went on in.

It was a small room, hardly space enough to turn around in. A gold cross hung on one wall, pictures of Jesus in gold frames on the others. In one picture Jesus, in a white robe that dragged on the ground, carried a long pole and looked down on some children that was clamoring around him for attention. Leon had stared at that picture a lot last night while Cora Mae's mama read the Bible, whispering the words to herself, and her daddy sat there wringing his hands. Looking at that picture was when he thought of Preston Dalton, who he hadn't remembered for the longest time. He didn't know why Preston Dalton should have come to mind at just this particular occasion. Didn't seem appropriate. Preston Dalton wasn't no Sunday school teacher, let alone no Jesus. Ain't you never done this before? Preston had asked. Why, you're big old boys. I bet you done this lots of times already. Ain't you, Joe Mack? Fess up, Elvin. Leon, I know you done it many a time.

The other picture of Jesus was just of his head. He had long brown hair pretty as a woman's.

Cora Mae was pressed up against the wall beneath the picture of Jesus and the little children. He hadn't cared to look at her a lot. Last night they'd had her in a light blue dress with a string of pearls around her neck. The coffin lining was a dark blue, and Cora Mae's sister Johnnie had said this outfit would match it nicely. When he had recommended the wedding dress, nobody took to the idea right off. It wasn't appropriate, Johnnie said, it wasn't right somehow. Over my dead body, her mama said. Her daddy stepped out of the room.

I got a say in this matter, Leon said. Ain't I her husband.

Ain't I her mother!

Now, now, Johnnie had said. Let's not fuss at a time like this.

Leon reminded them that he had a say in the matter.

I never heard such a thing, her mama said. She was a large woman, taller than Leon and for sure heavier, but he stuck to his guns. In the end they agreed to dress her in the blue outfit for the viewing and in the wedding dress for the burial. The funeral man said it was highly unusual and would mean extra expense, but he could certainly arrange things however they wished.

I won't pay a cent extra, her mama said. If he wants it that way he'll have to pay the extra charge.

Send me the bill, Leon said. And be sure and put her white shoes on her. She liked them shoes.

He felt good winning the argument, but then remembered he had no money. Well, maybe they'd let him pav on the installment plan. The layaway, whatever you called it.

Can't squeeze blood out of a turnip.

He shivered at the sight of that white dress. It would've been enough, seeing her in the afternoon at the service. What trouble this was, what could he possibly have to say to her, he hadn't wanted to come here. The white—had it been that bright on their wedding day? The hat looked like a crown, and the white veil over her face just made her red lips look redder.

Cora Mae, I got a bone to pick with you.

He was mad at her. Look here, he wanted to say to her, look here what I found hid underneath your underpants. This photograph—it's him ain't it. And look here at this letter I found. Why was you saving this letter if you didn't love him anymore, answer me that. Who do you think is here with you now, him or me. It's *me,* ain't it. Me, not him. You think he cares enough about you to even show up for your funeral? Answer me that, huh.

When *is* the funeral, Leon, she seemed to ask him.

Why, this afternoon. Three o'clock. By four o'clock you'll be in the ground, laid to rest.

And what time is it now, Leon.

Why, it's nine o'clock. Five minutes after nine in the morning.

Then he's got six hours to get here, doesn't he.

Six hours. What's that got to do—

He could be a long ways off and still get here in six hours, Leon.

He won't be here. I'm here and you don't have a idea in the world where he is. He won't be here.

We'll see, won't we.

Why had he come here. Mightn't he have known she'd get him in a stew again. The man wasn't going to come and that was that. Whoever heard of such a idea. This is what was true: him, Leon Udell. He might not have wanted to come here, maybe he had other things he could have done this morning that he would have liked better, but here he was, wasn't he, and didn't that mean nothing to her. What was a fellow supposed to do.

He realized he had the photograph in one hand, the letter in the other.

Well, here then, he said, take them. What good are they to me.

He dropped them into the casket. No, that wouldn't do. Someone would see them at the service and take them out. He wanted her to have them though. It seemed to him now that that's why he had brought them here, to give them to her. He wanted her to have that photograph and that damn letter. That's what he had meant by taking them out of her drawer.

Here, he said. You take them then.

He tried putting them along the side, but couldn't get them pushed down far enough and so he slid them underneath her waist, where he could work them back and they wouldn't be seen. She lay on a satiny smooth sheet and her dress was also smooth. The photograph, being stiff, slid under easier than the letter, but he got them both where they wouldn't be seen. He hoped she was happy.

She didn't look happy. Didn't look like she cared, one way or the other. She always looked that way. There was no figuring her out.

Sure looked pretty, though, in that wedding dress. If he was to die now, in the next six months say, he wanted to be buried in his CCC uniform. He felt healthy, however.

The thing was, he didn't have no memento, now that he'd given her the photograph and the letter. He wished he'd thought to take something of hers from the house. Well, it was too late for that. He sure wasn't going back to that house. Didn't she owe him something for his trouble, though. Maybe he could take her veil. Naw, he liked seeing her in that veil. The little bouquet she clasped in her hands? That wasn't of no significance.

He considered the shoes. Did she have them on her? He'd told them to be sure and put them on her. It was part of what he paid for. They better be on her. He raised the hem of her gown. Yes, by God, she had them on. They was white, just like the dress, and might have been made of satin too. They had little bows on the toes, studded with sparkling jewels, and high tapering heels.

He had no use for them, no, of course not, but that wasn't the point. The point was, she owed him something. He happened to know that she had liked those shoes. She wore them sometimes for no reason at all. Ain't those your wedding shoes, he'd asked her once. I wore them at my wedding, yes, she said.

Get that. *My* wedding. As if he'd had nothing to do with it.

Why are you wearing them now, he had asked her.

Because I want to, she said. I like them, she said.

Wasn't no skin off of his back!

They wasn't so easy to get off of her. He put them in the paper grocery sack, stuffing them down beneath the clean undershirts and socks he'd brought from the house. Then he pulled the gown back down over her bare toes—they hadn't even bothered to put stockings on her. Unless somebody bent down to look, they'd never know the shoes was gone. Showed that this funeral parlor was on the up and up, he guessed. Another parlor might have thought they could get away with leaving off the shoes. Of course, they hadn't put on her stockings.

He felt he had stayed long enough.

Her mother a devout pilgrim and for many many years a faithful Baptist, her father a decent, hard-working man. An older sister who mourns the loss, a younger who will long grieve, a little brother who preceded her in that ascent from this our vale of sorrow and strife and who welcomes her with open arms and a glad heart.

Surely the man was nearing the end. Her sister Johnnie, sitting next to Leon, held a handkerchief to her face, dabbed at her eyes. Cora Mae lay still, didn't give a sign of having lost her shoes. Well, but didn't she have her letter and that picture. A fair trade, by any light.

He had taken the paper sack with his clothes and her shoes in it down to the Union Bus Station and put them in a five-cent locker. He would pick them up later and take them with him. He didn't know where he'd go, but he wouldn't go back to her house. He might bury the shoes or he might not. He thought that he probably wouldn't.

He got back from the bus depot in plenty of time. Even had time before leaving to get him a hot dog. But he wasn't the first to arrive. When he walked into the chapel, he saw that a man stood over the casket. Was it *him*? Could it be that she was right and the other husband would show up, as if for pure spite. But no, this wasn't Don Temple. This fellow didn't have no little mustache. Leon stood next to him, introduced himself.

I'm the husband, he told the stranger, extending his hand.

The stranger took the hand, but didn't hardly squeeze at all. Leon's daddy had taught him to squeeze hard when he shook

hands with somebody. He'd had to practice it by shaking his
daddy's hand ever so often. Grip, Daddy said. Harder! Is that
all you got, boy? Come on now. That ain't nothing. You can do
better than that. And they squeezed until one of them called it
quits—usually Leon, the bones in his hand about to bust, but he
was getting better at it, and he liked to imagine that someday he
would force the old man to his knees.

The stranger let Leon shake his hand, but volunteered no information. The fellow might be a little slow.

I said I'm the husband: Leon Udell. Didn't catch your name.

Mildren, the man said. Mildren Bagley. I'm her cousin. I rode
on a train all night to get here.

Where from.

Arkansas.

Arkansas. I'll be. That's where I'm from. Whereabouts in Arkansas.

Danville.

I'm from Greenwood myself. Near Fort Smith. I was only
married to her for two months and now this. A heck of a note,
ain't it.

Others began to come in, and Leon thought that this cousin
should step aside so as not to be mistaken for the grieving husband. Much to Leon's embarrassment, tears was falling from the
cousin's eyes. Leon figured on shedding a few tears himself, for
there was nothing fair about none of this, and didn't he have a
right to grieve with the best of them. But just now his eyes stayed
dry.

Maybe we'd best sit down now, he told the cousin, and let
others have a look.

But the man stayed, his shoulders shaking he was sobbing so.

In the lobby Leon mixed with the other mourners, offering his
hand freely and gripping firmly. He didn't know these people.
They were members of her mother's church, he figured, powdery
smelling ladies with black lacy veils over their faces. I'm so sorry,
they told him. Oh, that's all right, he said, it wasn't your fault. It

wasn't no one's fault that he could see. Just a common cold, as far as you could tell, and then that coughing and the sore throat that wouldn't quit.

Nobody that fit the description of the former husband appeared.

Cora Mae's mama and daddy came in. They had the little sister Sarah Jane with them, but not the baby. Cora Mae's mama was not crying. She looked like she always looked, almost frowning but not quite, as if she had a thing or two to say to you but it could wait. She had on a black sacklike dress, a little hat and veil like the other ladies wore, and she carried a small white box in one of her hands. Mr. Monroe, wearing a white shirt and black bowtie, and a suit that looked two sizes too big, trailed behind her a little. Sarah Jane, though only nine years old, looked almost as tall as a grownup lady next to her daddy, who was short, even shorter than Leon. Sarah Jane waved at him, but her mama and daddy scarcely nodded their head in his direction.

He turned away from them. At the chapel door he saw that the cousin still was standing alongside Cora Mae's open casket, looking down on her with his hands clasped behind him. The chapel was filling up. Although a electric fan had been set up in the lobby, it was plenty hot. A hundred degrees in the shade, as they said.

Johnnie came in right after her parents, escorted by a man that Leon thought at first was Don Temple. Like Don, he had one of those thin mustaches such as movie actors wear, but he was a little too short to be Don, and slightly heavier. He looked flashy for a funeral, his suit a summery bluish gray, his silky tie blue with yellow polka dots, clasped by a shiny gold bar that had a big ruby stuck in the middle of it.

Leon, Johnnie said, this is Bill Haynes.

I've heard about you, Bill Haynes said, flashing a grin, extending his hand. Pleased to meet you, though sorry about the circumstances.

It's all right, Leon said.

Bill Haynes had a grip as strong as Leon's daddy, and Leon almost kept squeezing, wanting to see who would be the one to go down on their knees.

But Bill let up, took his hand back.

Where is the little one, Leon asked Johnnie.

Little one. Oh, you mean Gloria Clara? She's at Mrs. Perry's. She's too young to know what's going on. It wouldn't do her any good to see her mama . . . like that, would it. I thought it was nice of Mrs. Perry to offer to take care of her today. Good neighbors are a blessing. Oh, Lord. Is that who I think it is.

She was looking in the chapel, where the cousin could be clearly seen. How long was he going to stand there gaping at Cora Mae, Leon wanted to know. Was he going to notice she didn't have her shoes on?

It's Mildren, Bill. Cousin Mildren. You know, the one who—

Oh, yeah, Bill said. In the stable or something? When you all were visiting—

Hush. You don't have to tell the world.

Says he come from Arkansas, Leon said. But they went on into the chapel and didn't say anything else to him.

Behold, I show you a mystery. We shall not all sleep, but we shall all be changed.

The preacher like to never stopped. It was very hot. Leon sat by the aisle, with only Johnnie beside him. She kept her distance, but he felt the heat she gave off and smelled her sweet perfume. Next to Johnnie was her boyfriend Bill Haynes, who fidgeted with the program card. Nobody else in this row. Cora Mae's parents, with Sarah Jane, sat on the other side of the aisle, behind them the tall Arkansas cousin and the old ladies from Mrs. Monroe's church.

Leon worried a little, seeing the mourners pass one by one in front of Cora Mae's casket, but no one seemed to notice that she didn't have her shoes on. Mrs. Monroe opened the white box she'd been carrying and pulled a Bible out of it. This little Bible, black with a gold zipper to keep it shut, she set down in the casket, and Leon hoped she wouldn't see the letter and photograph he had slid beneath her.

She didn't. Or if she did, she didn't let on. She put the Bible down and walked away.

He was the very last to look, right after Cora Mae's daddy, who leaned down and kissed Cora Mae on the cheek.

See there, he thought, it's all over but the shouting and he didn't show up, did he. I'm here and he ain't. Doesn't that prove something to you, doesn't that go to show.

He had more to say, he wanted to bring up the matter of his weekly paycheck from the WPA, his hard-earned money and where it went, but the funeral man, his white teeth shining, said it had come time to go, and closed up the casket.

Was this when he was going to cry? He turned and began to walk towards Cora Mae's parents, who were almost to the door. The rest of the crowd would be waiting outside, lined up in their automobiles. He would ride in the limousine with Mr. and Mrs. Monroe, Johnnie, and Sarah Jane. They had told him that yesterday. The hearse would lead the way.

There was more. There had to be more.

He heard a rustling noise behind him, turned and saw the four pallbearers lifting the shut coffin. They were strangers, these four men. Leon had tried to get Darrold Peters from the CCC camp to be one of them, but Darrold already had something to do today. They were men Johnnie knew from the store downtown where she worked, and a deacon from her mama's church.

What was he doing here, with all these people he didn't know and who didn't know him. It was between him and Cora Mae, and then Cora Mae wasn't no more, and here he was with all these strangers.

Wait a minute, he said to no one in particular.

Cora Mae's daddy stopped in the doorway and looked around.

Wait just a minute here, Leon said, and now he was facing the coffin again, which the four strangers had just then lifted.

You put that thing right back down, he told them. Don't you move it another inch, you hear me.

The men stopped, one of them almost losing his grip. The funeral man began to walk towards Leon. He wasn't smiling now. His shoes squeaked. The men put the coffin down.

It's all right, Mr. Udell, the funeral man said, touching Leon's elbow. I know what you're feeling, and, believe me, I understand.

It ain't all right, Leon said, and you don't understand.

Well, then, maybe you can tell me. We can't keep people waiting. What is it, Mr. Udell.

Leon saw that Cora Mae's mama had come back into the chapel. Sarah Jane too. Sarah Jane held her daddy's hand. The mama stood behind them, tall and breathing deep, her black hat shining like metal. She had lifted the veil and was giving him that ugly look.

What was it he had meant to say. He remembered only that it didn't concern them. It was between him and Cora Mae. He wanted these people to know that, and to know she was his bride. He loved her. Sure, he loved her. Didn't they know that. Why, it was as plain as the nose on your face. He loved her like he loved his own life. He loved her from the first time he laid eyes on her. He would love her forever. That's what he wanted to tell them.

Maybe it was the way the funeral man begun to squeeze his arm. Maybe it was the expression on Mrs. Monroe's face, or the way that hat seemed to snatch up the light. Maybe it was the way Sarah Jane reminded him of Cora Mae. Maybe it was the way Mr. Monroe released her hand and began to move towards him. Maybe it was the thought that Cora Mae's other husband still had time to show up.

He wasn't right in his head and he knew it. Something dark was getting darker. It's a cheat, he heard himself saying. We been cheated. She ain't got her wedding shoes on. She ain't got *any* shoes on her feet. She is barefoot as the day she was born, and not a one of you was going to say a word, was you. You was

going to let her go to her grave in her bare feet, wasn't you. It
didn't make no difference to you, did it. Well, I'll tell you what.
It makes a difference to Leon Udell. Yes, it does. It ain't a matter
of money. I will pay what I owe. It is a matter of . . . it's a matter
of honor, that's what. It is a matter of honor, sure as the day I
was born. You can't cheat Leon Udell. No, sir!

Then he remembered. He was the one that stole the shoes.
He sat down. It was hard to breathe. He needed more air than
they had in this room. For a second there he imagined that the
pallbearers had surrounded him, hogging the air, but they had
kept to their places. It was Cora Mae's daddy that looked down
on him. He had thick black eyebrows and little black eyes set
back deep.

Come on, son, Mr. Monroe said. She's gone and there's nothing in the world we can do to bring her back.

Leon felt himself being assisted, gently, to his feet, and led up
the aisle towards the door of the chapel. He greatly appreciated
the help. He felt weak, like an old woman. He realized that he
was crying.

Outside, the hot bright air hit him hard. I stole them shoes off
of her, he wanted to say to her daddy. I took them myself, and
for no reason but spite and meanness. I robbed from the dead. Is
there anything meaner.

He didn't say anything. In the limousine, with her daddy next
to him and her mama and her sisters across from him, he was
facing backwards, aimed at the line of cars behind instead of
towards the hearse ahead. He might have talked to her daddy,
but not with the rest of them in earshot. Probably the cousin
from Arkansas rode in the next car. You couldn't tell for sure.

Johnnie commented on the heat. She couldn't remember a
worse August.

They're all bad, her mama said.

I like June best, the little sister said. In August you know summer's over and school's about to start.

Leon brushed his cheeks with his cuff, but the hot wind had already dried the tears. Maybe the women hadn't even noticed.

She sure looked pretty in that white dress, he said.

Nobody said anything after that.

The Sunnylane Cemetery was way out on the southeast edge of town. Trees was sparse and small, yet somehow old-looking. It was high, flat ground. Off in the west the two thirty-story bank buildings looked like gray stubs—Leon couldn't tell which was the one he'd jumped down the belly of.

It wasn't a crowded cemetery—plenty spacious, he'd say, though he figured they had them this big in Fort Smith and Little Rock. Cora Mae's gravesite seemed almost in the center of it, with a neat mound of red dirt piled high to one side. They had to stand in the hot sun, the dusty wind stinging their faces, while the preacher reminded them that they was all sprung up from the dust and would be returned to its bosom on a whim.

The man had not come. It was sure too late now. He would never be here. Leon felt sorry for him. If it had been him, he would've been here. He forgave Cora Mae for loving the poor man. Looking up from the grave, he seemed to see her rising up into the tall white clouds, bride of his life, beautiful and pure in her everlasting faithless love. *God is in the midst of her,* the fat preacher said. *She shall not be moved.*

XVI

. . . .

A Broken Jar

In the *Daily Oklahoman* Marshall read that the former fiddling sensation at the old Arcadia Ballroom, Plowboy Pink Miracle, remembered fondly by many Cityans, was starring in the latest Tom Mix movie. They ran a photograph at the top of the article, and Marshall saw that it was the same old Pink Miracle all right.

The movie played at the Rialto downtown, and then at the Blue Moon in Packingtown. Marshall saw it in both places. Pink wasn't really the star, of course. He was one of the cowboys on the trail with Tom Mix. On a horse he did not look comfortable, but around the campfire at night he played the fiddle and grinned just like he used to on those nights he came in late at the cafe to pick up Argenteen.

Once Tom Mix turned to Pink and said, Are you coming along, Plowboy. This was when Pink spoke the only line he had in the movie. Grinning, he said, I reckon not, Tom.

In other parts of the movie you often saw him in the background, leaning in the saddle as if he was trying to look beyond Tom Mix and see who was out there in the dark motion picture theater.

Still later, in the fall of '38 or '39, sometime in there just before the War broke out, Pink returned to Oklahoma City, playing at

the old Arcadia Ballroom, now called the Trianon. Plowboy Pink
and the Oklahoma Pioneers. Six straight weekends. He had become a RCA Victor recording artist and had a hit tune on all the
juke boxes, a pretty song, the kind that would have broken your
heart if Argenteen was singing it. Pink sang it himself though.
His voice had gotten smoother, deeper, but it was him all right.

Marshall was working for Morgan Ferrill Grocery at that time,
good regular hours, and so he had his weekend evenings free and
could get down to the Trianon easily enough if he wanted to. He
didn't want to. What would be the use. He doubted that Pink
could tell him anything about Argenteen, nothing he would care
to know anyway. He doubted that Pink would even remember
him.

And so he was surprised when one evening Pink called him up.

Say, Marshall, do you remember me, your old buddy Pink
Miracle.

Before Marshall realized what he was saying, he was asking
Pink what had become of Argenteen.

Oh, Marshall, Pink said. I wish I could say for sure. I believe
she passed away some time ago, bless her heart. She had long
since left me, you know. Many's the time, Marshall, I wished I
never did take her off to California. Pray for her soul, that's all
we can do. She was taken advantage of out there. They left her
out in the cold, and she wouldn't never come back to me—no,
sir, she was too proud. You know that for a fact. Say, Marshall,
I'd like you to come down to the Trianon Saturday night. I'll have
a free pass waiting for you at the door.

No, Marshall said. I couldn't do that. Thanks all the same.

Sometimes when he thought of Cora Mae, in her grave now
these half dozen years, he saw the face of Argenteen. He carried
a photograph of Cora Mae in his billfold, and at such moments
he had to take out the photograph and hold it before him until
the image of Cora Mae was clear and sharp enough to make Ar-

genteen's vanish. He didn't like it one bit that the two images should be so confused in his mind. There was no resemblance, just that Cora Mae had some of the same life in her that Argenteen had, a knack, a kind of gift, an ease of loving. How the life shone forth from them—why, they *were* life. And gone so soon. He might have known it all along, knew it as sure as he knew his Cora Mae was dead, knew it in his heart long before Pink told him, and that was why he kept confusing the two images in his mind.

Wanting more than you have, Argenteen said. It was that wanting more, the feeling of wanting more than the world can possibly give you, that made you hear Arkansas in Pink's music. *You know what I'm talking about, Marshall.* He guessed he did. At the time he didn't. Said he didn't anyway, because he knew what she was driving at. She wanted to talk him into going to Cromwell, or some place like it, when he had already pretty much made up his mind to do just that. Anybody tried to talk him into something, even if he had already made his mind up to do it, he would argue against it, he would resist it—that was his nature, stubborn as the day was long.

Still, Argenteen hadn't had it quite right. Going to Cromwell wasn't the same thing as Pink's playing the fiddle. It gave him time to think, that's all, it gave him time to try to forget he'd ever known anybody by the name of Argenteen Miracle. He was alone in Cromwell, alone in the midst of thieves and crooks, gamblers and whores. The money he earned there made him sick. He saw himself as just like the rest of them, opportunists, trying to cash in on a sure thing, black gold.

Argenteen should have added that it wasn't only wanting more than you can have that gave life to Pink's music. It was also knowing that you couldn't ever have what you wanted most. Knowing that even if by some quirk of fortune, some impossible chain of events, you could get what you wanted, you wouldn't deserve it.

When you got to that pass, you could get some Arkansas into your music.

And you could leave Cromwell as sure as though it were nothing but a burned-out husk of your former self, the false pride, the old bluster of your youth. Humbled, he had gone back home, to Jane and his sweet daughters, and he never felt better about himself. All the same, he never forgot Argenteen. Gladly never forgot, even while falling in love with Jane again and again, year after year. That was the way it was going to be. Once you start loving, there is no stopping it.

It made him smile to think of how Argenteen had taught him to blacken his eyelids and mustache. Oh, he'd been a dashing one though. Argenteen saw that, saw something in him that otherwise would never have been awakened. It wasn't vanity. Damned if it was vanity. Jane would say so, but she would be wrong.

Sometimes it came alive with Jane, a way she had of touching him, as if she knew him in spite of herself, better than she would ever admit, and this knowing pleased her, touched awake a joy that was the match for his own. If you didn't have that, maybe you did as Don Temple had done, you ran off. You hid yourself, you broke a woman's heart.

Sarah Jane was fourteen years old now and shapely for her age. All his girls matured fast. He hoped she had better luck than Johnnie and Cora Mae in finding a man that would do her justice. And there was Gloria Clara, Cora Mae's girl that had lived with them ever since Cora Mae's passing away. Seven years old, she was a sweetheart, fair like her poor mama, that Bagley paleness and the sharp nose. Like his own daughter she seemed, not Don Temple's, who was in jail, last anybody heard, in the State Pen at McAlester. Gloria Clara couldn't be as pretty as her mama, but she'd have her own beauty, you could tell, and some man would come along that wouldn't deserve her.

Last summer Johnnie had been named Miss Oklahoma City for a Day. They took her picture while she stood behind the jewelry counter at Kerr's and put it in the *Daily Oklahoman*. They didn't tell her her picture was going to be in the paper, and she was so surprised when she saw it. Can you beat that, she said. Now why do you suppose they picked me.

Drummed up plenty of business for the store, he'd bet you.

Then, years later, out of the blue, Marshall had a letter from Argenteen. This would have been sometime during the war, several years after Pink had told him that she was dead. The letter had her scent in it—not strong, but there all right—and at the end of it, down at the bottom of the second page, she had pressed her lips to the paper and left a bright red imprint.

The letter was postmarked Norfolk, Virginia, but she did not say what she was doing there or how she came to be there or whether she meant to stay. She wrote to him as if she'd never left. You remember what we were saying, she said, about immortality.

Damned if he did, not a jot, heaven help him. What could he have had to say on such a subject.

Whatever it had been, she wanted him to know she thought he was wrong. We *were* immortal, she said. She couldn't prove it, of course. But although she had agreed with him at the time, it hadn't set well with her ever since. Why, it was almost a matter of common sense. When she considered her life, for example, when she remembered all the events, brought forth memories and dreams, it was as if she did so over a gulf surely as vast as death. Yet, once called forth, the lost image leaped that deathly gulf, as easy as breathing.

And just now, the pen moving across the page (blue ink, he noted, on light blue paper), she called him forth, she saw him, she had before her, within her, the image of him, his dark eyes when she had stroked his eyelids with charcoal and showed him himself in the mirror. You look startled, she wrote, you look surprised by your beauty. You look away from the mirror and into my eyes. How helpless you look, Marshall. Do you think I might blind you. I would never do that. I want you to see. I want you to know the loveliness that is in you. Maybe you have to coax it—that is what I'm showing you how to do—but it is there to be seen and you know that. It wouldn't come forth so easily if you did not know, if you did not recognize it when you saw it.

That image will not die, Marshall, neither in you nor in me. It is what survives us, our beauty, our loveliness. You know that, don't you. When I look into your eyes—darling, such deep, dark eyes—I see your knowledge. It took some doing to call it forth, but now it glows, it warms you, it is your song, honey, and it ain't never going to end. Love, Argenteen.

He read the letter twice, refolded it carefully, not wanting to smear the lipstick on the page, and put it back in the envelope. No return address on that envelope. What was she doing in Norfolk, Virginia. Where had she been since he'd seen her—almost twenty years ago. Lord. Immortality! Life couldn't be short enough to suit him. What on earth was he doing, still around, his only son dead, his Cora Mae gone. Immortality. He'd have none of that. No, thanks. Argenteen had come along, she had been present, stirring his blood, quickening his soul. Then she was gone. That was the way it was, and how it should be. A beginning, and then an end to it. Sweet and swift, simple and merciful. Beautiful? God, yes. Downright painful, that beauty. Who could deny it. A mercy that could kill you. And that *should* kill you, if there was any justice—wasn't any. You lived on. Might as well be immortal. For sure it went on and on, God damn the luck.

After supper he carried the letter in his pocket out to the garden. It was July, plenty of weeding to do. Best time of the year, such long sweet light, warm well into the darkness. Sometimes he stayed out here, on his knees, the spade in his hand, until the sky got all starry and black. He could stretch out in one of these smooth rows and sleep, immortal as he ever cared to be, and never get cold, all through July and August too. Now he took the letter from his pocket, crumpled it without looking at it again, and set the match to it.

Anyway, he knew the letter by heart. How could he ever forget. *It is your song, honey, and it ain't never going to end.*

Perhaps he did sleep a while, stretched out on the warm furrowed ground of his garden at the foot of the incinerator. The moon was full, the stars bright, the crickets busy as the devil. When he stepped into the house, the darkness like to jump at him. In the closed-in back porch, where she put up her canned black-eyed peas, green beans, pickled beets, peaches, he stumbled and reached out for something to steady him, drew his hand back fast, a sharp pain, damn it, a splinter, and then the sound of breaking glass and a sour smell, the beets for sure. He reached for the string that hung from the light bulb—knew it was there somewhere, but couldn't feel a thing, just air, empty air, his eyes would adjust to the dark before he would find that pesky string.

He heard footsteps in the front of the house.

Marshall, what's happened. Marshall?

The light came on in the kitchen, flashing through the glass door pane, and he saw her coming towards him, the deep folds of her white nightgown flapping. Save me, he wanted to say. For God's sake, save me.

She looked through the door, couldn't see him, he knew, the light on her side not his. But she seemed to see something, drew back before taking the doorknob as if suddenly frightened—no, it wasn't fright. More like recognition. An instant, no more than that. Then she opened the door, and his hand found the light bulb string, pulled it so hard that it broke off. Still, the light came on.

Marshall, she said. I was asleep.

I'm sorry.

What is that—are you bleeding.

She pointed at his feet and he looked down, saw what she meant: the beets. He'd knocked off a jar of pickled beets.

Couldn't find the light, he said. Watch out you don't step on the glass.

I've got my shoes on.

He saw that it was true. She had put on her thick-heeled lace-ups. Looked kind of funny sticking out from beneath the white gown.

I'll clean it up, he said. Go on back to bed.

He took the broom and dust pan from the corner, began to sweep up the broken pieces of glass.

Pick up the big pieces first, she said, bending down, reaching for the large curved ones.

Then you'll have to scrub up that beet juice, she said. It'll stain sure as blood.

It's my doings. I'll take care of it.

I know how you'll take care of it.

You won't know anything ever broke here.

I'll be stepping on slivers of glass all winter.

Go on back to bed.

She turned, carried the slivers of glass to the trash can beneath the kitchen sink. He swept some more, saw that he was spreading the beet juice with the broom, and realized that she was right. He should pick up the bigger pieces first.

You won't be long, will you, she asked.

No, I won't be long.

I don't know if I can get back to sleep.

He picked up a sliver, cut his finger first thing. Here came the blood. Damn it all, what a God damn mess.

When I woke up, she said, I reached for you.

I wasn't there.

I saw that. Did you cut yourself.

Yes, he said, I guess I did.

I'll get a bandage.

It isn't anything.

Nothing's anything at first. Cora Mae had a sore throat. Next thing we knew, it was her heart. You have to take care of things first time around.

I know.

There's no second chance.

You go on to bed. I'll be there directly.

But she had already turned, and he heard her footsteps in the hallway and saw the light go on in the bathroom. She was opening the cabinet by now, she had the bandages in hand, the peroxide, the cotton swabs. He took out his handkerchief and wrapped it tight around his cut finger. Swept as much as he could see into the dustpan. Already she was there before him, in the doorway, ready to mend him.

XVII

. . . .

Fathers and Daughters

For many years Don Temple lived on North Broadway, in a hotel across the street from Norton-Johnson Buick, just a block up from the Southwestern Bell Building. To get to the rooms, you entered a doorway next to the Diamond A Drugstore, walked up a flight of stairs. There wasn't a desk or lobby. The Regal Hotel. The other tenants he did not know, nor care to. Sometimes he sat by his window, watched for the streetcar to come by, and when it did, with a clatter, sparks flying from the pole that connected it to the wires running all up and down the street, he could feel the chair tremble. This was peculiarly satisfying. After that, he moved to the bed, its mattress a narrow slab that smelled a little like medicine, and he lay still on his side, facing the windowless wall on the north, which had wallpaper with a pattern of entwined roses the color of old leather, and a black-framed print of a racehorse leaping a hurdle.

When he couldn't stand his room, he did some business, but strictly small time. He didn't need much money.

His mama died and his father died.

Once he went out to see what had become of his grandfather. He drove up the narrow dusty road to the frame house with the chicken coop off to one side, the soddy to the other, and saw

the woman first thing, a dark shape on the porch, her broad
shoulders wrapped with a shawl the very color of shade, long
fringe dangling. She sat still in a rocker, her legs crossed like a
man's, her black hair pulled tight, tied with a broad red ribbon
in back.

I'm Don Temple, he said.

I remember you, the woman said.

You're Rose, ain't you.

Minneola Choate.

Yes, Minneola.

He's dead. Your granddaddy's dead. Go out back and see him
if you want to. Back of the soddy.

Back of the soddy.

That's right. He wanted to be *in* it, but he don't know no
better.

I never knew him well.

Nobody did. That's the way he wanted it.

I'll just—

You go right ahead. It's marked. I done it right.

He lived a long time.

Too long, hear him tell it.

What'd he die of.

Heart.

I'll just—

Go right ahead. You can't miss it. I done it right, the way he
wanted me to, except he's outside the soddy, not in it.

The dirt house looked about the same as Don remembered
from that time he'd come here with Leroy, maybe sunk down
a little lower in the ground, the roof worn smoother, corners
rubbed almost round by the wind. Elzick's home place, cool in
the summer and warm in the winter. Tufts of grass stuck up in
places on the roof like clumps of unruly hair. Around in back,
tall pointed weeds grew up. He couldn't see a thing like a grave,
neither mound nor marker, until he almost stepped on it, a flat

stone level with the ground, no bigger than a piece of paper. But the letters was handsomely carved:

ELZICK ISIAH TEMPLE
d. 1932
A Sooner

. . .

In the summer of 1979 Johnnie took her mama to Arkansas for the funeral of Uncle George. Daddy had been dead ten years and Johnnie long divorced from Bill Haynes after bringing up three children. Aunt Mina, Daddy's youngest sister, came up to Johnnie and took her to one side.

Honey, she said as they made their way through the memorials towards the waiting cars, honey, your daddy was my favorite brother. He was older than me by a good sight—six years, you know—but he played with me when the others left me behind. Used to take me down to the Methodist church and we'd sneak in and he'd sit me up on that pump organ and show me how to play it. You didn't know your daddy could play the organ? He sure could. Never had a teacher. Didn't need one. It came natural to him. He knew I loved to sing, so he took me there and we sang the hymns while he played. I said to him, Marshall, I'd sure love to play that organ the way you do. Well, he said, you set right up here and I'll show you how. That's what he did.

They came to the car and got in. Mama was riding up ahead in the limousine with Aunt Billie and the twins, Monroe and Mildren. They were joined by Aunt Faye, Daddy's middle sister, and her husband U. S., who had the Chevrolet dealership in Danville.

You remember that time, Aunt Mina said, when Marshall came here on the train with that little boy, Faye, don't you.

Little boy? Aunt Faye said. Why, no, I don't believe I do. What little boy?

She remembers, said U. S. I don't think she heard you plain. You'll have to speak up, Mina. She's getting hard of hearing.

I heard all right, she said. I just don't remember.

You remember. It was Marshall's son. Isn't that the time you're talking about, Mina?

Yes, it is. Oh, it was years ago.

Well, of course. I do remember now. Marshall coming with his son. Why didn't you say so. Wasn't no little boy. His son, an infant. I remember it well, like yesterday. Carried him here in a white coffin, Marshall did, and buried him up on the mountain where our daddy is laid to rest. Uncle Charley is there too, and Aunt Esther. I believe it's Esther.

It's Esther, U. S. said.

Yes, I believe it's Esther.

I wonder, Aunt Mina said, who takes care of that Monroe graveyard?

Don't nobody take care of it, Faye said. Ben used to go up there once in a while. Now he's gone, nobody has the time. I can't keep up my own garden without my arthritis acting up something terrible, and U. S. here is worse.

I wish I lived closer, Aunt Mina said. Little Rock's just too far. Oh, yes.

People should be buried in regular cemeteries, U. S. said. They have perpetual care.

We have our plots, Aunt Faye said. Memorials and everything. All our children will have to worry about is filling in the dates.

It's a great comfort, U. S. said.

Yes, said Aunt Mina, I'm sure it is. But you know, there was something touching about Marshall and his little son. In a way—

You'd not get me up there, Aunt Faye said. No, sir. It's wild up there, all overgrown. There's snakes up on that mountain.

It's pretty though. I remember the view. Marshall loved it too, said he could see all of Arkansas on a clear day. And the blackberries everywhere, and wild plums, even grapes.

Blackberries was always too tart for my taste.

I do like a good blackberry cobbler, U. S. said.

You like the cream.

Well—

You was always a blackberry eater, Aunt Faye said to Johnnie. Why, I remember when you and your sister used to visit us at Mama's. Put a bowl before you two girls, Mama said, quickest way to get shut of them berries.

Turn your teeth black if you don't use plenty of cream. Isn't that right, Mina.

Mina supposed so. Conversation fell off then. They were back at the parking lot of the funeral home chapel.

You know what, Mina said as they unloaded from the car, we all should go up to that graveyard and see what condition it's in. It's not such a long drive.

I *know* what condition it's in, Aunt Faye said.

We've got to get back home, Mina, U. S. said. Duty calls.

Wouldn't you like to, Johnnie?

Johnnie certainly would.

We have regular cemeteries, U. S. said, because of the year-round perpetual care.

Aunt Faye and U. S. climbed into their Chevrolet and were gone.

Well, said Aunt Mina, you and me and your mama'll drive up there.

Mama was walking up to them at that moment. Johnnie remembers thinking how good she looked for a woman eighty-seven years old. She held her head high and her shoulders back. Uncle George's widow, Aunt Billie, shriveled and bent, walked beside her with the help of a cane, and the twins Monroe and Mildren, old men before their time in dark suits that looked several sizes too large, trailed along behind. You could almost have taken them for shadows, except that one was waving his arms in the air, and Johnnie realized that he was singing.

Daddy's favorite hymn, he explained. I'm the only one remembers it. "Little Cabin Home on the Hill." He used to sing it to me by the hour. Had a fine tenor voice. Didn't carry far, but always in pitch.

It's no hymn, Mildren.

He said it was. Daddy always said, Mildren, he said, come here and I'll sing you a hymn.

I never heard it before. Did you, Mama?

No, Aunt Billie said, I can't recall that I did.

Mama didn't want to go to the family graveyard on the mountain where Little Brother was buried.

I never wanted him put up there, she said. I told Marshall it was a bad idea. He'd see to it that the grave was taken care of, he said. Well, you see how it is.

Johnnie saw all right. She didn't go. Neither did Aunt Mina. If Mama cared so little about going, why should they? It was spite on Johnnie's part. She knew that, and wished later that she had gone, but it was too late then. She'd never go back to Arkansas. She knew that Cora Mae would have climbed that mountain though, would have climbed it in her bare feet if need be and washed the grave with her own sweat, whether Mama wanted her to or not.

After the stroke, Mama sometimes called Johnnie Cora Mae. Johnnie didn't bother to correct her.

The most important part was that coffin. Born of her daddy's grief, it came out beautiful. When Johnnie saw it, she knew it was made for her to see herself in. Turning from that deathbed, leaving the shaded room of her parents, she shook with the sweetness of her knowledge. The beauty of that coffin, made by her father for his dead son, she had in her bones. It was as if her life had just begun.

What was it like, Gloria Clara asked Johnnie, when you and my mother were growing up?

Cora Mae was the fair one, Johnnie said, and I was dark, like my daddy. I thought she had the beauty in the family, and she thought I did. And when Sarah Jane came along—your mother would have been ten and I was eleven—why, we thought that she was the one destined to be the great beauty. I don't know why we set such store on beauty. Certainly it was nothing our mama taught us, unless by negative example. Cleanliness she cared about, but beauty was strictly a matter of vanity. I believe she knew more than we did, but it didn't much seem so then. She *was* beautiful in her way, but she didn't give it a thought.

She was the same with me, Gloria said. She raised me up the same way.

She would have, yes.

And beauty mattered to me too.

Oh, it did to all of us. And look at what good it did us, every last one of us married by the time we were eighteen. Your mama was just fifteen.

It takes for some.

What takes, honey?

Marriage. Lasts, I mean.

Oh, yes. Took for Mama and Daddy. I guess it did. Seems to have taken for you too.

Seems to, yes.

My first marriage didn't take at all. Seems almost like a bad dream. Mama never told me a thing! Did she you?

Precious little. Said not to believe everything a boy told me. Said to watch out, come home early.

Come home early—I can just hear her. And see Daddy winking behind her back. He'd always let me in. I knew that.

Boys were dangerous. That much I gathered. Just why, I couldn't have imagined, not from what she told me.

Babies could have come from the moon, for all I knew.

I hope I've done better by my children.

Lord, I do too. Sometimes I wonder. Sometimes I wonder what you can teach them. Especially when it comes to love. Have mercy.

It can end. That's what I never was taught.

No, honey, it doesn't end. It just changes. I love everybody I
ever loved. Even poor Doyle Briggs, my first husband. I really do.
I believe that.

Gloria Clara didn't know what to say to that. She could have
said something rude, could have been insulting, but she knew
herself well enough to know that possibility, and so she said
nothing. Who was she to claim knowledge of love, after all. And
didn't she want to know about her mother and her father. Aunt
Johnnie knew things, had known her parents, who seem to have
become for Gloria Clara ghosts, as alive in her heart as her flesh-
and-blood children. Aunt Johnnie knew and could tell, if only
she, Gloria Clara, might learn to listen. What might she have
heard from her mother and daddy—her grandparents that had
raised her, she meant—if she had known how to listen.

Johnnie sat in a chair by the window, her hennaed hair given
a brilliance by the late morning light. Gloria thought her calm,
even serene, certainly a handsome woman at age seventy-one in
her neatly furnished apartment, with a new husband ten years
younger, a good man for her at last, everyone said, after her
long troubles with Bill Haynes. If Gloria Clara looked into Aunt
Johnnie's eyes, those hazel eyes, the Bagley eyes, for a glimpse of
Cora Mae in them, she also saw a freshness that was Johnnie's
own, an innocence surely as quick now as when she was a girl.
Could you save it, maintain that innocence, she wondered, or
conjur it up again when you knew it was lost—and if so, how.
It seemed to her that she had never had it, not the way Aunt
Johnnie so clearly had, that in spite of her grandmother's ag-
gressive silence on matters of love, a determination to keep her
innocent, she was always a grim child, cynical before she had
reason to be. She always knew in the worst way.

You want to know about your mother, don't you, Johnnie said.
You want me to talk about Cora Mae.

Tell me about yourself, Gloria Clara wanted to say. Tell me
who you are. I want to know you, Johnnie.

Yes, she said. I want to know about my mother.

• • •

When Don Temple made himself known to his daughter, he was seventy and she forty-seven.

His face is lined, the creases deepest across his forehead and around his mouth. Above his right eyebrow a white line, perhaps an inch long, gently curves downwards. The hair is thick for a man his age, though a stale yellow, the color tobacco makes when it stains your hands. He combs the hair straight back, parted slightly off center. With his broad fingernails, neatly clipped, he taps on the table as he talks. The teeth ride low in his mouth, seem loose, though uniformly so, and unpleasantly handsome, as if chosen solely for their beauty, fit be damned. Plenty of care has been taken with that mustache, so straight and thin, all along the edge of the lip, then made to turn sharply upward beneath the nostrils. He wears a gold watch, a gold ring with a ruby set in it, a gold chain around his neck, a small cross depending from the chain, nestling in thick silvery curls of chest hair.

I want to take up where I left off, he tells Gloria Clara.

She lets him talk. She imagines him saying more than he can ever have said. He talks to this day, this father that was loved by her mother, Cora Mae. He does not always say what she wants to hear. He is shifty, he contradicts himself, he sits there tapping the tabletop with his thick nails. His teeth shine. And the hand that she cannot see, the secret one beneath the table—does it rest, reach, does it clutch or clench, mark time on his knee.

He shows her a photograph of his mother, dead for some time, pulls it from his wallet, a snapshot in black and white creased at the corners, and as he hands it to her his lips form a smile so suddenly familiar to her that she starts and draws back.

It won't bite you, he says, go ahead and look. It's your grand-mother.

In his smile she has seen her own, no more than that.

In the photograph she sees a large stoop-shouldered woman standing next to an immaculately trimmed, egg-shaped bush that is exactly her height. She wears a polka-dot dress and white lace-up shoes like Mama's friends wore to church.

Your mother got along pretty well with my mother, he says. Must have. You got her name. Clara. That's your middle name. Clara.

He pulls out another photograph. In this one the same woman stands alongside a tall, thin man with white hair that curves outwards above his ears.

My grandfather?

Oh, no. No, this was a fellow named Lovell. A husband of hers for a while. She left my father, your grandfather, John Temple, and came out here to Oklahoma not long after I did. I respected her for that, though it put me to some bother. She did what she knew she had to do. It wasn't many women of that day and age would do that. They might know, but they would never dream of doing it. I might have been a better son to her. I pray for her soul.

He has not always been one to pray, he gives Gloria Clara to understand. Oh, he isn't the same man as in those days. He hopes she understands that. Nothing stays the same, no, not one thing, not even the dead, who won't stay dead, who pass from dust to grass and trees and, like as not, into clouds and rain.

Your mother's and my love, he tells her, was no flash in the pan. She married again, sure, but what difference does that make.

Where were you, Gloria Clara asks him, when she died. Where were you then?

He looks her straight in the eye, and she sees the pain in him so clearly it seems the very shape of his forehead, the thickness of his eyebrows, the neatly trimmed mustache that makes his lips look pink and full like a woman's. Pain moves across his features like a bunch of muscles flexing.

He can't explain nothing. He wants to see Gloria Clara again. He is her daddy, he keeps telling her, her flesh-and-blood daddy.

Don't call me again, please, she tells him. I can't see you again.

He keeps calling.

Mama never wanted to discuss Cora Mae and Don Temple. It did no good to dwell on things, she told Gloria Clara. You couldn't change anything that had already happened.

Daddy always sat on the porch glider and waited for the evening paper. Sometimes he smoked a cigarette. Towards the end, he withdrew to his room, said that the next time he went anywhere, someone would have to haul him. When Mama couldn't care for him anymore, Johnnie and Gloria Clara took him to a nursing home out on Western Avenue, where he received visitors in silence. Sarah Jane, who had never married and who lived in California, came twice a year and sat for hours by his side, holding his hand. He never said a word. It broke Gloria Clara's heart to see him that way. She talked to him, telling him about his grandchildren, who did so well in school, and although tears sometimes came to his eyes, he kept his silence to the end.

Her own children have gone their own way, one son in Illinois, the other in Louisiana. They call on Mother's Day and her birthday, and are sometimes home for Christmas. She believes she loves her husband.

Don Temple still calls every so often.

Tell me about your life, he says. I want to know who you are.

How far back, she wonders, would she have to go.